Ashyer

James Petrillo

Rocket Science Press

SHIPWRECKT BOOKS PUBLISHING COMPANY

IN®
DIE

Minnesota

Cover and interior design by Shipwreckt Books

For Jen,
and all those with true adventure in their hearts

Ashyer

The World of Ashyer

Olan

Castle City
Olan

Anden

Castle City
Anden

W · E
N
S

ddle

doms

Redim

Castle
Ilselm

Cool
Ferry

Castle of
Agethsa

1. The forbidden weapon

*F*rost heard the unmistakable sound of arrows leaving their strings and slicing through the air. Instinctively, he leapt from the forest path. *Thunk thunk.* Two arrows pierced thick oak bark just inches from his head.

Twilight gave way to blackness in the woods, but Frost used his heightened senses to investigate the black projectiles, quivering still, the shafts oily with a fetid residue reeking of goblins.

Strange, he thought, *the wizard had never before summoned foul beasts during training. Perhaps this session was meant to be more difficult?*

Just then, Frost felt knuckles against his neck as a hand grabbed his tunic from behind and pulled him into the undergrowth while a voice said, "Do you want to be a pin cushion?"

Frost spun to see Ty pointing across a field of tall grass at goblins armed with bows and knives.

"I count at least ten," Ty whispered.

Frost leaned close and whispered back, "What is Cirrus thinking sending goblins after us?"

Ty shrugged. "Maybe he's just stepping up the game."

"Something doesn't feel right. This does not feel like a game." Frost shook his head, then pointed. "Throw a decoy dart over there."

Throwing darts were Ty's weapon of choice. They were not as long as arrows and had short, feathered shafts with long, weighted, razor-sharp heads. Ty could throw one with some accuracy as far as sixty yards. Most were simple projectiles, but some were coated with colored potions and poisons. Some even glowed with magical enchantments.

Ty picked a simple dart and whipped it effortlessly into the undergrowth on the left side of the clearing. The goblins, hearing the rustle of thorn bushes where the dart had landed, stopped and turned to look. Frost and Ty watched the vile creatures grunting to each other in their guttural language. The creatures had mottled black-and-green skin, gnarled and wrinkled like a wart-wracked toad. They drooled from their sharpened teeth, and their eyes glowed in the dark like a cat's as they searched the spot where the dart had landed.

Quietly Frost gave his command. "I'll go straight in. You circle to the right."

Ty nodded and the two separated. Suddenly, the wind picked up and the air seemed charged with electricity. Frost noted the change. "The wizard is near. Let's dispatch these stinking wretches first. Then we'll deal with him."

Frost reached under his cloak and quietly produced his unique bow. His own design, Frost had worked closely with both the bowyers and the weaponsmiths to produce a bow made entirely of steel. His was the most powerful and accurate bow in the kingdom. A clever system of cables and pulleys allowed a steel bowstring to be used—an engineering marvel that had convinced some of his subjects that Frost might himself be a wizard.

He pulled three arrows from the quiver that hung from his belt. He saw Ty almost in position when the goblins turned back in his direction, their pig-like snouts twitching. *How can they smell anything but themselves*, he wondered, *putrid as they are?* He lightly planted two of the arrows in the soft ground at his feet and nocked the third to his string. Then he stood and revealed himself.

Upon spotting their quarry, the goblins triumphantly shrieked their earsplitting battle cry, but Frost was ready. Before they could begin their charge, the lead goblin was gazing wide-eyed at an arrow that had sprouted from the center of his chest. Before he had time to fall, two more were stung—one with a killing shot to the neck; the other in its knobby thigh, the arrow passing through flesh and sinew out the other side.

Two were down and a third was limping, but that still left eight goblins now scampering over their fallen brethren and rushing on him with their knives drawn. Frost well knew that once they fell upon him, it would render his death-raining weapon impotent.

As Frost continued to fire arrow after arrow on the advancing horde, a new volley began to whistle in from their left flank. Ty's darts found their marks with meaty thunks.

"Reap!" Ty yelled, a code word meant to signal Frost to close his eyes momentarily. The next dart he threw released its enchantment when it hit its target, sending out a spray of colorful but blinding sparks, similar to the magic fireworks they saw at the harvest celebration. The goblins hesitated in their charge, momentarily stunned and blinded.

"By the gods!" Ty yelled as he let fly yet another dart, "These buggers smell even worse when you fill them with holes and air them out!"

Frost cracked a smile, but his momentary amusement turned to panic when he opened his eyes post-fireworks display to see the shadowy silhouettes of dozens more goblins emerging from the trees *behind* Ty. Just as he was yelling a warning to his friend, an unusually large goblin—barrel-chested, nearly as tall as a man, and draped in rough hide armor—picked up Ty and tossed him through the air.

Ty, with reflexes that would put a fox to the test, swung his arm back even as he was being thrown like a rag-doll, slicing the goblin's hand with the dart that he was about to throw. Then he was sailing twenty feet through the air, further into the center of the grassy clearing. Like a seasoned acrobat, he rolled and was undamaged from the fall. He sprung to his feet again to fling the dart he still clutched at the beast that had just tossed him.

Unfortunately, the goblin's moldy hide armor turned aside the dart. It was not one of Ty's more graceful throws, heaving his projectile a goodly ways but lacking deadly force.

Fortunately, the enraged goblin suddenly became wobbly. Poison from Ty's initial slice was quickly taking effect. It staggered, taking a few more steps forward, grunted, and fell face-first to the ground. Only a ragged snore indicated it was still alive.

The others now hesitated. The remaining few backed off, as did the reinforcements behind Ty. They pressed around the edges of the clearing, taking stock.

"Leave me," Ty said to Frost with utter sincerity. "There are more coming in. We're outnumbered ten to one. I can hold them off while you make your escape, my Liege."

"Oh, don't get all formal on me now," Frost chided him. "I would never leave you, my friend."

Suddenly, lightning flashed above them, illuminating the hungry, greedy faces of the beasts all around. Frost shuddered at the sight of those faces, thinking, *They plan on eating us raw tonight.*

But the goblins' hateful faces began to register fear as the energy permeating the atmosphere intensified.

The wizard descended in an electromagnetic sphere.

Frost yelled, "Summoning goblins is a pretty dirty trick, Cirrus!"

"I suppose you had your eye on us the whole time?" Ty said. "Just waiting until the last moment to intervene?"

"I would never summon such vile filth!" The wizard boomed from above them.

His voice resumed, but only as a whisper in his student's ears. "This horde is not part of your exercise. Things are afoot that are well beyond my control."

Frost felt momentary vindication that his initial gut instinct about Cirrus' innocence had been right, but this was quickly quashed by a sinking feeling and an alarming thought: *We're surrounded by goblins in a situation that is beyond the wizard's control?*

"What do we do, Cirrus?" Frost muttered under his breath, knowing the wizard would hear him.

Cirrus' answer was not terribly reassuring. "The goblins are held at bay by fear at the moment, but their hunger will soon prod them to a desperate, bestial bravery. I cannot kill them all. If I strike, the survivors will likely rip you to pieces."

"We know all that," Ty whispered impatiently, "But do you have a plan?"

"Of course I do." The wizard's reply was tinged with mild annoyance. "When have you known me not to have a plan? When I strike them, Ty, throw your vial of fire potion straight up. Aim it at me. Put a good spin to it. Then, just before it hits me, Frost, fire an arrow directly at the center of its base. You must both be precise."

Ty shook his head as he produced the vial. "Sounds like a dicey plan."

"I didn't say it would work," Cirrus said. "Only that it is a plan."

Frost nocked an arrow. The goblins, seeing this action on the part of their prey, rallied. Breaking the stalemate, they rushed in.

"Now!" Cirrus' voice boomed.

Lightning crackled out from the wizard's sphere and roasted half the goblins. At the same moment, Ty tossed the potion up, putting a fast spin on it. Frost, honed by hours of practice shooting thrown targets, took split-second aim and let loose the arrow. The bottle exploded. Due to the spin, its contents flew outward, raining down in a fiery ring around them. The grass all about the remaining goblins was set ablaze. Their ragged clothes and greasy hair catching fire, most of the inhuman creatures scattered and fled into the forest.

"We provided them the fire but denied them their supper to cook over it," Ty laughed. His nonchalant sense of humor never seemed to ebb, even in the midst of a life-or-death situation.

The sphere encasing the wizard settled to the ground, then it flickered like a candle flame and vanished. Cirrus stepped over a smoldering body and raised his staff. "Don't underestimate the tenacity of the hungry goblin. They have not all fled."

Ty produced a dagger. Down to his last two arrows, Frost readied his bow. True to Cirrus' pronouncement, several half-dead and even burning goblins rushed forward, their rage and hunger driving them to attack even in their death throes. The three men cut down the remaining predators until the only movement in the clearing were wisps of smoke from the smoldering grass.

After a few minutes of rest, the two young men stamped out the last burning patches, lest the whole forest go up. Cirrus even cast a spell that produced a shower of water on a tree that had begun to blaze. With that taken care of, the three set about the task of retrieving arrows and darts before they made their way into the woods. The battle might have drawn more unwanted attention, and they'd had their fill of goblins.

Breaking the silence of the walk, Ty said, "Well, old man, next time we do that exercise could you cut the numbers of the goblin horde down by about half?"

"I told you I had nothing to do with that—" Cirrus began to protest, but Frost intervened.

"Cirrus, you know he is just trying to get your goat."

"Well," the wizard grumbled, "I do not have a goat, and if I did I certainly would not give it to him. He would probably just try to steal it. Either way, I will not be goaded." Cirrus frowned and looked severe, but both students could recognize the ever-so-slight flicker of amusement in Cirrus' voice. If it had been lighter out, they knew they'd see the tale-tell quiver at the corner of his mouth, indicating he was suppressing a chuckle.

A magician of some repute, Cirrus was actually not quite old enough to be their father. He felt like an older brother, or an uncle, perhaps. Although he tried to be firm and harsh with them, the wizard was fond of both boys. *Young men, now,* he thought. *Soon to be called upon to take on their responsibilities as men. Sooner, perhaps, than we thought. Xan, my King, I hope we have prepared them well.*

After the brief exchange, they fell into silence, as if the weight of the night was now settling in on them, and they turned inward to their own melancholy thoughts.

Frost's wavy, dark brown hair fell wildly down his back. He thought, *What would the ladies of the court think if they saw their prince in such a state,* and smiled. His tunic and cloak were black, since the training exercise was supposed to have been one in forest stealth. At nineteen, he was still sheltered from most of the pressures and responsibilities of state, and he generally had a carefree air of happiness about him. Ty probably had something to do with that—ever since he had come to live with Frost in the castle, that insubordinate thief from the streets was dependable for deflating any tendency toward pomposity or showy formality.

Ty followed close behind him, always alert even if his casual bearing did not show it. Ty, the same age as Frost, was shorter and slighter, but he was quite agile. His blonde hair was tied back tight so it would make no noise, and any but the most sensitive forest tracker listening to their footfalls would swear there were only two men passing through the woods.

The wizard led the way, a soft glow at the tip of his staff acting as a lantern. Though his dark hair was beginning to show streaks of gray and he had a slightly sallow look, he had only seen seventeen summers more than his pupils. He wore a dark blue robe that seemed to be sewn from the fabric of twilight itself. He led them carefully up a hill toward the Great Road.

The moon had started to rise as they cleared the forest, and they all stopped to look at it for a moment. As always, they were struck with wonder at its beauty coupled with dread at what it had brought to their world, the world of Ashyer.

The "moon" of Ashyer was, in fact, a planet. Its orbit had brought it ever closer the past few weeks. The time was drawing near when it would pass its closest to Ashyer. As it rose, the moon filled half the horizon with its sickly yellow light. Later that night it would fill most of the sky, and they would be able to make out some surface features of that terrible world. Then, the dragons would come on their yearly pilgrimage to kill and collect tribute.

Cirrus shook his head at the moon dismissively and continued walking. Pushing away their own thoughts of the coming Dragonshade, Ty and Frost followed.

"There are always a few living here on Ashyer," Cirrus said as they resumed their hike. "Dragons I mean. Some of them stay behind. I was just thinking about them."

Frost cast another involuntary glance at the yellow blight on the horizon. "How can you not, with that thing in the sky to remind us?"

"'Twas not always so, Fredris. Since your father is one of the last of the immortals, he can remember a time when that cursed moon did not appear in the sky."

"Can't you just call me Frost?" Frost replied with more irritation in his voice than he'd intended. "You did when we were in battle."

"Very well, Prince Frost, as you command."

Ty started to chuckle.

"*Prince* Frost? That's even worse." Frost deliberately modulated his voice back to a more casual register.

"Like it or not, Frost, you may be king someday. Whether your father be immortal or not." Cirrus' statement sounded rather enigmatic, but before Frost could prod him and try to unravel this riddle, Cirrus crested the hill.

Frost caught up and looked down. On the other side of the hill only a few miles to their left lay the eastern ocean and the capitol city of Olan; the castle, his home, on the top of a hill southeast of the port and south of Olan Bay. "Father *is* an immortal, so I don't think I have to worry about that."

Ty joined them, sounding much more serious than usual when he said, "There's a reason he is one of the last, Frost."

Cirrus glanced at Ty, then turned back to Frost. "I would not have put it quite that way, but Master Ty is right. Your father is an immortal, but he is not indestructible."

Frost frowned in thought. "We have had peace in Olan for centuries, though, since we made the deal with the dragons."

Cirrus looked ahead to the south. "Things change, Frost," he said quietly.

Frost turned to follow Cirrus' gaze. About a half mile downhill to the south, the Great Road crested a smaller hill. The road had existed since before the Kingdom of Olan and was therefore a mystery. Two parallel stone corridors, and wide enough to put three wagons across on either side, it stretched from one ocean to the other on its westward journey. Usually only a few caravans or adventurers traveled it, but on that night, it seemed the entire army of Olan streamed westward upon its ancient stones. From their vantage point on the hill, the three of them could see the column of men marching toward a camp just to the southwest of their position. The sound of horses and armor reached their ears.

"Who are we fighting?" Ty asked.

"King Xan Olan received intelligence about a massive goblin army approaching from the west only days ago. His scout confirmed the approach today. I did not expect to encounter the goblins during your training however."

"What do they think they are doing?" Frost said, perhaps a tad boastfully. "We will wipe them clean of this land without losing a single man."

"The goblins are allied with the dragons," Cirrus said. "We do not yet know what this may mean."

"We will join the army," Frost declared boldly and began toward the camp.

Cirrus grabbed his arm. "I've given my word to your father that I would keep you away. I am sorry."

Frost eyed the wizard suspiciously. "I suppose that means you would use magic if necessary?"

With no malice, Cirrus said, "Yes. I *am* sorry. We can camp near the road if you wish, so we may see what is to come."

"I suppose that's the best I can get, huh?" As if weighing the prospects and suddenly making peace with the situation, Frost shrugged, smiling, and said, "Come on, Ty."

The three walked south toward the Great Road, collecting scraps of wood for a fire as they went. When they were close enough to be identified by the passing soldiers as allies, they settled in. Cirrus produced a wine skin and some salted meat and passed it to Frost. Ty tended to the fire and then joined his companions, sitting down cross-legged in the grass.

"There in the distance, Frost, can your remarkable eyes see it?" Cirrus was pointing.

"Goblin Warfires. Maybe hundreds."

Ty strained to make out anything and shook his head resignedly. "I don't see a thing. I wish I had your bloodline, Frost. Or at least your *eye*-line."

"You can have it. Besides, you have long-blood in you. Your mother was long-born."

Ty shook his head again. "It doesn't make me long nor does it let me see any better."

Cirrus looked appraisingly at the two. "No one can predict the outcome of the mingling of the blood. Many have remarked upon your uncanny dexterity, Ty. As if your mother had been a cat."

Ty lifted an eyebrow. "A cat, eh? You know, I *could* take that the wrong way."

Frost, seeing an opportunity perhaps to pry some information from their normally private and tight-lipped teacher, chimed in. "So, I guess I've never asked … how did you end up with wizard's blood?"

"Well, let me think." The wizard produced a smoking pipe from a pocket in his robe, tamped in some tobacco from another pocket, and lit the pipe with a twig from the fire.

Ty rolled his eyes. "Great. Here comes a history lesson."

Frost punched him in the shoulder. "I want to know; shut it." Ty rubbed his shoulder and grinned. Frost didn't pull his punches much, but the gesture between the two of them was always friendly.

Cirrus cleared his throat. "Wizards come from the mingling of long and common blood, for it seems that in some common men and women lies the key to unlocking the magic of long blood. Sometimes it takes generations for the key to surface. For me it was two generations ago. My grandfather was of common blood. To my knowledge, that is how my father and I gained the ability to cast and to speak to the elements."

Frost stared intently into the fire. "Is my father the last one, the last Immortal, longest of long-blood?"

"I don't know, Frost." After a short silence, during which he took a long, thoughtful draw from his pipe, Cirrus added, "Your father is a good man, but not all Immortals were. Just as not all Giants were either giant or evil, not all Immortals were noble or honorable. Some of them were the worst tyrants this world has ever known. Sometimes … sometimes I hope he *is* the last."

Frost thought for a moment, then asked, "How long do you think I will live?"

Cirrus raised an eyebrow. "How long do you think I will?"

Frost caught the wizard's meaning and chuckled, "Point taken."

The fire crackled and started to die out. The fully risen moon provided ample light to see the progress of the army, however, and the three companions watched the slow march.

Cirrus knocked the ashes of his pipe into the remains of the fire, rolled onto his side and said, "Get some rest, boys."

Ty slapped his knee. "We're *men*, old man."

Cirrus smiled as his eyes closed. "As you will, Master Ty."

Ty and Frost continued to watch the dying embers as they winked out, one by one.

Lapsing introspective, Ty asked, "Do you remember the day we met?"

"You mean the day you stalked and tried to rob me?"

"I wasn't actually going to rob you. Someone needed to watch your back. What kind of prince wanders out to a forest lake alone to go swimming?"

Frost lay down on his side and muttered, "You had no idea who I was until you went through my things."

"I was just curious. I wanted to know what kind of things a prince might take swimming."

"Sure." Frost's eyes closed. He said something else, but it was an incoherent mumble that trailed away, weary exhaustion finally overtaking him.

Ty grinned. "Nothing very valuable unfortunately," he said to no one in particular. He lay down beside his companions on the soft grass in the sickly moonlight. For a while, he stared up at the moon. He could see tiny red mountain ranges, as if he were floating above looking down on them. He wondered what Ashyer looked like from over there, and then he was asleep.

Cirrus shook Frost and Ty until their eyes crept open to find the wizard crouched between them. The position of the moon told the tale of two sleeping hours. Frost looked toward the road—empty. There was a great rumbling in the west. He sat up quick. Cirrus held his shoulder tight.

From their vantage point the three could see, perhaps only a mile off, the army of Olan assembled at the base of the hill before a goblin horde, thousands strong.

The creatures were banging swords and growling, their inhuman voices carrying for miles. Knights were organized into ranks, with shield bearers in the front to protect the archers. The goblins stood like a mob, pushing and yelling. Frost thought they looked like a filthy ocean that was threatening to spill over the army. The gravity of the situation hit him—the goblins could win. Their numbers were enormous. Had his father wanted him out of the city in case they lost? Then he spotted it—his father's pavilion.

"He's down there!" Frost yelled at Cirrus.

"I know, Frost. Please, stay here," Cirrus said calmly.

A tear threatened to spill from Frost's eye, and he wiped at it. "We could lose. He could be killed."

"Your father is not so easily beaten, Frost."

Before any more could be said, trumpets sounded and their army loosed arrows on the horde. Hundreds of goblins died in the first volley, but the rest seemed unswayed. A wave of thousands of hideous creatures surged toward the army. More arrows flew, and the front line of filth fell again, but it was not enough. Swords were unsheathed, and man met goblin in combat. As the two forces clashed, the sound was deafening.

"Look!" Ty was pointing to the forest to the south.

The others saw what Ty had spotted. The mounted knights of Olan rode out from cover at full charge on their armored horses. Each horse was covered in razor sharp protruding blades. The Knights crashed into the ocean of goblins at full charge without slowing. They left a mangled trail of broken bodies in their wake.

The mob was thinning, and the goblins looked as if they were starting to scatter when there was a terrible *crack* from the sky. All looked up and saw it. An enormous dragon was streaking down to the battle.

Frost tried to leap to his feet, but Cirrus forced both him and Ty to lie down in the grass. They raised their heads only enough to see. The dragon was flying low over the battlefield as if assessing the state of affairs. Then, apparently deciding it was a lost cause for the goblins, it started breathing fire on everything, man and goblin alike.

Frost tried to wiggle free, but Cirrus held fast. The dragon circled around and inhaled deep. It was lining up behind the fleeing Knights of Olan. Just as the Knights reached the forest line, it exhaled, destroying trees and Knights as one, leaving only ash, more accursed Dragonshade. Frost dropped his face into the grass and began to weep. It was the voice of his father that made him raise his head again.

"Hear me, dragon!" Xan Olan stood on a small rise at the edge of the battle. His voice was barely audible over the chaos and fire. "Face me!"

The dragon turned in flight and landed in front of Xan. The battlefield was a scorched waste with very little movement.

"YOU HAVE VIOLATED OUR AGREEMENT," the voice of the dragon boomed.

Then Xan was talking, but his voice could not be heard from the hill where the three lay in hiding.

"SPARE ME YOUR LIES," the dragon answered the unheard statement. "YOU HAVE CREATED A FORBIDDEN WEAPON AND WILL BE DESTROYED!"

Before Frost could wonder what that meant, they heard another *crack* behind them. The three looked around and saw another dragon diving toward the castle.

"No—" Frost began, but before he could utter any kind of pointless plea, the second dragon enveloped the castle with relentless incineration. Frost was about to scream, but it was the scream of his father that echoed in the hills. The three turned to look at the battlefield once more. The first dragon was breathing fire in a steady stream. The figure of Xan Olan was silhouetted for a moment, then engulfed, and finally turned to ash.

Frost leaped to his feet. His blood quickened; the wizard too slow to stop him. Pulling his bow, the Prince ran at a non-human pace toward the dragon.

The appearance of the enraged archer caught the dragon off guard. Frost did not hesitate. He released two steel arrows almost simultaneously and struck the dragon in both eyes, piercing the soft ocular flesh easily. Fire erupted from the wounded sockets almost instantly, shooting straight at Frost, but Cirrus and Ty arrived in time to deflect the flames and pull Frost to the ground.

"Quiet, you fool," Cirrus hissed into Frost's ear.

The dragon roared and spit flame wildly as the furnace within continued to leak plasma from the blinded eyes. Tents and pavilions were engulfed all around. Finally, the dragon took off. Roaring in pain and smoking from the eyes, it flew toward the moon. The three watched as it was joined by the other dragon and disappeared into the yellow sky.

Frost buried his face in the scorched grass and wept. Cirrus and Ty continued to stare dumbstruck at the moon. When they were sure there were no more dragons coming, Ty and Cirrus sat up. Frost clenched his head with his hands and wept harder. Ty cradled his friend and wept himself.

Cirrus watched as the two boys cradled each other. His eyes were just as wet, but he stood on guard, lest they be taken in the open unaware.

After some time, Frost and Ty stood and walked toward the devastation. Cirrus followed closely behind.

Reaching the smoking mound of ash that had been his immortal father, Frost knelt, bowed his head, and wept openly. Ty and Cirrus turned away, giving privacy to the moment.

"I knew Xan well," Cirrus said flatly. "He sent me to the wizard school in the south, and I became his most trusted advisor."

The sound of rustling from behind them made Ty and Cirrus turn around. Frost was sliding his hands into the ashes. Ty cringed, but Cirrus quickly started walking toward Frost.

"Frost—" Cirrus began.

Before Cirrus could finish, Frost pulled a longsword of incredible quality from the ashes. Deep blue steel with a twinkling sharp diamond edge, the weapon emitted a light fog as he lifted it.. Frost turned the marvelous blade, aglow with powerful magic, in his hands, and reached to touch the blade.

"Stop!" Cirrus yelled. "One touch could kill you!"

Frost fixed Cirrus with an accusing stare. "The dragon said a forbidden weapon…. How much do you know? Tell me wizard!"

Cirrus put his hand up in surrender. "I will tell you all, my King, but not here. We need to hide that sword."

At the words "my King," Frost dropped the sword. Ty, always with an eye for value, delicately rolled the beautiful weapon tight in a fallen Olan banner and tried to return it, but Frost's eyes scanned the battlefield. The Prince walked toward the dead. Ty turned and offered the sword to Cirrus.

"Carry it for him Master Ty. A time will come that he will take it up on his own. Until then, remain his true friend and keep it safe."

Cinching the blade on his back under his cloak, Ty asked, "What is it?"

Cirrus kept his eyes on Frost. "A sword, Master Ty, a sword that could alter the destiny of Ashyer."

H ours passed before Frost returned to his companions on the hill. He held out his hand to Ty. In his palm was the symbol of the Captain of the Royal Guard—a small white shield pendant with two down-pointing crossed green swords. Ty accepted it without a word. Frost then held his other hand to Cirrus, in it a dagger of the Order of Knights. Cirrus also accepted without a word. Frost then produced a scrap of purple fabric rent from the battle cloth worn by Xan Olan and tied his hair in the back using the token.

"So we shall not forget the sacrifices of this day," Frost said in a somber tone neither Cirrus nor Ty had ever heard from him before. Frost sat by their re-lit fire and looked at Cirrus. "Now my teacher, teach me. What has transpired this day?"

Cirrus rubbed at his forehead for a moment, collecting his thoughts. "Your father knew the peace with the dragons could not last. He saw how greedy the dragon-kind are and knew they would continue to demand more each year. He saw the toil of the people to keep up with the demand. He did not want the people of Olan to suffer their entire lives with no end. So, he began to plan. Other kingdoms have gone to war with the dragons, but all have fallen. As you know, if you kill a dragon, the furnace within explodes destroying everything.

"He needed to battle a dragon and survive, so, secretly he commissioned the best swordsmiths and enchanters from the land to make a weapon. The sword that master Ty has on his back is eternally sharp and can pierce even stone. The reason I told you not to touch the blade is because of its enchantment. Whatever it strikes, is frozen solid. This is a dragonslayer blade, the only sword of its kind ever imagined—one that can pierce the heart of a dragon and extinguish its fire as well as its life."

Cirrus paused to gaze out at the battlefield. "This carnage was not part of the plan. The dragons must have spies in Olan. The destruction of the castle caused King Xan to hesitate, I think, for otherwise he would have slain the dragon. In that hesitant moment, the dragon killed your father. You, Frost, are what the dragons failed to consider. I'm sure they would have gathered up the sword and destroyed it had you not attacked. But now, we have cold blue steel that can end the Dragonshade nightmare and change the destiny of our world."

Frost looked into the fire for a long moment before speaking. "You didn't try to stop me from attacking the dragon because you knew what was at stake." His gaze shifted from the fire to Cirrus.

Cirrus looked away. "Yes, my king. I knew, if the dragon destroyed the blade, we were all as good as dead anyway."

Silence fell, broken only by the cawing of distant crows and vultures gathering on the field, and the crackling of the small fire.

Ty chuckled half-hearted and said, "Well, at least you're a good shot, Frost. Saving the world … that could take some time."

Frost looked east with tears in his eyes. "My mother was in the castle."

Tears rose into Ty's eyes. He buried his face in his cloak. Cirrus lowered his head and nodded. Frost lay down and closed his eyes. Ty put his hand on his friend's shoulder.

Cirrus watched over his former students and spoke to himself, "Rest now boys, for tomorrow you must be men."

2. The child Vigo

efore the birth of Prince Fredris "Frost" Olan, half a world away in a land called Redim, a boy named Vigo lived in a small farming village. Different than the other children of the village, Vigo was born a wizard. Villagers worked long hours every day to feed the livestock in preparation for the yearly offering demanded by the dragons. Vigo, who was tall for his age, lacked the muscle for most of the work.

He served an important role for the village, however, after his father broke his leg. Village men had carried Vigo's father into the house from the pasture and laid him in the bed. Wanting to help, Vigo simply touched his father's leg—there was a flash of light— and his father was healed.

In the years following that incident, Vigo honed his skill as a magical healer to the inestimable benefit of both the villagers and their livestock. In the land of Redim, wizardry was forbidden, and any child born with the magical gifts was put to death, so Vigo's talent was kept a secret from all outsiders.

Vigo's village was encircled by a wall that stretched all the way to the northern sea. One morning, he perched on one of the shorter sections of the wall, a favorite spot to watch workers in the fields to the south. His father, Arthur, had told him that the village was once a great city called Tenir, and that the northern water was actually an inland sea that stretched to the eastern ocean of Redim. Tenir had boasted one of the most prosperous ports in all the land but was destroyed when the dragons came centuries earlier. The sea itself was no longer usable for travel, nor as a source of food; it was putrid and filled with horrible creatures. Therefore, the farming village was concentrated in the southernmost region of the old wall. The fields and pastures lay south of the wall. Some still insisted on calling the village Tenir, but most could not, or did not want to, remember.

With long black hair and a slight figure, Vigo resembled a girl, a very tall nine-year-old, having reached the height of many of the men. His height did not stop the other children from taunting him whenever possible.

"Gonna start growin' bosoms soon, aren't ya tall girl?" yelled one of the mean children from outside the wall.

Vigo glanced down to see a boy with a shovel, his hands bloody from field work. Vigo looked at his own hands—completely unmarked by labor—and quickly looked away. He understood why the other children hated him. He did not have to work like they did, and they felt it unfair.

"Well?" The insistent boy on the ground yelled again.

A sudden idea popped into Vigo's head, *Maybe I could incinerate him with a thought.*

A trickle of blood ran down the boy's palm on his wooden shovel handle. Vigo stood up and shaped his hands as if he held a ball. Between his fingers, light glowed and became a sphere of energy, which, without warning, he threw at the boy.

The boy flinched when the light struck him. In an instant, his bleeding hands were healed. The boy looked down at his palms in wonder. Many emotions flashed across his face. He couldn't decide what to say or do.

Finally, the boy looked up at Vigo and said, "Bah." Then he turned and tramped into the village.

Just as a self-satisfied smile began to emerge on his lean face, the voice of his father rang out. "Vigo! *Viiigo!*" From the tone, it was clear he had angered his father. He jumped down and ran to his home.

Arthur stood in the doorway, his arms folded across his barrel chest. He scowled at his son—not *down* at him, because Vigo already nearly matched his height; nevertheless, his father's gaze made Vigo feel small and helpless.

"Vigo, you must never show your powers in the open. If anyone from the outlands were to see, they would surely report you to the lords."

"I'm sorry father."

"Get inside and eat your supper before I decide to give you a reason to heal yourself."

Vigo obeyed. He knew his father would indeed hurt him, as he had done before on several occasions. Vigo did not question any beating; they were for his own good. The village itself could be destroyed for harboring and raising a wizard. He knew that some of the families in the village were already of the opinion that turning in Vigo would profit them greatly. It was only his father's brute force that convinced them otherwise.

Supper was mostly a silent affair, only the sounds of slurping as the three ate what little soup they had. But then, just at sundown, there came a knock at the door. Vigo looked up from his bowl, feeling a terrible misgiving. He always feared that one day, the rest of the village would band together and take him. Was tonight the night?

Arthur stood and went to the door. There was no mob, only a single man holding something small and wrapped in cloth for Arthur. With a short glance to Vigo then back to Arthur, the man departed. For a time, Arthur just stood at the door looking down at the package without opening it. Then he returned to the table, slipping the object into a pouch on his belt.

Silence fell again. Slurping slowly continued. Arthur finished his soup and folded his hands on the table. He regarded his son with an impassive look Vigo could not decipher. "So young," he muttered.

"So young for what?" Vigo was a very intelligent boy. He knew something was amiss. "Does that bundle have something to do with me?"

"Your display of magic today will not have mattered, my son," Arthur said with resignation. "The time has come."

Vigo opened his mouth to ask questions, but his father put up a hand to silence him.

"You well know of the sickness that burned through the livestock this past year. It was worse than anyone could have predicted. The few you were able to restore with your … your gift … it was not enough. Only a fraction of the herd survived."

Across the table, Vigo's mother put her hands over her eyes.

Arthur continued, "The portion that remain are too few to satisfy the dragons. Our village will be destroyed."

"We can escape—all of us!" Vigo cried, nearly knocking over his empty bowl with the sudden passion he felt.

"The men of the village discussed running away, but we have nowhere to go. To the south lies the undead bloodtree forest that would consume us all. To the north and west lies the poison sea, and to the east are impassible mountains. It is true that the lords of the land live in those mountains, but if we were to ask for protection, they would offer *us* as tribute to the dragons in exchange for their own wretched hides. No, there is no escape, not for all of us."

"What are you saying, father?"

"There is only escape for you, my son. You are a wizard, and you could change the world. You must survive and grow strong, for someday you must end the tyranny of the dragons."

"How can I do such a thing in a land that would destroy me for being who I am?" Tears began to form in the young boy's eyes.

"From what few books I've been able to study, you know about the expansive trade conducted in the port city of Tenir long ago. There were great wizards throughout Redim and the world of Ashyer. The greatest of these used crystals to channel and amplify their power. About a month ago, digging inside the wall, we found just such a crystal." Arthur reached into his pouch and produced the bundle. He slowly unwrapped a small, ten-sided red crystal. "Hold out your hand."

Vigo did as his father bid. Arthur placed the crystal in his palm. At once, it began to glow. Then, it began to *float*. It was longer than wide, like a dial, and it began to spin slowly, an inch above his palm. Vigo could feel it connect to the magic inside himself.

Raising eyebrows, Arthur said, "It is true then. This is a crystal of power. It seems it will work for you quite well, however, you cannot take the chance of losing it. I am sorry, Vigo, but we will have to place it inside your body."

Vigo withdrew his hand quickly and the crystal dropped to the table. His father scooped it up.

"Don't worry, my son. It will only hurt momentarily, then you can close the wound."

Arthur produced a knife from his belt and grabbed Vigo's arm. "Hold steady now."

Arthur made a cut just below the inside of the boy's right elbow, not too close to the wrist. He then slid the crystal inside the wound. Vigo felt a surge of power in his body. His eyes felt hot. He heard his mother gasp. Almost immediately the wound began to knit itself up and vanished without so much as a white scar. Then Arthur shifted his gaze to his son's face. A wide white flame rose from the bottom lid of each of his son's eyes, crawled up his forehead, and flickered above his hairline in two wavering streams.

"Spellfire." Arthur's hushed voice was barely a whisper. "I thought it was a myth. You will be powerful indeed, my son."

Vigo closed his eyes and the two small fires winked out. "I feel so tired," he whispered.

"Rest now," Arthur said as he wiped off the knife and put it away. "Tomorrow is our last day together, for the dragons come at nightfall. They are never late, and we must prepare you for your journey."

Vigo's strong, stout father—such a contrast to his lanky son— carried the boy in his arms to a bunk. Vigo frowned, but his eyes remained shut as he nodded to sleep. He awoke the next morning with an odd headache. His eyeballs hurt, eyes that had burned white-hot the evening before with a heat that should have melted them. Slowly, the events of the night before swam to the front of his mind.

Unusual sounds issued from all directions—inside the house, slamming and sharpening, and outside the ring of steel. Vigo slipped out of his bunk and into the small common room where he found his father honing the edge of a sword.

"I can't wield that. I haven't the strength, father."

Arthur looked up at him for a moment and went back to sharpening, "This is for me. The dagger on the table is for you. I will be staying here with the rest of the village. If Tenir is to fall again, we're taking one of those bastard dragons with us."

Vigo realized the sounds from outside must be the other villagers preparing to fight. "Why don't you come with me father? Together we stand a better chance of success."

"Together we stand a better chance of being spotted and killed. No, I will stay and make sure there is nothing for the lords to rummage through. If successful, the dragon will explode when we kill it and nothing will remain. Your escape will be complete. Besides, I'm the only one in the village who actually has the nerve to attack a dragon. If left to the rest of these cowards, the people would be harvested for food."

"I'm afraid father." Vigo's gaze dropped to the floor, feeling ashamed to admit as much to this man who was preparing to face a dragon head-on knowing it will be his death.

"Don't you think I am? Use that fear son. It will keep you alive." Satisfied with the edge on his sword, Arthur stopped sharpening and turned his full attention to his son. "I want you to leave this afternoon. Head east toward the mountains. Find some cover in the small woods. It's not far. There you can see if we are successful in slaying the dragon. If we are not, you are in greater danger and that you must know. Always remember, the more intelligence you have, the better your advantage. If we slay the foul bastard, head toward the mountains. There, you must gain entry to the lords' keep. Infiltrating undetected would be best, but you could pretend to be a kitchen slave if needed. There will be old books of learning held within. There, you can start your studies in secret. If you need to steal to survive, do it. If you must kill to survive, do it. There is so much more at stake than your morals." He paused for a moment, then said in a more reflective tone, "I never wanted a life of toil for you, but I did not want this hardship thrust upon you either. I love you, my son. Avenge my death and destroy the dragons for the good of all Ashyer."

Vigo's mother emerged with a small bag filled with journey provisions and fixed it to his back. Arthur attached the dagger to his son's belt, and his mother produced a black cloak with a green interior. She turned the inside out and draped it from his shoulders. The green side would hide him in the day, and the black at night. The cloak hung down to Vigo's ankles.

"You were to be older when we finally gave this to you, but the time is upon us whether we wish it or not," Arthur told his son. Then, he embraced the boy for the last time, hugging him so tightly, Vigo felt the air being squeezed from his lungs. Vigo was about to start gasping for breath when his father released him, took up his own sword and walked purposefully out of the house. Vigo's mother embraced him, less roughly, and started to weep. The boy just stared blankly at the door where his father had gone from his life.

Vigo left his small home and walked the streets of the village. No one spoke. Everyone wore grave expressions as they went about their respective tasks. Vigo felt even more an outcast in his own village. From this day forward, he would be a stranger wherever he went. Tears threatened to run freely. As the sun started its slow decline in the afternoon hours, Vigo left Tenir and began his journey east.

It took only two hours to reach the small woods to the east of the village. There, Vigo rested with his back against a tree deep enough within the woods to not be seen, but near enough the edge to provide a clear view of the distant village. The weight of the situation suddenly hit him, and he began to weep again. He could no longer hear the men readying for battle. Only the birds of the forest kept him company. When he would sit on the wall in the village, he always wanted to venture to these woods and feel their embrace, thinking the trees would keep him company. But in reality, he was alone. There was no peace for him as he drifted into sleep.

night had fallen while he slept. *Crack*! The sound woke him from troubled dreams. He knew the sound—it was a dragon approaching. A sick yellow moon filled the sky. Silhouetted against it, a dragon slowly descended toward the village, soon landing. The dragon no doubt expected to be greeted with the usual offering; but even from a distance Vigo could tell something was different.

The dragon began roaring curses that carried to Vigo's ears. It became enraged, then exploded with a concussive fire blast that shook all the trees around the watching boy. He could even feel the heat from the distant blast. It was over.

Something landed in the grass about twenty feet in front of him, just at the edge of the forest. He knew he should lay low as to not be spotted, but he had to know what had fallen from the explosion. He flipped the cloak to the black side for night, and crept out to the debris, grass all around singed. Vigo discovered a dragon's scale, reddish-black in color, about the width of the boy's head. He picked it up and quickly combed the grass to leave no trace. He ran back into the forest for cover and sat by his tree, turning the scale over and over. It was light but hard, possibly as hard as steel. Perhaps harder? He did not know. Anger boiled within him. He looked toward the ruined village and felt his eyes burning. The trees around him were illuminated by white flames issuing from his eyes and burning tall—the Spellfire his father mentioned the night before. He had to make it stop, his burning white eyes were surely visible from a great distance. He shut his eyes and concentrated. After a moment, the burning sensation dissipated. He opened his eyes. The glow was gone.

Crack! The sound made him jump. *Another dragon must be approaching!* He thought. He slid the scale under his tunic and lay flat in the undergrowth. A dragon swooped low over the wreckage of the village and turned in his direction. *Could it know? Can it smell me?* It was too late to do anything. The dragon was fast. It passed over him in seconds and flew to the east. *What can it be up to?* He wondered. He had to know.

For a second time he left the cover of the forest to look over the tops of the distant trees toward the eastern mountains. Then it all made sense. The dragon had attacked the mountain keep. The people of the lords' village had slain the dragon's kin. This was retribution. Vigo watched as the distant towers and walls were bathed again and again in Dragonshade. The mountain glowed. After several minutes of attack, the dragon flew into the sky, back toward the wretched moon.

Now what? Vigo asked himself. He looked from the burning remains of the village to the blazing mountain. He considered for a moment. There was nothing left in the village, but perhaps there would be something of value left at the mountain. It was at least a day's journey, but what was the alternative? The trees to the south? He had never seen a blood tree, but he knew they were always thirsty and would drink him dry. No, he would continue to the mountain as soon as dawn arrived. He sat by his tree again and watched as the fire in the village burned itself out.

The next morning, Vigo took one last look in the direction of the smoldering remains of his life and began his trek into the forest. After a few severe tumbles in the undergrowth, he realized that being raised in a farming village had not prepared him for the rigors of the wild woods.

Traversing the "small" woods turned out to be no small task. From time to time, he was able to glimpse the distant mountains through clearings in the trees, but each time, they seemed no closer. Indeed, after the first day of the treacherous hike, he thought he would never see the end of the forest.

He stopped for the night in the driest spot he could find. There he was able to examine his battered body. Despite his slim form, Vigo felt that he must have bumped every tree and thorn bush in his path. His limbs were covered in cuts and bruises. He closed his eyes and concentrated while passing his hands over the injuries slowly, healing them all. The job of healing was complete, the pain gone; he was almost too tired to breathe but forced himself to eat a small amount of the rations in his sack before passing out just as the sickly yellow moon began to rise.

He awoke still tired, but with a new idea. Perhaps the crystal could help him fly? He rolled up his sleeve and gazed at his inner right forearm, concentrating all his will on the idea of flight. Suddenly, his arm burst into white flame and rocketed straight up. The arm pulled Vigo, as if by an invisible giant, above the tree line, where he hung for a few seconds before panicking. His concentration broken, the fire went out and his body crashed down through the trees with several loud cracks until he collided with the forest floor.

Vigo opened his eyes. He had broken both legs and one arm. He blocked the pain as much as he could and concentrated his healing magic, first on the arm then on his legs. *What a foolish thing to have done. I could have been killed. I hope I was not seen.*

As chance would have it, he had been seen, by a small girl hiding in a tree a half-mile to the south. She was shocked to see the figure of a boy shoot into the sky with a burning arm, then fall like a rock. The girl in the tree had been tracking the thrashing noises from the north all the previous day and was now sure that the flying boy was heading to the mountains. The girl in the tree decided to stay quiet and track the flying boy to their common destination.

After tending to his serious injuries, Vigo was exhausted. He spent most of the day after his first flight napping. If it were not for the loud snoring, the girl might have thought him dead from the impact. When night came, Vigo decided to practice flight again. This time he concentrated on gently floating. His body rose a few inches off the ground and hovered. Heartened by this accomplishment, Vigo focused on moving forward. His body started to move slowly eastward. This accomplishment made Vigo's heart leap. Unfortunately, the spike in emotion amplified his magic and Vigo was propelled forward at great speed into the trunk of a particularly large tree. On the ground and bruised again, Vigo decided to call it a night. *Tomorrow I will pay more attention.*

The next morning, the girl in the tree could tell the flying boy was moving because she could hear faint noises of parting branches, but the progress was at greater speed and with much stealth. She tracked her quarry as fast as she could.

Vigo had risen early and practiced flying. He found that concentration and emotional control were all he needed. He could now float in any direction easily, so he resumed his trek to the mountains brushing against only the smallest of branches where his flight path was too narrow to steer clear.

By the end of the day, both children had reached the base of the mountains. Vigo decided to rest until morning, since floating with magic proved just as exhausting as the other magics.

The girl saw Vigo emerge midflight from the dense woods—his speed and relative silence now made sense to her. She decided this was going to be her only chance to catch the flying boy; if he went up the mountains using flight, she would never catch him. Now was the time to make an introduction.

Vigo was about to nod off when he heard footsteps approaching from the south. He stood and pulled the dagger from his belt. A moment later, a girl came into view. Covered with leaves and forest debris, she was shorter than Vigo. He noticed she had beautiful golden hair. Vigo guessed she was no older than he; more likely a year or two younger.

"My name is Victoria," said the girl, "I have been following you through the woods. I'm sorry if I startled you."

A sweet and kind voice, Vigo thought, but he could not take chances. "Why are you following me?" Vigo raised his dagger.

Victoria stopped. "You seem to be the only other survivor of the attacks the other night. I am … I was a kitchen slave in the keep. I know my way around, so my masters sent me to gather mushrooms in the forest the night the dragons came. I was going to return to see if anything was left of my home when I heard you. What is your name?"

Vigo lowered his dagger. "My name is Vigo. I am also going to the keep to see if there are any survivors."

"Shall we go together in the morning?" Victoria asked. "I know where the stairs are."

Vigo thought for a long moment. "Very well. Know this, Victoria, I am a powerful warrior and will not tolerate betrayal."

"You mean you are a powerful wizard." Victoria smiled.

Vigo was shocked. "How—"

"Don't worry—I think magic is amazing. I saw you float out of the forest a few minutes ago. Only a powerful wizard could have done that."

"You don't blame me for the dragon attack then?" Vigo frowned.

"I don't know why the dragons do the terrible things they do, but I had no family up there, only owners. As far as I'm concerned, those monsters did me a favor." Victoria's eyebrows furrowed, an involuntary gesture that unsettled Vigo. He got the impression that she took some pleasure in the wholesale burning of the keep. And it occurred to him then that his life in the village—sometimes taunted by his peers, mostly ignored—was perhaps not so bad after all.

Vigo couldn't help giving the girl a half smile. He believed her, but the thought of his village consumed by the explosion quickly wiped the smile away.

"I'm very tired." Victoria said. "I don't know if you have some kind of wizard alarm, but I can sleep without a guard if you don't. I am pretty sure we are the only two around here anyway."

"No alarm. I need rest too. But stop calling me wizard. You know what they do to wizards."

"Sure, okay Vigo. I don't think there is a *they* anymore, but you're right. You must be cautious." Victoria sat down, leaning back against a wide oak tree.

Vigo nodded and settled back where he had almost fallen asleep before the girl appeared. Before long, both children were fast asleep.

In the morning, Vigo was awake first. He considered leaving Victoria behind, but then reasoned that the girl might be useful.

Victoria had lived in the keep, so she must know some of its secrets. Also, he found something intriguing about her—this child whose life and experiences were so foreign to his own—and the thought of leaving her behind made Vigo feel ashamed and a little sick. He started to rummage through his supplies.

"Mushroom?" Victoria said.

Surprised, Vigo spun around.

"You're jumpy. Sorry, after seeing dragons I'm always on edge too." Victoria smiled.

"No thank you." Vigo pulled some bread out of his bag.

"Suit yourself." Victoria shrugged and started munching on a large mushroom. She watched Vigo eat. He seemed sad and distant. "Do you come from the keep too? I don't remember you."

"The village, my family …"

Victoria's face darkened. "Sorry. I heard the blast. I didn't think anyone made it out."

"I was already out when it happened." Vigo stared at the bread.

"Someday Vigo," she said, her voice tense and serious, "someday, we will put an end to the dragons." Vigo smiled wide. The smile made Victoria feel a little uneasy; there was more than a little bloodlust in that smile. She took a deep breath and said, "To the stairs?"

"Lead on."

The two climbed the base of the mountain. After an hour climbing, Victoria pointed ahead. "There!" Before them, carved from the face of the cliff, stone stairs wound upward to the blackened keep above.

Climbing the stairs took almost two hours, but when they reached the top, Vigo could see the entire forest below. He had never seen such a beautiful sight. In an instant he knew why the lords preferred to live so high in the air. Then he spotted the black crater in the distance that was his village and again he quietly spilled tears until his eyes burned and he looked away to examine the keep. Victoria was already at the front gate. The doors were completely destroyed, and the flat stone walls were scorched.

"Hello?" Victoria called. Vigo waited. After a few more greeting calls were met with no response, Victoria looked back at Vigo and shrugged her shoulders. "Should we go in?"

Vigo nodded and joined her. The two entered the main courtyard where they saw several mangled bodies strewn around piles of wreckage and debris. The smell of burnt flesh made Vigo's gorge rise, but he felt self-conscious at the thought of vomiting in front of the girl and held it down. The doors and windows of the inner structure were all destroyed. Wood still smoldered, but the major fires had all burnt themselves out. They went to the main door and Victoria called out. Again, only silence answered.

The two began a careful search of the keep, moving from room to room, looking for survivors. They found only the dead. When they arrived in the kitchen, Victoria paused beside the corpse of a burned woman lying face down near the ovens. It was not fire from the ovens that had consumed her flesh.

"She was always nice to me," Victoria said, the first time she'd shown any emotion other than gratification that the keep had been destroyed. Vigo put an arm around her. Contact made her jump and draw back. Again, he wondered what cruelties the young girl must have known in her short life. She flashed an apologetic smile at him, silently communicating that she had not intended to convey fear or disgust of him. She put her head against his shoulder and accepted his comforting pats on her back—human affection that she was likely not well accustomed to. They continued their search.

By day's end, satisfied the keep was empty, Victoria broke open the stone protected lower vaults and found food provisions undamaged. The supply could last two children years if properly managed. Then, Victoria broke the lock on a lower trap door in the vaults. "You will have to go first here Vigo. I'm too scared."

Vigo looked frightened too. "What's down there?"

"I don't know. This is the secret vault where the lords stored all the things they weren't supposed to have. Some of the other slaves said it was magically cursed by the lords to protect it. I don't know anything about magic."

Vigo's face changed. He looked almost happy. "I will go alone. Stay here."

"Fine with me." Victoria took a few steps back.

Vigo thought, *light*, and his hand glowed white. This show of power caused Victoria to back away further.

Vigo aimed his palm down below the trap door. There was a ladder. He got on his knees, swung himself down onto it, and disappeared into the hole. At the bottom, Vigo aimed his hand around, directing the light like a bullseye lantern around a dank storage room lined with bookshelves sagging under the weight of precious tomes. Some of the books looked rotten, but many were still sound. He walked deeper into the room. He noticed books about magic, history, and lineage. At the end of the room sat a table piled high with objects. Many looked valuable but not useful. As Vigo investigated closer, he noticed containers for creating potions and a forge for enchanting. Indeed, he had discovered the treasure he was hoping for. He grabbed one of the larger rubies on the table and returned to the ladder.

Vigo emerged from the trap door. Victoria rushed over to help him out. "Any curses?"

"Nope." Vigo handed Victoria the ruby. "Magical stuff for me, and riches for you." Vigo thought Victoria's eyes were going to fall out of her head as she gaped at the ruby. He found her expression so funny, he laughed for the first time in many days.

That night, the two gorged themselves on delicacies they had before only dreamt about. The food, reserved for the lords, was the best to be found in the keep. After their banquet, they discussed what they would do next.

"I intend on studying," Vigo said. "There are hundreds of books down there. I will read all in which the pages still turn."

"I can't read, so have at it," Victoria said, "I think I will try working on making swords and armor. I want to be a knight."

"Perhaps we should only burn small, hidden fires at night." Vigo suggested, "We want to go unnoticed up here. We may be the new lords of this keep, but people are bound to find us after enough time passes."

"We should set traps," Victoria suggested, "Leave the doors destroyed so the place stays uninviting; but we must set snares at all the entryways."

"Then maybe I should work on magical traps first. I can reinforce your trail craft with magic."

Victoria considered. "When winter comes, it will be cold up here. Perhaps we need to find a way to warm the lower vault by magic first?"

Vigo nodded. "You're right. That first, then traps." Vigo shifted uncomfortably, "All right, I have to get rid of this thing." He reached under his shirt and produced the dragon's scale and plopped it on the floor.

"Is that what I think it is?" Victoria's eyes were wide again.

"If you think it is a scale from one of those fire breathing bastards, then yes."

"Can I have it?" Victoria looked excited.

"Why?"

"I want to … I don't know … study it, I guess. Figure out what makes it so strong. I mean, can you imagine armor made from whatever that stuff is?"

Vigo smiled at the idea of a kitchen slave, this little girl, undertaking such a task. "Have at it then. Good luck."

Victoria frowned. "I can do it. You're not the only great thinker person here."

Vigo laughed, and Victoria pretended to be offended. Before long, both were laughing themselves to sleep.

3. Vigo the Wizard, and the Black Knight

igo and Victoria began work immediately. Together, they laid traps and commenced their studies. Vigo spent most of his days cleaning the lower chamber and reading. After a time, he moved all the useless treasure out of the room and created a wizard's laboratory. As planned, he first studied permanent enchantment to heat the lower level of the keep during the coming winter. Victoria thought they would freeze to death as the days got colder and no spells were being cast, but when the first days of winter arrived, Vigo cast a permanent charm on the walls of the vault that radiated an exact temperature. He explained that the stone would do so in the summer as well; the constant temperature would be cooler in contrast.

Victoria returned to kitchen duty. She moved the useful equipment to the lower level and created a new kitchen. Then, she inventoried their supplies. There were a few items that needed to be refreshed from time to time, but she could acquire them down in the forest.

Perusing the books of magic, Vigo found he had an innate gift for research and scholarship. Not yet ten years old, he found himself quickly mastering concepts that had proved challenging for students twice his age.

Vigo learned the art of magical traps and set them in early winter. He gave Victoria a charm that allowed her to pass through without harm. Victoria unintentionally tested the traps only once. Pursued by a fierce bear back to the keep after gathering supplies in the forest, Victoria sprinted through the opening in the wall where doors once stood; the bear was roasted by magical flame as it entered. That night, Vigo and Victoria agreed that bear meat was not so tasty.

Years passed. Victoria began to feel conflicting emotions about her friend. She was sure a feeling of affection—what adults called love—was growing between them. But it came with an equal measure of loneliness. Vigo spent more and more time in his lab. Victoria learned it could be dangerous to disturb him. One night, while investigating strange noises, Victoria crept toward the ominous whirring sounds that issued from the trap door and poked her head in.

"Hey Vigo," she started to say. Then there was a magical explosion that almost completely burned her long golden hair. Despite Vigo's assertion, Victoria believed even more thereafter that the room was cursed.

Vigo started to ignore her. Victoria began to daydream about leaving for parts more populous, but the image of an isolated and lonely Vigo pulled at her heart and would not leave her mind, so she studied armor and swordsmanship to occupy her time.

She became skilled at making armor after a few years of tinkering. It was then she returned to the dragon scale. Piece by piece, she started to chip away at it. When Vigo heard the strange noises, he came to investigate.

"You'll never figure it out that way," he told her. "Wait here." Vigo disappeared into his lab in an excited manner Victoria had not seen in years. He reemerged with a floating box in tow. "Here. Some proper equipment for you," he said with a genuine smile.

He gave her magnifying lenses on stands with tiny tools. Victoria set up the examination equipment at one of her worktables and continued chipping at the relic. The lenses allowed her to see the various intersections of materials in the scale, and the tools allowed her to extract each piece individually.

Months of toil later, Victoria discovered tiny black flakes of a metal-like material that held the outer plate together. The material was stronger than steel but lightweight.

Vigo reminded her about the dragon that exploded in his village. There would be tons of scales there, if time had been good to them. He knew no one had occupied the village since that fateful night, because almost every night he stood on the ruined upper floors and looked out empty windows toward his destroyed childhood home.

Victoria began salvaging immediately. It took her weeks, but she gathered every scale she could find, and brought them back to her shop. There, she started the work of extracting the dragon metal from the scales. When she could stand the tedious work no longer, she studied her other passion. She learned to read the training manuals for swordsmanship and erected combat dummies. Using an old sword Vigo found in the lower vault, she practiced until she was sore.

Vigo had moved on from the greater conjuring spells and started to work on enchantments again. From time to time, he picked up the history books and pored over the pages with wonder.

"Did you know there were once bird-women that people called angels?" Vigo asked one night at supper.

"Think I heard a fairy tale once," Victoria said absently.

"Three races—Angels, Immortals, and Giants. That's all there were to begin with."

Victoria stopped chewing and looked up. "That's just superstition. Some people live longer than others, and people give birth to people."

Vigo frowned and continued eating. Sometimes he hated her. He had no apprentice for proper learning. Victoria was smart, and remarkably creative, but infuriatingly narrowminded as far as he was concerned.

Vigo had grown well past six feet but remained lean and lanky. He didn't get much physical exercise and ate at infrequent intervals. He would remain engrossed in his studies until he could no longer ignore the disruptive hunger pangs from his body. Sometimes, he would eat to appease Victoria, who would periodically hound him about his absence from supper. Dining together was one routine they kept from their very first night, even if they simply ate in silence—or one-sided silence, Victoria sharing her day, trying to break in on Vigo's preoccupied thoughts.

Victoria was still much shorter than him, the average height of a woman, but she was incredibly strong. The hours of labor and practice made her a formidable fighter. Indeed, Vigo knew she could easily best him in any physical competition. Only in magic did he have mastery. She had also begun to look less like a girl and more like a woman—a change that he did his best to not notice. He considered her maturity another distraction from his purpose, like food, like sleep, like any of the little pleasures or comforts life could offer. He found pleasure, great, unbridled joy, in mastering the aspects of magic, gaining ever more control over the unpredictable chaos of the world.

Despite their differences, the two companions stayed together in the keep, leading their separate lives. They still, at times, found common cause. Vigo had been studying the magic of change and wanted to try it on something difficult. At supper, Victoria mentioned that she had nearly completed the task of extracting metal from the dragon scales, but she didn't know what to do next as it could not be pounded or melted. Vigo asked for a sample and told Victoria to design whatever it was she wanted to use the metal for.

After many months, both finished their work. Vigo learned to manipulate the metal with magic, and Victoria finally finished designing a suit of impenetrable armor. Her design required Vigo to fashion the metal into thin interlocking strips no wider than one inch, each strip capable of sliding up and down as well as flexing on hinges. The result would be a head-to-toe plate of armor that covered even her eyelids by attaching to her lashes with tiny hooks. When she closed her mouth and eyes, the dragon armor could not be pierced. Vigo was very impressed with Victoria's specifications and began work at once.

"It will look beautiful on you," Vigo said with a blush. Though magic was seductive, he could not help but notice how alluring she had become.

To Victoria's dismay, Vigo took an entire year to create her armor. He'd done more than just create the design, however, he'd improved it. On the day he finished, he handed Victoria a long, thick-chained necklace with a large pendant the color of ebony.

"What?" Victoria asked, bewildered that he had promised a suit of armor but was handing her a piece of jewelry.

Vigo grinned. "Put it on and press the side of the pendant."

The chain fit perfect. Victoria pressed a tiny button. Narrow plates extended out from the neckpiece and like black curtains covered her chest before flowing down her arms and legs, ultimately covering her feet and hands.

"Now press the other side."

Victoria flexed her arm, experiencing the exquisite sensation of dragon armor, and touched the opposite side of the neckpiece. Plates extended upward, forming a helmet that covered her face and head. The armor featured dragon wings protruding upward from the helmet.

"One more surprise," Vigo said. "Press your thumbs to your palms."

Victoria did so. A strange sensation flowed down her body. The weight of the heavy neckpiece transferred into her hands. She looked down and saw a sword made of dragon metal forming in each hand. Both swords were attached to the armor, but the blades had firm hilts as well. She stood in shining black armor more beautiful and deadlier than any ever before forged by humankind.

"You are the Black Knight!" Vigo said triumphantly.

"It is ... unbelievable," Victoria managed to say.

"I know," Vigo said, staring at her with unguarded admiration. He began to blush and quickly turned, returning to his lab.

Victoria spent the next few days admiring the armor and using the swords to destroy the combat dummies.

till more years passed. Using the marvelous suit, Victoria became a master sword wielder. When it became impossible to further her skills by smashing more practice dummies, she began making overnight excursions to the nearest traveling routes where she intentionally ran into highwaymen and bandits—a helpless young maiden lost in the wilderness. As soon as their evil intentions became clear, the armor, with its deadly stingers, would blossom from her magic pendant. But she found these real encounters to be nearly as one-sided as fighting training dummies stuffed with straw. Her armor was meant for far more formidable foes.

With the passage of time, Vigo became ever more secretive about his studies. Late at night, Victoria could hear strange chanting coming from the lower chamber. Sometimes the keep thrummed with unknown power.

Together, and with trepidation, the couple watched the death moon come and go. Every year, the sick yellow orb drew close, then retreated. Once a dragon circled their keep. They agreed that the best course of action was to hide. Vigo was certain that Victoria's armor could deflect dragon fire, but inside the suit, Victoria would be cooked like meat for the evening meal. For her part, Victoria wondered if Vigo would actually eat her if she were roasted. Vigo became more and more isolated, and cruel in his manner. The changes occurred slowly, but she could tell. Her loyalty to Vigo grew strained, and the voice of love in her heart began to wane.

After two decades since their first night in the keep—the night they feasted and began a new life together as the lords of nothing—Victoria decided to move on. Vigo had not spoken about plans to raise an army, or any plan for that matter, yet he had claimed he wanted to destroy the dragons.

One night at supper, everything changed—the same night, coincidentally, and unbeknownst to them, that Xan Olan was consumed by Dragonshade half a world away. Vigo and Victoria were eating their nightly meal in brittle silence when Victoria looked up at Vigo, ready to broach the subject of departure, when she noticed Vigo's eyes. Dark and sunken, in the center of each pupil she noticed a faint white glow.

"Your eyes Vigo, they—"

"It's nothing." Vigo stared at Victoria for a long moment. "We should start our journey, Victoria."

Victoria's face brightened. "Our journey? I was just about to—"

Vigo unrolled a large map on the table. "I have pieced this together from my study of the histories. It is a map of the land of Redim." He began to point at different places on the large scroll. "We are here, in Tenir Keep on these mountains. To our north lies the putrid sea, which we cannot cross, we must, however, go north. The books I have studied mention an ancient city—the seat of power in these lands. The Castle Redim was located in the northeast tip of the continent—here." He pointed. "The sea cuts the land in half, but to our southwest, it narrows to a river. There we will cross into the desert land and travel north around the western edge of the inland sea. Then we turn east. We must begin by traveling south through the realm of the blood trees. Beyond the trees lies a castle carved into the side of a mountain, and a city called Acamea. Whether anyone still lives there, I do not know. But our ultimate goal is the ruin of Castle Redim. In Acamea, there might be another option…"

"Will we find something in the northern ruins to help us destroy dragons?"

Vigo smiled. "Long ago, when the dragons first arrived, the land of Redim conducted commerce with them. The tower of Redim had a floating bridge that permitted sky-travelers from Ashyer to visit the dragons once every year. If the bridge still exists—one text tells of the dragons' attempt to destroy it, to no avail—we can use it. The attempt to destroy the bridge led to a war between the worlds. The dragons abandoned their plan to destroy the bridge and instead laid waste to the castle and all of its inhabitants."

After pondering Vigo's disclosure for a moment, Victoria asked, "Should we raise an army to follow us?"

"Perhaps, once we have taken back Castle Redim. You see, If we were to march with an army, the dragons would hunt us at every turn, and a grand target we would be."

While they studied the map, a strange noise came from outside the keep, growing in volume.

Vigo's head snapped up. "What is that?"

"It sounds like people—lots of people. The villagers must have climbed the mountain." She frowned. "Oh no."

"Villagers?"

"They've been living in the forest and farming the old village land for years now. Have you never noticed them as you walked the upper levels?"

"No. I've been too lost in thought."

Taken aback, Victoria asked, "For years? That's a lot of thinking."

Vigo started to smile ruefully, but the emotion was interrupted by the sound of an explosion. One of the old magical traps had been triggered. A roar of fear and anger went up from the people above.

"We'd better get up there," Victoria said, activating her armor. Vigo went to the corner and grabbed a black metal pole carved with strange runes, slightly taller than himself. He also pulled a hooded black cloak over his head. Dragon metal plates, similar to her armor, were fastened to the cloth in tight patterns. Victoria then realized that the pole was also dragon metal. "Had extra material?" She smiled.

"Just a little. Let's go see what the angry mob wants. Probably our heads."

The two climbed the vault steps into the main keep. Outside, they could see the flicker of torches. At the main door to the courtyard stood roughly fifty men and women. *They brought the women too; this must be serious*, Victoria thought. The group fell silent at the sight of the two black clad strangers.

"What can I do for you good people?" Victoria shouted.

"Give us the vampire!" One of the men shouted.

"Vampire?" Victoria was a little amused.

"The vampire who plagues these lands, kills our children, and poisons the sea!" a voice shouted back. "We have seen the lights up here for years. We have seen you before—the Black Knight who guards the vampire. You stand on the walls, looking down on us, and in the still of the night you come to the village and kill our children!"

Victoria was about to laugh when she felt Vigo's hand on her shoulder.

Vigo spoke with a magically magnified voice, "I am your vampire." Vigo stepped in front of Victoria and raised the pole. "You have come to destroy me, but I will allow you to leave safely. I am not a vampire, but I am a dangerous creature, even more rare in these lands—a wizard." The pole began to glow intensely. "Now I am afraid that, for your own good, I must erase all of your memories. If you return to this keep in aimless wandering, you will find it empty. I do not wish for you fools to become a target of the dragons; I wish to liberate this world from them!"

Beams of light shot from the staff and struck most of the villagers, causing them to relax and become unfocused. The few who were not struck grew enraged and began throwing torches into the keep. Victoria pulled Vigo to safety as he cried, "Idiots! Why would you do such things? Ignorant fools, don't you understand I am your only hope?"

"Let them go," Victoria hissed through her armor. "They are ignorant, but it is not their fault. Perhaps it is ours. We could have guided them all these years, but instead I ignored them. It does not matter. The upper keep will burn; but we are leaving. Let's descend into the safety of the lower keep and prepare for our journey."

While they scurried to the lower level of the keep, the remnants that had survived Dragonshade two decades earlier re-ignited with flames from the villagers' torches.

Vigo produced a wand that looked like a writing apparatus. "Behold, my greatest accomplishment," he announced with a bit of a flourish.

"A pen wand?" Victoria asked, arching an eyebrow.

"It opens a pocket dimension." Vigo dropped to the floor and drew a trap door that became real. Victoria could not believe her own eyes. The door was an exact replica of the lab entrance with a ladder descending into faint light below.

"The entire lab?" She asked with wide eyes.

Vigo grinned. "Indeed. I have also put your working supplies and treasure in there. Grab anything else you want, and we can be on our way."

"And when we close the door?" Victoria asked.

"It's gone. We can draw it anywhere."

"It is a marvel, Vigo," Victoria whispered in awe. In the depths of her mind, however, Victoria feared the wizard for the first time since she followed the floating boy through the forest all those years before. She had just witnessed him best fifty people … and of course he'd fabricated her armor … and now an amazing device that conjured up spaces, separate but parallel. *Just how strong has Vigo become?* She wondered. Victoria had maintained a fantasy that if either of them went too far, one would stop the other, but now she doubted her own power. It was quite probable that she could not match her longtime companion.

Victoria quickly left her thoughts and gathered her things for the journey.

4. New Olan

Ty could sleep no longer. He knew it was still early in the morning by the smell of the air, but there was a gnawing pain in his back that would not stop. Rolling over, he found the icy longsword of blue, the source of his aching sleep. He sat up and slid the bundle to one side. Cirrus stood a few yards away looking toward the city of Olan.

"Can't I," Ty started to complain but was silenced by a wave of Cirrus' hand. Ty stood and joined the wizard. At the sound of his friend's voice, Frost woke and joined the other two. In the early morning light, they could see a cloud of smoke hanging over the city. The castle on the hill lay in ruins.

"What happened?" Frost asked.

"In the night," Cirrus said, "I cast a sleeping spell on you both because there was nothing to be done. A dragon arrived and crushed the remains of the castle and declared the city his. He brought several garrisons of goblins in to control the population. The dragons want more production from Olan residents. Goblins are to be the taskmasters."

"Look there!" Ty pointed at a line of wagons and people streaming out of the city on the great road.

"They are being led to the battlefield to scavenge, and to the watchtower in the west to bring tidings from their new masters," Cirrus explained. "If we are to enter the city, we will have to employ stealth."

"We don't have much time," Ty said as he turned toward the battlefield. "We need some goblin rags or cloaks … whatever they wear."

The three covered the remains of their campsite and rushed to the battlefield. It took them no time to outfit themselves in the stinking garb of the enemy. There were ample corpses to choose from. Dressed as goblin warriors, they headed back toward the hill, tracking north to avoid the great road teaming with travelers—thinking it best not to test the effectiveness of the disguises until necessary.

Cresting the hill, Frost looked to the northern forest on the edge of Olan Bay. "I wish I was swimming back at that lake," Frost mumbled as the trio began their downhill walk toward the city.

Ty slapped Frost's shoulder. "I tell you what, as soon as we get this whole thing sorted out, we can go swimming all you like. How long could it take to defeat the dragons anyway ... three, maybe four days? We'll be swimming in no time." Ty's good-humored nature reasserted itself in defiance of all that had befallen.

"I will join you!" Cirrus' sudden proclamation surprised them, and they both chuckled. Cirrus simply shrugged. "I am interested in this lake you talk about. It sounds refreshing."

"That clinches it," Ty declared. "Let's go to the lake instead." His remark was met with a half-hearted grunt by his companions. They all understood there was no going back.

"Cirrus, how do we begin?" Frost asked after some time.

"When we reach the city, we'll rest until dark. Then we will employ Ty's network of, ahem, friends to sneak us into the under-passages of the old castle."

Ty pretended to be insulted. "Just what are you implying? My friends are the most honorable bunch of scoundrels you'll ever know."

Frost barked a short laugh.

"Only if you know that bunch and no others," Cirrus said gruffly. "But they will help you, Ty, that much I am sure of."

"Sounds solid," Frost said, "But why the under-passages?"

"I am hoping they are intact, and that I might find something we need. In one of my laboratories I have a key to my old school.

We will need the wizards' help, and one does not approach the wizard school without a key."

Ty stopped walking. "Hold on. The wizard school? That has to be days south of the city."

"Do you think the school survived the attacks?" Frost asked.

"We must hope so, or our journey may be in vain. The only other useful information about dragons was in the castle Olan."

Their gazes shifted to the distant hill crowned with the ruins of the once great castle.

Cirrus turned and addressed the two youths. "Do not despair, boys. Come what may, we carry a weapon that is, to my knowledge, unique in the world. It may change our destiny."

They reached the edge of the city while the sun was still high in the sky. A few small houses lining dirt roads surrounded the city's outer wall.

"We will find an empty house to stay within until dark; then we will attempt to gain access to the interior," Cirrus whispered. "Hopefully, the goblins are not well-organized enough to have posted guards at the wall."

"I'll kill every one of those bastards that get in our way," Frost said earnestly.

"I understand your anger, however, with the moon still in the sky for another week and their prized weapon missing ..." Cirrus trailed off.

Ty finished the thought, "There will be nightly visits from the dragons and instructions to look for the sword."

"Indeed," Cirrus agreed, "and anyone who carries the sword will be set upon by all the forces the dragons can muster."

Frost smirked. "When you put it that way ... guess I'll only kill the ones that won't be missed."

Ty nodded wryly. "That's the spirit, Frost."

Cirrus found an empty house and kicked in the front door. "Quickly, inside! And don't use that name out loud if you can manage it, Ty. The name of Frost is known to some and will draw attention in the city."

Ty saluted the wizard as he entered the house followed by Frost. Cirrus closed and barred the door behind them.

"I thought you said we were looking for an empty house," Ty said.

Cirrus turned quickly, readying his staff. Ty pointed at a nest of rats feasting on what looked to be the remains of a dog. The wizard cleared his throat. "Perhaps we should find a different room."

Ultimately, the front room proved to be the least infested space in the house, and the three huddled in a corner away from the grotesque supper party.

"When we clear this city out," Frost said, "remind me to make an ordinance to exterminate rats."

Cirrus grimaced, "Yes, my lord."

Ty said, "And the first rats we'll start in on are the goblins and all the other vermin that have thrown in with the dragons."

Frost's spontaneous laughter tapered quickly at the thought of the road ahead. Once again, he looked crestfallen, his face a portrait of despair.

Cirrus regarded him and spoke gently. "Frost, the mission we have begun may seem insurmountable, but do not despair. We will be victorious in the end. When you think of how far we must go, also think of a world free from the tyranny of the dragons. Make a shining vision in your mind and hold on to that. We will find allies, and we will change the world."

Frost nodded, but he turned his face and looked away into the dark shadows of the room.

Ty grinned. "A world without dragons ... think of the business opportunities ..."

Cirrus shook his head in mock exasperation. "I'm sure it will be quite profitable."

"And beautiful ..." Ty continued in his reverie. The wistful expression that spread over his face made Cirrus and Frost both take notice. But then Ty added, "All those women falling at my feet—hero and all. I'll have a different one for each day of the week."

Cirrus shook his head in disgust.

Frost punched Ty in the arm and said, "For a second there, I thought you might say something wonderful."

Ty raised his eyebrows. "Tons of women would be wonderful, thank you." Frost shook his head and laughed.

They waited, bunched in the corner of the rat house until the sun had fallen below the western hill. Frost peeked out a window to see the evening glow—the gloaming—from behind the hill. It was the hill from which they had watched their destiny change. On its other side, still washed in the rays of the setting sun, lay the battlefield where his father was slain. He sat back down and muttered, "Not long now."

Cirrus stretched his cramped arms and legs. "Let's get ready. Don't say anything, even if forced. Your voices will give you away. If anything, grunt and spit on the ground. Keep your heads down so your hoods cover your faces."

The three prepared themselves, tightening the goblin disguises and covering their heads. Ty went over to the rat feast and grabbed one of the dead rats off to the side.

"For luck," Ty said.

Turning to the door, Cirrus said, "Master Ty, sometimes you are truly disgusting. You will make a fine goblin."

"Ha!" Frost blurted out, covering his mouth. Ty smiled. Cirrus studied the two, confirming in his mind that they looked the part, and opened the door.

The companions shambled out of the rat house and onto the main road. They meandered toward the wall. When they got close, they noticed that none of the torches were lit—the guards of Olan always lit the approach to the city. Through the open gate they could see the city beyond. An ominous orange cast washed over everything, which meant the fires still burned.

They did not attempt stealth when they encountered a goblin asleep at the gate—merely stepped around it as they passed, the smell of ale wafting from the snoring creature.

They continued onto a side street. Once they were out of sight, Cirrus turned to Ty. "Where can we find your friends?" he whispered.

"They will have hidden themselves in the tunnels and blocked the entries," Ty whispered in response. "The only way in will be through the back room of the tavern."

"The tavern? Surely not—" Cirrus began.

"Dragon Snot!" Ty exclaimed in a voice that echoed down the street. Frost covered Ty's mouth. The three waited. There was movement.

"Great," Cirrus whispered.

From above them came a voice, "My lucky night! Three more pillaging bastards to be sliced."

All three looked up, foolishly revealing themselves. A woman jumped from the rooftop to the street without effort, landing in front of them without losing stride. She wore skin-tight scale armor of purest black, a suit flawless from toe to fingers, and all the way up to her chin, covering her neck. Her straight black hair hung carelessly over her right eye, razor cut along at her jaw line. She smiled. With a twitch of her shoulder, honed blades sprung from the armor covering her body, and suddenly the long edges of daggers lined each limb. Spikes sprang out down her spine. Even her fingers had dual blades. The three companions stood dumbfounded.

She stopped and frowned. "You're not goblins at all." She looked at each of them in turn. "Why are you dressed like that? Why have you come here?" She focused on Frost. "Your name is Frost. You are the son of—" She turned her gaze to Ty. "—and you carry a fearsome weapon."

"She can read our thoughts!" Cried Frost, each of his words a slap to the armored woman's face. Her head jolted to one side, and she took a step back.

"Not anymore," she said. "It only works if you don't know that I'm doing it. But you are—"

"Quiet!" Cirrus said as loud as he dared. "What you saw is true. You know what we carry and who we are. Will you help us, or will you step aside and get out of our road?"

"Oh, I'm in, grandad. I think you'll find I can handle myself quite well, and I have no love for our enemies."

"I'm thirty-seven. I'm not old," Cirrus complained.

"I'm Nightshade," she responded, twitching her shoulder again, causing the blades to retract back into the armor. Nightshade leapt to a rope hanging down the wall and climbed up with incredible speed. After a moment, she jumped back down wearing a shoulder cape on her left side and a bag on her back.

"Nightshade? What kind of name is that?" Frost asked.

"You tell me, Frost." She smiled.

"I'm Ty ... Tycanerrious, um, Master Tycanerrious that is." Ty extended his hand.

She gave him a sly smile and shook his hand.

"The wizard Cirrus," Cirrus said flatly.

"Wizard huh, it shows. Well, grandad, grab the boys and let's get off the street. Patrol is due any minute. Goblins are dumb, but there are a lot of 'em."

Under his breath Cirrus said, "She's a dangerous woman."

Following, a dreamy glow in his eyes, Ty whispered, "I know …"

Cirrus shook his head and rolled his eyes. "This will not end well."

Nightshade led the three into a nearby building and up a flight of stairs. From there, they could see the patrol she had mentioned, thirty strong and led by huge war goblins like the ones they had seen on the battlefield. Nightshade quickly ducked out of sight and leaned against the opposite wall. The trio of would-be dragon slayers followed.

"If your father has died, that makes you the king then, doesn't it?" she asked Frost.

"I guess," Frost affirmed, speaking to the floor. "King of Goblin City."

"Don't say that. We will destroy them all and take back the city."

"Dragons first," said Cirrus.

"No big task there, wizard sir," she replied with a slight hint of sarcasm.

"Where are you from?" Ty asked her.

"Here, Olan; I've been here for years, and I have heard of you three."

The men grimaced in unison.

"Come on, don't be so naïve," she scolded. "I would've known who you are even if I hadn't had a few seconds to pry into your minds. Ty, you are one of the ringleaders of the city's underground market—some would call them thieves, but I'm not judging. Ty is childhood friends with the prince, who goes by the name of Frost, and both are taught by the court wizard. There's a bounty on your heads, you know." She smiled.

"And you are a bounty hunter, I assume," Cirrus said accusingly.

"Sometimes. But not today. I guess now I'm a freedom fighter like you." She twitched her arm and one blade emerged. She pulled a stone from her bag and started sharpening the edge of the lethal steel.

"Not sharp enough yet?" Frost asked.

"I killed twenty goblins already today. The bones don't treat my steel well." She continued sharpening. "What's the plan old man?"

"We—" Cirrus started.

"Dragon Snot," Ty interrupted. "We're going to Dragon Snot Tavern."

Cirrus responded by covering his face with one hand.

Ty continued apologetically, "Although I probably shouldn't tell you our plans since we've only just met, right Cirrus?"

She laughed. "Going to meet your friends, huh; the survivors? Well it's a good thing you ran into me. You can't get into the tavern. It has been claimed by the goblins. Without a castle, they decided the tavern would be the best place to run their operation. I don't know the fate of your friends, but it might not be good."

Ty's head drooped.

Nightshade turned to Cirrus, "Look, wizard, why don't you tell me what you really want, and I can help you. You must be hard up if you were going to trust the underground. I mean, half of them were likely to turn you in for a profit." She glanced at Ty. "Sorry, but your friends are not the most honorable folk."

Ty continued staring at the floor.

Nightshade stopped sharpening her blade and it disappeared back into her armor. She folded her hands in her lap and looked at the wizard calmly as if to demand a straight answer.

Cirrus sighed. "I need to get into the under-tunnels of the old castle. I must retrieve an object. After we have it, we will leave the city."

"Leaving the city?" Nightshade looked angry. "You would leave the people to be cruelly butchered by goblins? You have your blade; you needn't fear the dragons! Stay and fight—we can make a stand! Why would you leave like thieves in the night when Olan needs you?"

Cirrus let her cool a bit before answering, "We could do that. But what happens when the dragons come in force? What happens when they find out that the blade is being used? They will destroy everything from the air, goblin and human alike. They will sift through the ashes until they find the blade and destroy it. If we make our stand here and now, we serve only to destroy Olan forever."

Nightshade cast her gaze up to the ceiling in frustration. "So what then? How do we defeat the dragons? You really think we can end the terror that has plagued Ashyer since time before memory?"

Time before memory ... Cirrus was struck by the phrase. Had he heard it before? No matter now. He spoke quietly, "I intend to bring us to the wizard school in the south. There we will find allies, or at least knowledge to aid us in reaching the moon where we will destroy the dragons."

After a moment of contemplation, Nightshade regarded the three ragged companions sternly. "Fly to the moon, eh? Sounds like a longshot, but if anyone could do it, it would be the wizards. So be it. I will go with you and destroy the dragons, though I think it will most likely be the end of us all. But what else am I going to do?"

Another goblin patrol marched past outside. The night had blossomed in full darkness leaving the city utterly black except for the dim glow of uncontrolled fires.

"I know an exposed tunnel just east of the city wall south of the bay," Nightshade explained. "We can get there over the rooftops, but we should move quickly. The moon will rise soon, and another dragon is likely to visit this night. But heed me, there was much clamor coming from the castle area and the tunnel today. I don't know what the goblins have been doing, but what you seek may already be lost."

"We must recover it," Cirrus said. "Frost, Ty, let's go."

Now four, the adventurers ascended stairs to the third floor and climbed out a window onto the roof. Nightshade led them eastward toward the bay. Glimpsed only twice by goblin eyes that were not keen enough to recognize enemies, they reached the eastern wall just as the moon began to rise. Above them on a hill to the south of the bay, just outside the city, the remains of the castle smoldered and glowed. They all stood on the wall for a moment transfixed by a sickly yellow moon creeping up the horizon. Then they made their way to the ground and followed Nightshade to the tunnel entrance.

"I'll go first from here," said Cirrus, taking the lead.

Inside the tunnel, a loud clamor of metal and rumbling greeted them. They crept deeper into the narrow tunnel originally designed as an escape from the castle. They walked single file behind the wizard whose staff glowed like a lantern in the darkness. Finally, at the end of a long, straight corridor, the tunnel widened. Other passages branched off. At each junction, Cirrus stopped and looked around the corners to get his bearings.

"This is it," the wizard said, and turned down a corridor to the left. "My lab should be—" He stopped short when he observed the empty room beyond.

Frost looked inside. "Looks like you've been moved to better quarters."

"We shouldn't have come here." Nightshade looked around nervously. "I think that sound—"

Ty cut her off from around the corner. "Hey, check this out."

The other three quickly ran down a light filled passage to discover Ty peering over the edge of a chasm. The passage ended and opened onto a great chamber. Nightshade, Cirrus and Frost dropped to the floor and crawled to the edge. The great chasm was in fact the remains of the under-castle, hollowed out by great dragon claws and made into a den. At the bottom, some thirty feet below, a dragon lay on a pile of Olan's riches. Tunnel exits surrounded the chasm, and goblins streamed to the edges to throw more treasure down into the dragon den.

"The spoils of Olan," Frost said through clenched teeth. "Look, directly below us! It's the wreckage of Cirrus's wizard table. There's the glowing key. Ty, give me the weapon."

Ty did not hesitate. He unwrapped the hilt of the sword and slid it toward Frost.

"Wait," Cirrus hissed. "This is madness." The wizard's warning came too late. Frost slid down the edge of the pit, the great sword in his hands.

"Who wants to live forever anyway?" Nightshade said as she extended her blades and followed the son of the dead King.

Ty bounded after them, tossing a smile back over his shoulder to Cirrus. He opened his cloak and grabbed two darts. The wizard screwed up his face in exasperation and started climbing down toward the key.

Near the bottom, Frost stopped sliding and ran at the dragon only to learn that running on coins and jewels was much harder than he had imagined. But his heightened reflexes made sure his footing stayed true. The dragon was not asleep, but it paid no attention to Frost—too busy watching treasure pouring into its den.

Suddenly, a goblin tending a delivery pointed at Frost and screamed. The dragon craned its head around in time to see the blue steel sword leveled at its chest. It had barely opened its mouth, allowing smoke to escape, when Frost plunged the sword deep into the scales beneath its neck. Time stood still for an instant. The dragon did not move; Frost did not breathe. Only then did Frost wonder if the sword actually worked. *Cirrus had assured him it worked, hadn't he? Had anyone tested it? What if it doesn't slay dragons? How foolish I feel in the split second before I am blown to pieces.*

Then the dragon fell sideways with a huge thud, clattering treasure spraying everywhere. Ty and Nightshade arrived at Frost's side. The dragon began to crackle, the sound of ice. Slowly the body shriveled inward as if it were deflating, like a balloon. Frost yanked the sword free and waited for whatever might come next.

"Nice one!" Ty exclaimed.

"Thanks." Frost watched with grim satisfaction as panicking goblins fled from every entryway, roaches skittering away from a light.

"How many is that?" Nightshade asked.

Frost arched an eyebrow. "How many what?"

"How many dragons you've killed with that thing."

Frost grinned sheepishly. "One."

She regarded him with a startled expression. "So—so you didn't even know if it would work? Or if, you know, ka-boom?"

Ty slapped Frost on the shoulder. "Successful test!"

"Time to leave." Cirrus pointed to a tunnel exiting the den southward. He held the key in his hand.

"We could make our stand here," Nightshade insisted again. "This would be a good start."

Cirrus tripped on bits of treasure as he joined the others. "What we have done is tip our hand. You know what happens when a dragon is slain. It goes, as you say, ka-boom. Now, do you see that?" He pointed to the giant desiccated corpse of the dragon. "That has never been seen before. I think the dragons will notice. And they will soon direct every power at their disposal down upon this unfortunate city."

The others looked at the dead dragon and nodded. It was time to go. They grabbed some coins as they walked to the passage. Frost found a scabbard for the sword. He sheathed the blade and strapped it to his back.

The four companions made their way out of the southern tunnel, yet another escape route from the castle. Because it did not exit into the city, but instead to the southern fields, it was a much quicker route than the tunnel they had entered by.

Emerging into the darkened farmland of South Olan, they heard the strange mix of angry and fearful goblin screams echoing in the distance. Frost smiled grimly. *They will get terrible treatment from their cruel masters when their failure is discovered.* Then he thought of his own people. *Would they suffer with the goblins? Could it be that the goblins were just as much slaves of the dragons as they were? Would the terrible retribution be his fault?* He stopped smiling and shook his head.

"Will they suffer for what I've done?" Frost asked Cirrus.

"Serves them right," Ty interjected, spitting and adding some choice curses. Nightshade smiled darkly at him.

"I am afraid they will," Cirrus said. "And yes, probably the citizens of Olan as well. Two wretched races bound together in chains."

"Why do the goblins hate us?" Frost asked. Ty looked at Frost in disbelief.

"Do they?" Cirrus asked. "We don't know. For as long as anyone can remember, they have served the dragons, so is it by their will that they fight? Was it ours that we toil?"

Frost frowned and watched his footfalls as they hiked through the tall grass of the southern fields.

Cirrus continued, "The goblins are by nature more violent than humans, but perhaps that is due to the way they are treated. Suppose the dragons killed all the farmers and tradesmen in Olan and left only the warriors. How would those men be put to use? Farming? No, war of course. Perhaps that is what has been done to the goblins. If we are victorious, a new world will be made, and goblins will have to find their place in it."

"Perhaps their place is with the dead," Nightshade suggested.

"It could be; who can tell?" Cirrus agreed. "You know, in ages past, common and longmen thought the same of each other." He glanced up at the moon. "Such terrible wars ..." They all fell silent and continued through the rough fields.

After walking for hours, they were all stopped in their tracks by a sound from the north. *Crack!* The sound was unmistakable. A dragon had arrived in Olan. The four companions found tall scrub bushes to hide under and watched the north. They did not desire a witness of devastation but needed knowledge of its intent. An unmistakable roar of anger erupted from the city. Though many miles beyond them, the sound carried to the horizon, echoing back from hills and canyons. Then they saw distant fire. Surely, the dragon had flown into a rage when it found its dead kin.

Then, a silent darkness fell. They waited. After a long time, Frost tried to stand but Cirrus held him down.

"Listen!" Cirrus whispered into Frost's ear. From the north, very faintly, came the sound of large wings. The sound grew louder. They buried themselves deep into the vegetation. They could hear the dragon approaching. Then, the grass began to sway and thrash. The dragon sped back and forth, sweeping across the fields, slowly making its way south, searching for them.

How could we have been so stupid? Frost thought. *Of course we were seen leaving to the south, and the goblins would have told the dragon anything to save their hides.*

The dragon passed directly overhead several times, creating a wind torrent, but they went unnoticed. The wind died out as the dragon progressed south.

Ty scrambled to his feet and spoke. "How long do we have?"

Cirrus stood up with a groan. "Only a matter of hours, if that. Then, when it has not found us, the dragon will reverse course and begin burning everything."

Frost stood and drew his sword.

Nightshade stepped in front of him. "Frost, stop! Each time we intervene, we only create more clues to our whereabouts. If you slay another dragon, it will be like a sign saying, idiots fleeing this way!"

"She is correct, Frost," Cirrus said. "We now head east to the sea and follow the coastline south. I am afraid the southern fields will be burned to a crisp, but sacrificing the fields will allow us to escape." Frost sighed and sheathed the forbidden blade.

With haste, they started east. Before long, they could smell the salty ocean air and slowed their pace. In the distance, they could hear the rumble of fire. The fields burned as the dragon, making its way north again, made pass after pass breathing fire.

"Come on boys," Nightshade said, "let's get to the beach. That way if the dragon gets too close, we can always go for a swim." She spun on the spot, her shoulder cape flaring for a moment, and darted to the east with the others racing to keep up.

When they reached the sandy beach, they walked near the water's edge to allow the gentle waves to cover their tracks. The sun began to rise over the ocean. Daylight brought with it the ability to see the terrible vista that now spread westward. The dragon had burned all of Olan's farmland as far as they could see. Frost walked slowly toward the scorched ground and stopped at the edge of the blackened terrain. He looked to the north where the city lay. They were too far away to see it, but the dragon had created a black landscape that extended all the way to the northern horizon. Frost knelt in the ash and touched it. Ty arrived at his side and planted his hand firmly on Frost's shoulder.

Cirrus joined them. "There is one thing we can be grateful for in seeing this." The two regarded him skeptically. "If the dragon went to this much trouble to locate us in the fields, it must be sure we are not in the city. The reprisals will be minimal on the people of Olan." Frost nodded and looked at the black ground again.

Ty glanced around. "Where's Nightshade?"

Cirrus gestured toward the ocean. "She went for a swim." Ty's head snapped so quickly the direction of the water it made Cirrus chuckle. "She still had her armor on when she went in, as strange as that sounds," said the wizard. "She said it needed cleaning, Master Ty."

Ty looked slightly disappointed, but a smile spread across his face when Nightshade surfaced and walked out of the ocean toward him.

Cirrus rolled his eyes. "As if we didn't have enough trouble already." Nightshade joined them. Cirrus pointed to the south. "Only a bit further now and we will reach the barrier of the mountain."

Nightshade followed his gesture. "We should be able to see a mountain from here if it is close."

"We should," Cirrus agreed, "but we won't."

The four made their way south with Cirrus in the lead, passing the end of the scorched ground soon after they departed. Frost turned to gaze north. The dragon had burned a great black road into the land.

Cirrus rummaged in his bag.

Ty joked, "I didn't take it."

Cirrus looked up at Ty and raised an eyebrow. "No?"

Ty smiled innocently.

Cirrus smiled back. "Master Ty, you are welcome to try anytime you want. Anyway, I have it right here." Cirrus pulled a small hat, pointed, no brim, from his bag. The wizard fixed it to his head, and the point fell to one side.

So childlike, Frost thought. The small hat made Cirrus look almost like a boy again. There was one rune stitched on the front of the hat. "What does it mean?" Frost asked.

"The hat is that of an apprentice, and the rune is my sigil. I am Cirrus, Apprentice Storm Wizard."

"Apprentice?" Ty asked.

"Yes, Master Ty. Here I will most likely be the least powerful wizard you see."

Nightshade spoke up. "And just where is here?"

Cirrus took the key from his bag and held it to the sky. "I am Cirrus Storm, and approach with three companions. We request entry."

The key began to glow blue, emitting small electric bolts. Then, as if an invisible cloth wavered in front of them, the grass terrain of the south changed to a mountain. Near the top of the mountain stood a black tower carved from the mountain itself.

The key continued to discharge energy, but Cirrus returned it to his bag. "Come on, let's get to the lift."

Both the statement and the mountain puzzled Cirrus' traveling companions, but they followed the wizard, passing through the spot where the terrain had changed before their eyes. They felt like they were walking through a cold waterfall. Ty touched his hair to check, the sensation of walking through a wall of water was so real, but his hand came away dry. Soon, they spotted the lift. At the base of the mountain, a caged platform sat with a steel rope disappearing to a dizzying height above. The four companions entered the cage. The door shut on its own power. Cirrus whispered something to the bars, and the enclosure began its ascent toward the tower. Progress was very slow. Thinking the lift would take at least an hour to reach the top, Nightshade sat on the floor, leaned against the bars, and closed her eyes. Cirrus calmly meditated. Frost moved toward the part of the lift that faced north. Ty joined him to observe the devastation far and wide below on a grand scale.

"My first day as King," Frost muttered.

Ty stared silently.

"Behold, Ty," Frost said grimly. "The New Olan."

5. The Lost Kingdom of Redim

Vigo and Victoria stood before an ominous line of trees. Sprawling behind them, the fields of Vigo's youth. They had traveled down from the mountain, passing unnoticed through the small wood, continuing into the night across open fields under the sick yellow light of the dragon moon until they reached the forest of blood trees.

The trees, unusually thick in the trunk, had thin branches that resembled creeping vines. Each tree had a faint red tinge to it, and the bark shined as if it were polished. No undergrowth filled the spaces between the odd trees; feathers and bones littered the ground. The companions realized that the trees were not rooted in the ground, rather they slithered above the dirt on thick snake-like wooden tendrils.

Vigo cleared his throat, lowered his hood and stepped closer to the blood trees carrying his staff over his shoulder like a blunt weapon. "I know you can talk. The people of my village spoke of the unfortunate souls that strayed into your midst. I am traveling south, and I would have you grant me safe passage. What say you?"

The faint sound of giggling arose from the trees, reminding Victoria of the sound of distant children playing in the small wood. A quake of shivers shot down her spine—*The children,* she thought.

"What say you?" Vigo repeated.

On a whisper of wind, a voice came from the trees. "Come in, and we shall consider your request." More unearthly giggles followed. Victoria decided the giggles did not resemble the sounds of children after all, but more like the tittering of a madman who has committed a terrible deed and can't wait to see what happens next.

Vigo slid the staff off his shoulder and planted it straight up on the ground. "We have the power to make you comply with our request, however, we would prefer safe passage."

The only answer—more titters.

"So be it." Vigo thrust the staff upward, murmuring an inaudible incantation. A red rune glowed brightly on the staff and the top end of the staff, now high above Vigo's head, began to radiate red heat. Flames shot outward in a circular fan. The outlying trees were ignited instantly. Giggles turned into screams of horror and cries of rage. The trees began to retreat, but Vigo walked forward, the staff emitting regular pulses of circular fire—deathly heartbeats. Victoria followed close behind Vigo to avoid the flames. As they progressed into the forest, trees moved into the void behind them, careful to stay just out of reach of the flames, waiting for the power of the spell to dissipate so they could encircle their tormentors.

If they do that, we will find out what it is like to be eaten by trees, Victoria mused.

"Come close," Vigo barked to Victoria, his eyes bursting with Spellfire. Victoria drew near, and Vigo thrust the staff into the ground. The tip of the staff glowed white hot. Walls of yellow fire fifteen feet tall appeared all around. Vigo uttered a guttural incantation, and the walls shot outward in all directions. The trees screamed in pain as fire shot from the staff. In seconds, only ashes and bits of charred bloodwood remained. Victoria stared at a scorched vista. Nothing moved, nothing whispered. There was not even smoke, just blackened and twisted stumps.

Vigo straightened, breathing heavily. "I know what you're thinking, Victoria. Why kill them all when we could have passed through with circular fire?" Victoria gave no clue as to what she was thinking. "This land has been poisoned by foul creatures that bend to the will of the dragons," Vigo continued. "Wherever we go, we must purge it. We must restore Redim and destroy the agents of the dragons." After a moment's thought, Vigo added,

"The putrid sea to the north, for example. Would you not want to see it cleaned and usable for travel by ship once more?" Victoria nodded. Vigo smiled. "To do that, one would have to kill hundreds of times the number of creatures we just scattered to the wind, for the sea teems with them."

Victoria lingered a moment looking at the charred ground. Vigo headed south, his staff again propped upon his shoulder.

Victoria understood the logic in Vigo's words. But still she wondered. *Am I the "Black Knight"? A being the people fear rather than look to as a protector? Is there nothing but more devastation in our future? Is killing all there will be, and in the end, death for us as well?*

"You coming?" Vigo shouted back without looking. Victoria sighed and hurried to catch up.

By midday, they escaped the blackened ground and emerged into scrub land. Cresting a hill, they stopped to savor a marvelous sight. Below, perfectly groomed farmland swept down the hill to a valley cut by a river. A pristine stone bridge crossed the river, connecting the many farming communities on one side with a walled city on the other at the base of a mountain.

The castle proper, looking like it had seen better days, was carved into the face of the mountain. It had fallen into ruin in some places, and greenery took hold in others. Flags still flew from the main keep.

"Acamea," Vigo muttered. "I have never seen a real city before."

"Nor I," said Victoria.

Vigo turned to her. "There is something I must tell you," he said. "There were more recent books in that vault at the keep, tomes written by the old lords. I read about light trade the lords of Tenir Keep had with Acamea, claiming that this city at the base of the mountain was under control of the dragons—as I suppose many if not all of them are. General Krenn commands the Acamea Keep. He reports directly to the dragons. He is described as a dark-skinned man of short stature, with a keen military mind. He wields a curved sword that glows slightly and is suspected to be an ancient blade of great power. All who have faced him in battle have fallen to its edge. We need that blade, with or without the General."

"How do we convince him to give it to us?" Victoria asked.

"First, we shall find a room for the night, as it will be dark when we arrive in the city. Tomorrow we can ask for an audience with the General. The writings did not say where his true allegiance lay. Even if he secretly desires the end of the dragons, there may still be a fight."

Victoria pointed at the farmland. "It looks like a road begins over there."

The two resumed a more casual walk toward the city. As Vigo had predicted, it took until dark to reach the city gates. Their passage through the outlands did not go unnoticed. Several farmhands gave them good hard stares when they passed by clad in their black garments. No one spoke, nor dared to impede their progress—too menacing a look about them, the apparent wizard and his black knight.

Several horse-drawn wagons laden with goods passed them on the road en route to a clearing in the center of the farmland. Vigo commented in a low voice that the central spot must be where the dragons come to collect their tribute. Vigo also pointed out several wagons that had emptied their loads and continued on to the city. The presence of two more strangers might not be a surprise. At the city gate, they were greeted by a couple of thuggish-looking men.

"What business you have 'ere?" the uglier of the two men barked.

Vigo remained silent long enough to make the man feel uncomfortable before replying, "Our business is none of your concern, peasant. You impede the progress of the lords of Tenir. How dare you speak to me in such a manner!"

A long silence followed. Indeed, the city itself seemed to be listening to the conversation at the gate. Finally, the second ugly man straightened up and spoke. "We apologize, m'lord; we were not told to expect you. Please enter quickly, as night is upon us and the dragon comes tonight." The two men moved aside to allow Vigo and Victoria passage.

Vigo did not drop his stern, commanding tone. "Where might the best inn be these days? It has been many years since our visit, and I will rest before speaking with the General tomorrow." Had she not grown up with him, Victoria could have believed he was one of the Lords of the Keep by the way he spoke.

The first man answered, "The Ghost Whisper Inn, m'lord; but m'lord, no one sees the General anymore. 'Tis been years."

"He will see us. Which way to this inn?" Vigo answered without missing a beat.

The man pointed to a sign on the main street. Vigo and Victoria set off at once. They were quite aware that the news of who they claimed to be would reach the inn well before their arrival. The whispers and the gaze of hundreds was tactile. They kept to a slow pace, enjoying the click of cobblestone beneath their feet. Vigo looked up only once at the castle. No lights burned in any window, though guards stood watch on the walls.

At the arched doorway of the inn a short man stepped in front of the two companions and spoke quietly, "M'lords, you would find better quarters in my establishment, and better women. This place is haunted, so they say. That's why it is called thus."

Victoria responded, "Do you take us for cowards? The whispers of peasants do not concern us. Now out of our way!" Victoria pushed the man aside and the pair entered the most dazzling room they had ever seen—clad in velvet and gold. Patrons inside dressed in the noble fashion. Conversations stopped. Men at the bar turned to look at the newcomers.

A tall man dressed in clothes he was obviously uncomfortable wearing approached them. "Can I help you my lords? I hear you hail from the mountains of Tenir. We have not had a visit from your house for many years, I am told."

Vigo had drawn his hood up before entering and spoke from inside its moonless shadow. "A room, your best." He then produced a gold coin.

The tall innkeeper swallowed with greed but appeared nervous. "My lord, our best room—that is, the room that is the most spacious and sought after, is ..." His words trailed off. Vigo waited. The man found his tongue and continued. "Well, you see my lord, some people complain of strange noises from that room. It is on the fourth floor, the top floor—"

Vigo cut him off. "We care not a whit about the rumors of haunting. Give us the room." He slapped the gold into the innkeeper's sweaty hand.

The man looked at the gold for a moment with glassy eyes, then reached into his pocket. After a considerable amount of jingling, he produced a bronze key and handed it to Vigo. He led Victoria to the stairs, taking great strides all the way up to the fourth floor. Both were well aware that all eyes followed them. The conversations did not begin again until they were out of sight.

The door at the top of the inn was dusty, an indication that they were the only ones brave enough to stay there in a long time. Vigo used the old key to open the door and reveal an expansive room that included the entire fourth floor. Furnishings were plush, but dusty. The beds were the softest either of them had ever lain upon. A huge mirror, easily eight feet wide, spanned one of the walls from floor to ceiling.

Vigo went to the front window. "This is why I asked for this room. From here I can easily observe any changes in the state of the castle."

Victoria joined Vigo at the broad opening. Only then did she realize that the Ghost Whisper Inn was the tallest building in the city. One could easily see any activity from its vantage point.

"Victoria, I want you to go down to the tavern. Buy some drinks for people. See if you can gain any more information about the General, but be discrete," Vigo put a finger to his lips.

"Yes, m'lord." Victoria smiled and winked.

"Ha." Vigo too thought it funny that everyone referred to him as a lord. "Be careful, m'lord." Vigo smiled and winked.

Victoria strode out of the room with a few coins for drinks. Vigo pulled a small wooden chair over to the window and watched the castle.

Conversations stopped again when Victoria entered the room. She crossed to the bar, sat next to a scholarly-looking man and threw some coins on the bar. "I'll have an ale, and I'll get this gentleman whatever he would like." The man looked shocked.

"Do I know you?" the scholarly-looking man asked.

"Not 'My Lord'? You surprise me," Victoria grinned.

"I listen to no rumors unless I know them to be true."

Victoria smiled her most winning smile and asked, "Then why listen to rumors at all if you already know them to be true?"

The man laughed. "A good point. My name is Cidric. I don't believe we've met before."

"Victoria is my name. Indeed, my companion and I are lords of Tenir, but we don't stand on protocol there. I find it all amusing."

"We are well met, Victoria," Cidric said, raising his glass. "There are some here who still stand on protocol, but I am not one. I find it tiresome."

Victoria sipped her ale and pressed, "Are you from a different region of Redim? I don't imagine this is a popular place for local merchants."

Cidric raised his eyebrows. "Redim ... there are not many who still use that name for these lands. You must be a learned woman, Victoria."

"For my part. And you?"

Cidric looked at his glass for a few moments. "I come from the land west of here, now known as the Sand Sea of Sorrow. We had an order of scholars in the mountains there dedicated to preserving the history of Redim. Alas, the dragons have now taken the mountains for their own. The order was driven out and the desert is now impassible. Many wyrms live there year-round." Cidric noticed a slightly crestfallen look cross Victoria's face. "What is it?"

Victoria straightened. "It's nothing. We had hoped to visit the desert soon ..."

"I would not recommend it, my dear. The dragons are unwelcoming at best."

Victoria waited for the right moment. "What brings you to Acamea then?"

Cidric examined his glass again, as if the answer were written there. "I had hoped to see the General and ask for permission to begin the order anew in the castle, but alas, again there is no hope."

"No hope?"

"I have been told the General sees no one except messengers of the dragons. By order of the dragons, only the General and his elite guard are allowed to live in the castle."

Victoria had what she needed, but for a while longer she entertained Cidric with bits of the history of Redim she had learned from Vigo. In truth, Victoria was having a wonderful time conversing with someone other than Vigo for the first time in her adult life. The drinks kept flowing.

While Victoria enjoyed conversation three floors below, Vigo lost his battle with weariness. His head bobbed forward onto his chest and he fell sound asleep in the chair facing the open window. He began to snore loudly. Suddenly, he was pulled violently out of the chair and onto the floor. His arms and legs were bound and stretched apart. He heard giggling.

"Now we have our revenge for our kin," whispered a small voice.

Vigo recognized the whisper. He looked at his wrists; they were bound with red vines. Some small remnants of the blood trees had survived. The creeping vines and sinewy roots had scaled the outer wall of the inn to his window. Stabbing pain pricked the skin all over his body. Snaking, wormy branches penetrated his flesh and sucked his warm, red blood.

Vigo was about to scream when he heard a second whisper quite different than the hissing trees. The room vibrated with the power of a mere whisper echoing in his head.

"This place is protected," said the strange voice in an extreme low register.

At that, the blood trees stopped. Vigo turned his head and saw the mirror rippling like water. Suddenly, fire shot from the mirror, turning the trees to ash. Vigo rose slowly, his body aching, and approached the rippling mirror. He couldn't see his reflection for the silvery undulations. Behind them he could see a large silhouette with red glowing eyes.

"Whom shall I thank for this rescue?" Vigo asked.

"Remember me—Sarcarrion."

Vigo pressed for more. "What are you? Where—"

The image faded. The mirror was just a mirror again. Vigo gazed at his own reflection.

Hours later, Victoria returned to the fourth floor to find Vigo sitting in the chair by the window. She noticed a strange sheen to the floor in the middle of the darkened room. Approaching the shiny spot, Victoria asked, "Is everything all right, Vigo?" Vigo stared out the window and said nothing. Victoria bent to touch the shiny place. "What has happened? Vigo, what is this?"

"Blood."

Victoria pulled her hand away without touching the spot. "Your blood?"

No reply from the wizard. Victoria examined the mirror. Blood had been tracked right up to the looking glass.

When she reached out to touch the mirror Vigo cried, "Stop ... just in case."

"In case of what? Vigo, what happened?"

"It matters not. Go to sleep, and I will wake you when it is your turn to watch. Do not touch the mirror. I fear it is the reason the room is haunted." Vigo turned back to his silent vigil.

Victoria stared at the wizard for a moment in disbelief, shook her head, and walked to her bed, feeling dazed from the effects of the drink.

"One more thing," Vigo said without looking around, "sleep in your armor ... just in case."

Victoria glanced from Vigo to the blood, to the mirror, then back to Vigo. None of it made any sense. She lay down fully armored and fell asleep immediately due to the amount of ale she had imbibed. When Vigo roused her to watch, it seemed only minutes had passed.

"Wake me if you notice any changes in the town or in the room," Vigo instructed his groggy knight.

Eyes half open, Victoria saluted Vigo as a joke. She climbed from her bed and walked on wobbly legs to the chair beside the window.

Vigo carried his staff to bed. *There must be something dangerous for him to sleep with the staff*, Victoria thought, vowing to stay extra alert … just in case.

The night passed slowly. Victoria watched sleepy guards patrol the streets and castle walls. She eventually nodded off, unaccustomed to drinking ale. When her head snapped back up, the first brushes of morning light on clouds drifting through the eastern sky greeted her bloodshot eyes.

Without warning, three loud *cracks* thundered off the mountain, although there were no thunderheads in sight. Victoria did not need to wake Vigo. Before she could spring from the chair, Vigo stood at her side.

"Dragons," Vigo whispered. "That's the thunder of dragons arriving in the skies of Ashyer."

The companions strained their necks out the window to see flying beasts capable of turning the inn to ashes.

Three dragons circled the city gliding slowly over rooftops, creating turbulent wind gusts in their wake. Once the dragons decided that everything looked in order, they headed over the north wall to collect their tribute. Mere minutes passed before the dragons were again airborne clutching the bundled goods, flying hard toward the setting moon.

"Guess that's it," Victoria said quietly.

"It makes no sense," Vigo muttered. "How many dragons would that amount of food feed, and for how long?"

Victoria frowned in thought.

Vigo continued, "There's something else going on. None of this makes any sense. What did you find out about the General?"

Victoria told Vigo of her encounter with Cidric who had explained to her to enter the castle disguised as messengers of the dragons.

"Excellent," Vigo said, "we shall gain our entry then."

They waited for the sun to rise before leaving the inn. The streets of Acamea were filled with cheerful people, many drunk from celebrating the annual tribute. The threat of Dragonshade was gone for another year. Vigo restrained himself from telling boisterous revelers that the dragons might return any time, determined to take the castle.

The closer they moved to the castle wall, the harder the progress. Townsfolk congregated just outside the walls where several pavilions were erected for formal festivities. Many gathered around the statue of a man brandishing a sword skyward. Vigo tarried to read the inscription on the base—*Sir Roland the Demon Slayer.*

"Who is Sir Roland?" Victoria asked.

A man standing nearby holding a tankard of ale spoke up, "You must not be from around here."

"Forgive our ignorance, we are not." Vigo said.

The man grinned like someone who is usually the one asking the questions, thus overjoyed to be the one imparting knowledge. "Well, Sir Roland was a great knight of the realm and city leader more than a thousand years ago. It is said that the last of the demons continued to terrorize the people, so Sir Roland set out to the cursed valley where the beast was hiding. There he defeated and banished the last of the demons from our world."

"How adventurous," Vigo said with a hint of mockery that the man did not catch.

"Yessir. Unfortunately, Sarcarrion had mortally wounded poor Sir Roland, and he died on the road."

Vigo's face became pale. "What was that name?"

The man took another swig from the tankard and laughed, "Sir Roland!"

"Not the Knight, the demon," Vigo demanded impatiently.

The man appeared more than a little drunk. "Don't think anyone knows; not sure I've ever heard it."

"You just said—" Victoria started, but Vigo raised a finger to her lips and shook his head.

"Thank you, kind sir," said Vigo. He pulled Victoria aside. "You heard him say it didn't you?"

"Yes—Sarcarrion."

Vigo again shushed her with his finger, which she found to be annoying although he didn't notice. He cautioned, "Don't say it again. I fear it is a secret that leaks into our world at times. You heard what the drunkard said—Sir Roland banished it. That means the demon still exists somewhere. Let us not tempt fate by uttering its name again."

The pair continued toward the castle proper where they were greeted by two guards, entry doors closed tight. These guards looked battle hardened and deadly calm.

From under his hood, Vigo said quietly to one of the guards, "We come bearing a message from the dragons of the sand sea."

The guard regarded Vigo and Victoria shrewdly for a moment, his eyes passing over their attire. He pressed his lips together. Deciding they were telling the truth, he raised his arm and signaled a guard on the wall. There was a loud *thunk* and one of the giant wooden doors cracked open. The guard pushed it hard, and it opened only enough for Vigo and Victoria to squeeze through. Once inside, they heard the door rumble shut behind them.

They crossed a courtyard overgrown with scrub bush but otherwise empty and entered the castle keep.

At an earlier time, the castle must have been a marvel to see, Vigo said to himself. *I much admire the artwork, though faded, and intricate stone carvings, now weathered and crumbling. To fulfill my purpose, as my father has foreseen, the original beauty should be restored.*

A guard led them up an echoing stairwell to the throne room where he opened a large iron door. The hinges were the only parts not covered in rust. The guard gestured for them to enter but did not follow. Inside, the throne room appeared to have been converted into some sort of planning office. The main chamber was cluttered with long tables filled with scrolls. There were few chairs. At the far end of the vault sat the throne, immoveable, carved from the mountain itself. On the throne sat a dark-skinned man with greying hair. Clearly an old man, he wore the look of someone who could kill with one stroke of his sword—a sword, incidentally, that rested across his lap. Vigo and Victoria passed the tables and moved within ten yards of the throne.

"What do you want? Be quick." General Krenn droned with disinterest and disdain.

Vigo and Victoria stood silent.

Krenn noticed Vigo leaned on his staff, then glanced at the guard behind them and slowly nodded his head.

Before the iron door slammed shut, Vigo leapt into action, throwing his cloak up over the top of his staff, the supple cloth growing solid as iron as it fell in folds like a drape.

Krenn rushed at Victoria with unnatural speed, leaving her no time to react. She was paralyzed by fear. Krenn had crossed a considerable distance in a split second, his body becoming a glowing blue blur. He swung his sword downward, tearing the fabric of reality itself. Victoria could see her own back, as if Krenn had conjured a reverse mirror. *Or*, she thought too late, *a teleportation portal!* Krenn disappeared into the tear and it vanished. Victoria felt the collision of a sword slamming against her back, but unable to penetrate the dragonmetal armor. That gave Victoria enough time to activate her helmet and swords.

Indeed, Krenn had opened a portal in space. She spun around to face Krenn, noticing a pyramid erected beside her. Vigo had created a defense. *Am I betrayed? That makes no sense.* The thought of betrayal stung her heart.

She squared off against General Krenn, who was startled that the sword he gripped with two hands had failed to dismember the black armored knight. The sword had a slight curve to it and dissolved in blue light whenever it moved. Victoria found the weapon quite disorienting to look at, so she focused on the man instead.

"How have you done this?" General Krenn asked in a commanding tone.

"Yield or we will take the blade from your corpse," Victoria said.

"I demand to know," Krenn's commanding tone softened. "Who are you?"

The pyramid reverted to cloak form, and Vigo emerged with several glowing staff runes and Spellfire rising out of his eyes. "You will surrender and join us, or you will die. We have come to put an end to the dragons."

Krenn lowered his blade. "Spellfire ... you are a wizard of enormous power. I must yield of course, but I do not understand.

How can anyone possibly bring an end to a thousand years of suffering? It will take thousands of armies and magic of your ilk a hundred-fold."

"We will be victorious, but we need your blade. Do you join us, or will you be a counting-house coward, General?" Vigo asked.

Krenn slung the sword on his back. "I will come, but do not think that your attempts to insult my courage have anything to do with it. I have always wanted an end of the dragons; I have lived so very long. I have been doing the only thing any of us can do when faced with the overwhelming power of dragons." The General slumped in a wooden chair at one of the tables. Victoria relaxed her stance but kept the swords at the ready.

Vigo blinked out the Spellfire, the staff runes winked out, and he pulled up a chair beside Krenn. "General, do you know what that blade is?"

"I have always wondered about its origin. I only know what it can do. I am a master of its powers."

Vigo smiled. "That is why we would prefer you come with us. My studies have taught me that your sword is one of the five blades of legend. It is the blue Blade of Time and Space."

Krenn nodded. "As I have suspected for many generations. I have never let the dragons see it, for it is a treasure of Ashyer and would be greedily sought by their kind. But I do not understand how I can aid you. What would you have me and my rare blade do?"

"We seek the lost city of Redim, the tower to the moon," Vigo confided, though unsure of Krenn's real intentions. "From there, we can cross over and attack the dragons. No more defending ourselves from sky invaders. We will take the fight to them."

Krenn frowned as he pondered. "It is true that the dragons have a king, but merely killing him will not stop them. The dragons only hold loose fealty to their king. They are more like wild beasts than men." He sighed and stared hard at Vigo. "I was sick of this anyway." He made a dismissive gesture at the tables, the throne room, the city—at the world. "Better to go out fighting than counting. What do you want from me?"

Vigo grinned. "We have determined that we cannot cross the desert now, and it would take too long to walk even if we could. We need you to open a portal to the northland, beyond the putrid sea. Redim is in the northeast region of the kingdom."

Krenn shook his head, "Folly. When do we leave?"

"Immediately. Time grows short. The nights remaining with the moon in alignment arc few. I am the Wizard Vigo of the house of Arthur, and my companion is Victoria the Black Knight."

Krenn stood. "I would say we are well met, but I think it is a little too late for formalities. Sorry I tried to slice you in two, Miss Victoria."

Victoria withdrew her swords and lowered her helmet. "Sorry I offered to repay you in kind."

Krenn withdrew the blade from the sheath on his back, "This trip through time and space might be a bit rough. It is relatively simple to cross a few feet, but the distance we are going to attempt is greater than I've ever traveled. First, we must decide upon our destination. I have seen many lands in my lifetime. I visited a town on the northern ocean near the east where they tell of a strange ruin filled by an army of goblins. It is called North Port now; none remember its original name. I am guessing it was once the out-lands of Redim itself, and that the army guards the old castle and tower. I will attempt to take us to North Port—the sword requires sight of destination, in life or in mind. But beware, Vigo and Victoria, the portal will be as unstable as my memory of that place is. I assume you two are fully prepared, since you came here today to take the sword one way or another."

Vigo nodded slowly. Krenn closed his eyes, spun in circles and listened to something the other two could not hear. The sword began to glow fiercely. He raised the blade over his head and pulled it down with all his might. The muscles on his arms stood out as if he were trying to cut through stone. The tear in reality was jagged and unstable, waving like a mist. A town in a swamp sprawled within the tear. The portal edges sizzled with electricity.

"Now!" Krenn howled. The three plunged into the portal. A great cracking noise erupted from the castle, causing the celebrants of Acamea to freeze—they heard the exact same sound as an approaching dragon made.

Wind and electricity was deafening as the trio ripped through space, stung by bolts and debris in the void separating the castle from the town in the swamp. They each felt as if they were caught in thick mud, as they were pulled forward without moving. Cuts formed on their faces. Just as the pain became unbearable, they fell face down in the swamp. The tear closed behind them with another loud crack that quickly went silent with no mountains to generate an echo.

They lay upon flat, wet land. One by one, they looked up to see the ruins of a small farming town long abandoned. The swamp had claimed the surrounding farmland; the people evidently dead or gone. Clouds filled the sky above, and the air was moist with a light mist.

"North Port," Krenn managed to sputter, gruffly wiping a clot of mud from his chin. "The inhabitants must have moved on." He stood and looked around. Down by the oceanside, small boats rotted in their moorings.

Vigo got to his feet and approached the remains of a stone wall and wiped it with two fingers. "They went nowhere." He held up his hand and showed the other two. "Soot. The inhabitants were burned, probably because they failed to make their tribute. I've seen it before." He turned and began walking south.

Victoria and Krenn quickly joined him, making slow progress over soggy terrain. After an hour's slog, they heard low rumbling to the south. They crested a berm that had the distinct markings of centuries earlier having been a wall. In the valley below lay the tracery of ruins with a tower at its center. From their vantage, the city plan appeared to have been circular, miles across. The remains of a huge cylindrical keep had a single tower at its center. Above the tower, unbelievably, suspended in the air, giant rock fragments floated like clouds.

"Larger rocks will arrive with the moon, and our way across the bridge will be clear," Vigo said. "Behold, my companions, the lost Kingdom of Redim."

6. Cloud forest

Hours after they had napped in the lift, Frost could feel fatigue pressing hard again. Despite the yelling of old men around the long table where he sat with Ty, Nightshade and Cirrus in a dim-lit dining hall, his tired eyes kept slipping shut.

Their initial jubilant welcome to the wizard school degenerated into shock and horror when the travelers revealed that Olan had been scorched by Dragonshade and that Frost was the son of its slain king. They explained their quest and asked for support and aid from the wizards. None were prepared for the outrage and outright resistance that met them.

How dare you possibly ask wizards to do something so risky?

How can a young, untested king defeat the dragons without an army?

And so on into a free-for-all that dragged on for hours without resolution.

Now, Frost thought to himself as eyelids melted down over his irises, *maybe when I wake up there will be some agreement to help us. These old men are all cowards. That much is clear to me. Cirrus is by far the bravest of the wizards' clan. Perhaps fear comes with age?* His eyes slammed open as the debate heated up once more.

"Madness, I tell you, madness!" yelled a wizard seated beside Frost.

Frost glanced to his left. Nightshade slept, her head on Ty's shoulder; and Ty was starting to drift off with a drowsy but contented look on his face.

Frost slid his chair back, stood and climbed upon the big table. One by one, the old wizards stopped arguing and looked up at him. When the room fell finally silent, Frost spoke.

"Gentlemen, I thank you for your interest, but if you would be so kind as to show my companions and I to our rooms now, we must sleep, regain our strength. I withdraw our request for aid as your young, untested king. Despite your fealty to the sovereigns of Olan, it appears to me that, with the exception of Cirrus, there is little courage remaining among the wizards of this land. Therefore, after we have rested, we will leave you in peace to cower in your hidden wizard fortress while we attempt, without your help, to right the ills of this ill-fated world."

Frost stepped down from the table and helped Ty and Nightshade to their feet. "Which way to the barracks?"

One of the wizards—all of them shocked into speechlessness by Frost's admonition—pointed to a door at the far end of the room. The three weary companions shuffled from the dining room.

Not an hour after the three had fallen soundly asleep in soft beds, Cirrus woke them. "Come on, my sovereign king. Your words have swayed the old cowards." Cirrus disappeared from the doorway, then reappeared for a moment to add with a wry smile, "Well done, by the way."

The questers reëntered the dining room to find it empty save two wizards, Cirrus and a much older man whose mien gave the impression of an authority figure. The two wizards pored over scrolls stretched out on the table where Frost had scolded the wizards and withdrawn his request for help.

"Come, sit," Cirrus bade them. "This is Master Omegas. He is the headmaster of the school and will join us for part of our journey." The three travelers sat opposite the two wizards.

"I apologize for the lack of prudence in my fellow mages," Omegas said in a slow and serious manner. "They are cowards, all, as you said, but they are right to be fearful. What you propose is likely to fail. That said, I will assist you, both in person and in supplies, to undertake your mission." Omegas then fixed a stern gaze directly on Frost. "I'm sorry for your loss, son. With Xan dead, the last immortal is gone, and a fundamental balance has shifted in Olan. We are now all in danger of the wrath of the dragons. This school will not remain a safe shelter for long. Unless they are stopped, the dragons will demand an end to all wizardry in Olan as they did in the land of Redim."

As Omegas said the name, he pointed to one of the maps stretched out before them. Frost regarded the world of Ashyer with amazement. He had never seen a map so rich in detail and information.

Omegas continued, "Yes, this map is unique. The dragons have gone to great lengths to destroy the histories of this world, including charts, but there are still treasures like this that survive to teach us about ourselves." He pointed to the upper left landmass. "We are in Olan. To our south is a continent named Anden, where the last of the great power crystals still stands in opposition of the dragons; but that land is not our concern." He moved his hand over two great landmasses in the center of the map. "These are the middle kingdoms. Their names have been lost to time, as they were obliterated soon after the dragon's moon first arrived. A sea divides them north and south. It is through that sea we will pass to the great eastern ocean, and there ..." his hand moved back to Redim in the lower right of the map, "we will reach Redim, where a great city once stood, and exists the only bridge between this world and theirs."

Frost gently smoothed the map and tapped his finger upon the city of Redim. "A journey across the world will take weeks. We have only a few days before the moon fades. How do we get there in time?"

A sly smirk twitched the white whiskers around Omegas' mouth. "You shall see. I have many wonders to show you, my young king." He reached into a pouch and produced a crystal with ten sides, taller than it was wide. It rose up out of his hand and began to spin slowly. "This is one of the ancient power crystals, not a great one like that in Anden, but powerful enough for us."

"Powerful enough for what?" Ty asked, gazing intently at the glowing crystal.

Cirrus beamed with anticipation. "Let's find out."

They all rose from the table. Omegas gathered the scrolls into a case before leading them to the far end of the hall. There, he waved a wand at the wall, which slid open to reveal a metal staircase to a lower level. Each tread shook as they made their way below.

With unfinished rock on her right, Nightshade looked over the railing on her left upon an opening to unknown blackness. She could see nothing, but asked in a voice that echoed as if from a deep chasm, "What exactly is down there?" The old wizards chuckled. Nightshade shook her head at Ty and whispered, "These magic men are starting to get on my nerves."

Ty assured her, "I've got everything under control."

She smiled cynically. "Oh, that's a relief."

Overhearing the exchange, Frost let out a "Ha!" before he could stop himself. Ty punched him in the shoulder.

After hundreds of dusty metal steps, Omegas stopped, raised his wand and pointed it into the darkness. Tiny orbs flickered and began to glow. The orbs grew steadily in brightness and illuminated the giant chamber. Above them the stairs wended back into darkness, and below spread more darkness. They stood on a platform attached to an enormous *something* suspended next to them. As orb light brightened, details of that *something* revealed a mariner's ship. But where sails would have hung from masts, this ship had giant balloons with metal blades attached to them. The front of the vessel was curved, glass windows wrapping the edges of an airship. Omegas waved his wand again, and a hatch opened on the side of the airship; and the platform on which they stood extended until it docked with the vessel.

"This is the *Azure Sphinx*, the last airship of Ashyer. It's been in our care for centuries. The power crystal will give it life once more, and we shall endeavor to reach Redim before any foe crosses our path. The dragons long ago destroyed the rest of the great airships; as you can see, the *Azure Sphinx* barely escaped." He pointed to black scorch marks on the rear of the ship. "She is fast, as are the dragons."

"How do you know it's a she?" Nightshade asked.

"Because she's beautiful," Ty said without looking away from the ship.

Frost rolled his eyes. "Come on you two, let's get on board before the wizards decide to leave us behind."

On a lower deck made of wood and metal, Omegas used his wand to ignite lights set into the walls. Frost regarded one of the orbs. It emitted a dim yellow light and appeared to be made of glass. He rubbed off a thick dust layer to allow better light. He could see their footprints on the floor. "When was the last time this ship flew?" Frost asked.

Omegas answered from the darkness ahead, "I am long blood and have lived for centuries, and I have never seen it fly."

"This is a great plan, guys," Nightshade said sarcastically.

"Keep up, you three," Cirrus chided from an aft doorway.

The adventurers joined the wizards in the rear compartment where Omegas turned five small metal handles in a circular pattern and opened a small floor hatch about six inches in diameter. He then took the crystal out of his pouch and carefully lowered it into the hole. Immediately, the crystal started to glow and spin rapidly in the small cylindrical chamber.

Omegas closed the hatch and the entire ship began to vibrate fiercely. He screwed the handles back down tight. More lights began to glow from almost every surface. The vibration of the vessel whipped up a cloud of centuries-old dust thicker than fog, and all five onboard began to cough. A loud hissing noise—an air handling system—slowly removed dust until the features of the chamber, huge in diameter, became clear. Despite its great size, space was tight in the engine room filled with giant gears and clockwork devices. Tubes ran every direction to and from the walls. Shafts, glowing white, snaked the spot in the floor where Omegas worked to rouse the long-unused airship. Smoke rose from them as the last of their dusty coating was burned off. Smaller cogs and gears came to life.

Omegas stood. "Let us go to the bridge—the command center— there we can find out how bumpy our journey is going to be."

He led his passengers down dusty hallways and up two flights of metal stairs, emerging into a glass room at the front of the ship, dusty but well lit. Frost looked out to the main deck. Tiny orbs, glowing faintly, lit the platform. Omegas studied a console glowing with arcane runes. "All propellers are operating properly. Shall we take her up to the top to be cleaned and supplied?"

"Just when I was getting used to the dust?" Ty quipped.

"Wait, you mean you could have cleaned this thing before taking us down here?" Nightshade groused. "If there is another dock, why did we walk down all those stairs?"

Ty chuckled. "It's more *magic* this way … right?" Nightshade shook her head slowly wearing a "don't mess with me" expression.

Omegas ignored the exchange. "Up we go!" He pulled a lever. The ship shook violently. The propeller blades rotated with creaks and groans. The airship shuttered and began to move. The upward progress of the ship pressed on everyone's stomachs. After a minute of flight, the ship steadied. Omegas glanced back at his passengers, his eyes full of triumph. With a youthful cheer that belied his advanced age he declared, "The *Azure Sphinx* flies again!"

Ty looked a little green. "At least someone's having fun."

Cirrus handed Ty a potion, which he drank in one swig. His color quickly returned. "We're really going to do this," Ty whispered loudly to Nightshade.

"It appears so. We're all crazy. I can't believe I'm still hanging out with your lot." She smiled. "But, I do admit this airship transport is encouraging."

The *Azure Sphinx* rose to the top of the chamber and stopped. Omegas locked a brake lever and turned to face his four passengers. "Normally, I would guess, the ship would be readied outdoors, but as we want to keep the possibility of detection to a minimum, we shall do it here. We can all get a bite to eat while others clean and stock the ship. I will commission apprentices to serve as the ship's crew, that will free us to focus on our main objective."

The five companions exited the ship through the ramp that extended to the doorway at the top of the chamber. Frost peered up in amazement at propellers slowly rotating. Never did he think he would ride in an airship. *In fact*, he thought, *I didn't believe they actually existed.*

A sumptuous meal on the large table greeted them as they returned to the dining room. Everyone ate greedily, as it had been some time since any of the travelers had eaten properly and no one knew when they might eat their fill again. The secret door at the end of the room remained open enabling Omegas and his team of adventurers to watch the workers lading the airship. At one point, a brief, violent gust sent clouds of dust drifting into the chamber. Then, bright light began to stream through the open doorway. Men outfitted for travel started to arrive with additional supplies.

Omegas did not linger long at the table. After checking the ship, he returned to report, "If we are all in readiness, it is time to leave. You will all have sleeping quarters onboard the ship." He gestured to the door. The four companions exchanged glances in silent confirmation of their single purpose, then stood and strode through the door.

The sight of the lighted ship was breathtaking, cleaned from stem to stern. The balloons of a thin metallic material gleamed; and the propellers spun silently. The glass had been cleaned so completely that it disappeared, revealing many apprentices moving around and organizing the ship's interior.

"*Azure*," Frost observed. "Of course, the ship is blue. If it flies high enough it will be nearly invisible to anyone on the ground."

Omegas smiled. "Yes. And when we are over the ocean, the same is true from above. We are well cloaked. Now, let us embark."

They all entered the ship. The hatch closed behind them with a muffled click. They passed their sleeping quarters and climbed the stairs to the bridge where colored runes adorned the surface of tables and consoles they hadn't noticed on their first dark and dusty tour. An apprentice stood at each worktable. In the center of the bridge, a world map covered most of the large navigation table along with several other unrolled scrolls.

"We are ready," announced Omegas after a brief discussion with one of the apprentices. "We will descend to the bottom of the chamber and open the berth for this ship. It has not been used in some time, so we may have to be persuasive."

Cirrus raised his eyebrows in exaggerated disbelief. "Persuasive?"

"Onward!" Omegas barked to the crew, and the ship started down. Frost, Ty, and Nightshade braced themselves for the violent vibrations they had felt before, but none came. The ship flew flawlessly.

The *Sphinx* descended into the darkness for a short time before a crewman pulled a lever effortlessly and brought it to a halt. Omegas went to the front windows and raised his wand. The wall in front of them began to slide open, allowing blinding sunlight to blast in. All onboard shielded their eyes for a moment, allowing them to adjust. Slowly, the great portal yawned open to reveal the Southern Ocean reaching to the distant horizon. The *Azure Sphinx* emerged from the base of the hollowed-out mountain and rose into the sky in one fluid curve. Their speed increased greatly as they climbed into the clouds and headed east. Even the wizards were awed by the ground disappearing below.

The airship leveled off. Whenever possible, Omegas, now the Captain, used the clouds to mask their flight. The crew busy with flight, the adventurers wandered about the ship.

Ty meandered the lower decks for a while before going to look for Nightshade. He saw her climb a third set of stairs he had not explored and followed to a hatch on the upper landing. When he opened the door, the sound of turbulence created by the propellers shocked his ears. At a railing on the uppermost deck, near the bow of the ship, he saw Nightshade gazing out into the clouds.

"Just a little windy, huh?" Ty said loudly over the roar of the wind.

Nightshade faced away from him.

Ty tried again. "What do you think of the view?"

Her shoulder cape flapped wildly, and her hair blew backwards. "The most wonderful land one can imagine." she said. "The cloud forest."

The ship *Azure Sphinx* soared between two cloud layers connected by wispy columns, so many pillars they appeared to be flying through a forest of great trees. "You know, you can see anything when you stare long enough—" Ty stopped speaking when he realized that Nightshade's cheeks were wet with tears.

"Are, are you crying?"

"Please, Ty, just leave me be." She turned away.

Ty puzzled for a moment over whether he had done something wrong. Finally, he shook his head and headed back to the hatch to find Cirrus climbing onto the upper deck. Ty walked past the wizard and grumbled, "Women. Who knows?" He returned to the quiet of the interior.

When Ty was gone, Cirrus approached Nightshade. "A cloud forest. *Time before memory*," he continued, "I knew I'd heard that saying before."

"You will not tell Ty?" Nightshade asked in a slightly threatening tone.

"He will eventually find out, but not by my admission. You should tell him, for a time will come when such things matter greatly."

Nightshade's stern visage drooped into a sad frown. "We're all going to die on this quest anyway, so it won't matter." Suddenly, the airship braked. She and Cirrus spun around expecting danger. When none came, they rushed to the hatch and descended to the bridge at a run. Frost and Ty arrived at the same time.

"What has happened?" Frost asked, his hand on his sword's hilt.

Omegas studied a bright, glowing compass-like apparatus. "I know we are short on time, but we must investigate something. It may be very important." He looked at his stunned passengers. "Ah, yes, the magical energy detector. It has indicated a source of extreme power nearby, more powerful than I would have thought possible. We must risk descending below the clouds for a few moments to have a look." He nodded to one of the crew before anyone could object.

The *Azure Sphinx* slowly descended through the lowest level of clouds. Far below, two landmasses covered in mountains separated by water were visible. *We must be in the narrow sea of the middle kingdoms,* Frost said to himself as he gazed through the glass prow. The mountains seemed odd, however; like someone had used a gigantic shovel to pull up miles of land and drop it back onto the ground. *Had the mountains been pulled out of the ground by force?*

"There!" Omegas pointed at a mountain on the seacoast at the southern end of the northern landmass. The entire mountain quavered like heat rising through haze.

"Did you see that?" Ty exclaimed.

"Yes!" Omegas shouted, "It is as I thought; we have found the lost laboratory!" He ran to the map at the center of the room, Cirrus at his elbow, together plotting their location. "We must remember this spot," Omegas mumbled, "for it is the greatest lost wonder of the ancient age." He was very animated. The other wizards crowded around him.

Frost and Nightshade stood with their backs to the window shaking their heads. Ty gazed out the window. "Hey guys," he said, "what's that valley to the northeast up there?" Frost and Nightshade turned to look at a wide valley blanketed in a yellow fog or a cloud.

"That yellow," Frost began, "It reminds me of—"

"—Dragons!" shouted Ty, pointing wildly at five dragons streaking out of the fog straight toward them. Menacing specks in the distance at first, their incredible speed brought them closer at an alarming rate.

Omegas began shouting orders to the wizards. The ship lurched forward and upward into the clouds faster than the dragons; but as the airship slipped out of range, the clouds behind transformed into an inferno.

"Dragonshade!" Frost yelled.

"No matter," Omegas said. "We are well out of their range. As long as the clouds hold out, we will—" As he was about to congratulate them on their daring escape, the clouds that cloaked their progress dissipated. Shooting out of cloud wall like an arrow into wide, clear space, Omegas mumbled, "Well, we are still faster—"

"—Dragon ahead!" cried Ty, sounding the alarm again as a giant red and black dragon bore down on them faster than they could react, letting loose a stream of fire broadside at the *Azure Sphinx*, which began to vibrate. The airship slowed. Dragonshade had damaged the rear propeller so badly it stopped spinning. In the distance, the red and black dragon banked and turned for another attack.

"I must repair the propeller!" Omegas shouted, pulling out his wand and running to the corridor. The adventurers followed him to the upper deck. The burned propeller pumped a steady stream of acrid, black smoke into the air. Omegas climbed the propeller mast, his wand clenched in his teeth.

Frost spotted the dragon approaching up fast through the trail of smoke emitted by the damaged propeller. "Catch me!" Frost said to Cirrus as he pulled out his sword, rushed to the stern and jumped onto the railing. His sword raised over his head, Frost leapt off the ship in a deadly, fluid movement. Nightshade ran after him, but Cirrus put out his arm and stayed her.

"I have this one," Cirrus said.

Suspended in free fall, his sword clutched in both hands over his head, Frost plunged as the dragon passed below him. The dragon did not see him drop through the smoke that masked its impending doom until it was too late. Frost landed on the mighty dragon's neck and with the momentum of the fall he plunged the sword downward, slicing into the base of the beast's neck. At once, Frost felt cold spreading below his feet as the dragon withered. He pulled the sword out and pushed away, leaving the dead dragon to spiral downward into the sea below. Instead of plunging after his slain foe, Frost hovered in midair. He looked to the ship and saw Cirrus standing on deck with his staff brightly aglow. Then, as if reeling in a fish, Cirrus pulled the staff up and Frost flew toward the wizard. The two collided and went sprawling to the deck floor.

"Thanks, old man," Frost laughed almost fiendishly. Cirrus laughed too, releasing pent-up relief that his magic had worked. Nightshade helped them to their feet. She couldn't help but smile.

"We need to hurry," Ty shouted over the wind. He pointed back at the clouds they had emerged from only moments before. Five dragons streaked toward them.

Frost readied his sword, Cirrus held up his staff, Ty drew some darts, and Nightshade activated all the blades in her armor. The fearless quartet prepared for the worst at the stern. Then, with a sudden bang, the ship lurched forward and left the dragons in its wake. Omegas had repaired the damaged propeller.

The Captain descended the propeller mast and regarded the four warriors ready for battle. Perplexed, he waved his wand at the empty sky and said, "Did I miss something?" Frost shook his head in relief and signaled the others to relax their guard. Omegas grinned through his bushy beard. "Well, we're on our way again. Cirrus, it is time to prove you are no longer an apprentice and earn your title. Summon your rune to mask our approach."

Cirrus nodded. He adjusted his bent hat, walked to the spot Omegas indicated and thrust his staff forward. Clouds began to curl in around the airship. Before long, they were flying in the eye of a storm that moved with them. Cirrus knelt and held his staff firmly.

"What is his title?" Frost asked Omegas.

"Cirrus of the Storm, of course. Didn't he tell you?"

There's a lot Cirrus has not told me, Frost thought. "How long till we reach Redim?" Frost asked.

"A few more hours. Please do not disturb Cirrus. He will cloak our approach from now on. Perhaps you should get some rest. I fear we have some fierce fighting ahead of us."

Frost, Ty, and Nightshade went below deck, leaving Cirrus to concentrate. Weary, they each went to separate rooms, small sleeping cabins. All were tired, but none could keep their eyes shut. Every time they tried to sleep, thoughts of the coming battle woke them. Ty and Frost decided to rest at least, staring at the ceiling; but Nightshade opened the ancient curtain and gazed out her porthole at the cloud forest swirling in storm.

7. Forbidden weapons, forgotten past

Vibrations began many hours into the flight; Ty and Frost were deep asleep in their quarters when violent tremors rousted them from their beds and sent them dashing into the hall where they almost collided. They hurried to Nightshade's room—empty. They found her on the bridge, clutching the rail at the bow to steady herself. All the wizards held on tight to navigation tables as the *Azure Sphinx* lurched nauseatingly.

"What is going on?" Frost shouted.

"Appears that a magical field protects the city of Redim," Omegas shouted back. "We are passing through it now."

"Where is Cirrus?" Frost yelled.

"Holding fast; doing his duty!"

Without hesitating, Frost bolted from the bridge and up the stairs to the outer deck, emerging into incredible turbulence and pelting rain. Eyes asquint, he spotted Cirrus, thrashing like a rag in the wind, one hand on his staff, the other desperately clinging to a small wooden bollard fixed to the deck for mooring lines. Frost, drawing his dagger, ran to Cirrus and thrust the blade into the deck up to the hilt, wedged between two close-fitted deck planks. The dagger in one hand, Frost wrapped his free arm around the wizard. Cirrus reacted by releasing the bollard and gripping his staff with both hands. Soon, the staff began to glow brightly, and the airship steadied.

Omegas quickly joined Frost and Cirrus on the upper deck. He looked to the sky and said, "That is enough, Cirrus. You have brought us to Redim safely. Now we need to see the lay of the land."

With that, Cirrus collapsed into Frost's arms. The wizard, fully spent, let the staff fall from his badly burnt hands to the deck and shatter like a glass tube.

Frost glared at Omegas. "Listen, old man, I care about Cirrus. If he has been harmed—"

Omegas put a hand up. "He did what was needed and he is not permanently damaged. He volunteered for this task, both to aid you in your quest and to complete his final test."

"Test?" Frost teetered on the edge of full-blown fury, his teeth clenched.

"He is no longer an apprentice." Omegas reached down and removed the bent hat from Cirrus' head, the rune on his mentor's forehead fading until it was gone.

"Rise, Cirrus of the Storm, Wizard of Olan," said Omegas solemnly.

Cirrus smiled and put his hands on Frost's shoulders to pull himself up, standing on the deck. He faced Omegas. "Thank you, old man."

"Ha!" Omegas chortled. "Old indeed!"

Everyone returned to the bridge in high spirits. Everyone except Frost, whose temperament often matched his name. He felt it cruel to send Cirrus to complete the task of righting the airship alone, wizard test notwithstanding.

Sensing Frost's icy mood, Omegas said, "Young king, there will always be moments in life when you must face danger alone. That is why the test is always solitary. You helped Cirrus overcome the unforeseen defensive field protecting Redim, and for that I am grateful."

Frost remembered his father, who stood alone before the dragon who killed him, and decided not to respond. *Perhaps there is wisdom in the wizard's words.* Frost reluctantly admitted to himself that headstrong brashness did not always serve him well. *If you want to learn, you have to pay attention to—and, yes, sometimes even heed—the counsel of one's mentors.*

On the bridge, Frost found Ty and Nightshade standing before a giant, adjustable lens focused on dead swampland and ancient ruins.

Nightshade panned it slowly to the right and a particularly ugly goblin came into view.

"There!" she said, punching Ty in the shoulder, "I told you I saw goblins. I wasn't imagining it."

Ty rubbed his shoulder. "Fine, you were right."

"Move the glass further up," Omegas instructed. "You'll see there are hundreds of goblins."

Apprentices took over aiming the lens when Ty and Nightshade rejoined Frost and Cirrus. Omegas slipped into a small antechamber and returned carrying another staff made of wood and metal with a slight blue sheen. The rune of Storm shone prominently along with several others. The Captain presented it to wizard Cirrus with solemnity.

Omegas explained," I can think of no one better skilled than you, Cirrus, to wield the Staff of Storm."

Cirrus bowed his head. Omegas pointed out a strange rune toward the bottom of the staff. "This symbol summons the *Azure Sphinx*. Your staff is connected to this airship."

Cirrus' eyebrows arched in amazement. "My staff …"

"It is yours." Omegas said. "Use it well."

"The tower!" one of the apprentices shouted. Omegas and the four companions hurried to the lens aimed at center of the ruin where a tall tower stood. Above the tower, giant floating rocks were aligning slowly to create an intricate combination of interlocking natural rock and chiseled stone masonry that stretched into the sky like a spire connecting the two worlds.

Omegas stepped forward. "Magnify second rock, please."

An apprentice added a second lens, which clearly defined the figures of three people on the surface, two armed with swords, and the third with staff and cloak. "Looks like we have more friends; perhaps more enemies," Omegas said as he slung his cloak over his shoulders, "Let's find out. Bring us within a half mile," he ordered, turning to the others. "Are you ready?" They all nodded gravely. "Then above deck we go."

The group of adventurers emerged onto the upper deck just as the tower drew closer. As the airship approached the floating rocks, the bridging structure completed its combination, establishing a corridor from Ashyer to the accursed yellow world.

Omegas produced a glass orb from his cloak and held it up. "Everyone stand close." They did as they were bid. He released the orb, but instead of falling and shattering as a normal glass sphere would do, it grew in size, engulfed the party, and began to float. Omegas put his hands on the front of the glass, and they sped toward the rock where they had spotted the strangers.

The journey through Redim had been rough for Vigo, Victoria, and Krenn. Each bore the marks of battle as they rested on the second floating interlock. Sneaking through the loose groups of goblins in the ancient city had been easy, but the tower was crawling with the foul creatures—or at least it had been before they had come knocking. The trio left piles of corpses in their wake, clearing the tower of all save one or two goblins who still possessed some stunted sense of self-preservation and found places to scurry and hide. But the task had been exhausting.

Victoria thought she might close her eyes for a few minutes, catch her breath, but then she heard a strange sound approaching from the north. She lifted her head, alert again. Vigo strained to search for the source.

"What now?" Victoria whispered. "Is it a dragon, Vigo?"

"No." Vigo did not turn. "You will want to see this wonder yourself."

Victoria and Krenn joined Vigo at the northern edge of the rock and beheld something that no one had seen in a thousand years. A blue airship on approach, quickly at first, faster than a dragon's flight, then slowing gracefully.

"Enemies?" Victoria asked, transfixed.

"Doubtful," Vigo said. "Our enemies destroyed all of the airships a thousand years ago."

Krenn corrected him. "All but one."

The airship came to a full stop some distance away; an orb appeared and flew toward them.

Victoria extended her blades. Vigo put a hand on her arm. "Look—there are people in the sphere, five in all."

"On your guard. We do not know their intention!" Krenn drew his blade.

The sphere landed on the rock with a gentle *clink*. Inside, Omegas, Frost, Ty, Nightshade and Cirrus stood motionless. The sphere retracted into a small glass orb that rested in Omegas' hand.

The two groups regarded each other, curious but suspicious.

Ty spoke first. "We've come to kill dragons. Are you with us or do you stand in our way?"

Frost cringed at his friend's bluntness.

Krenn laughed. "I like him."

Vigo and Omegas stepped forward in unison, two emissaries sensing the other's power and authority, silent for several heartbeats, sizing each other up, neither breaking eye contact.

Finally, Omegas said, "I am Omegas, head of the order of Wizards of Olan. We are on a quest to end the rule of the dragons. And you, sir?"

"I am Vigo of the house of Arthur from the lost kingdom of Redim. We pursue a similar quest."

Frost clutched the hilt of his sword by way of a formal salute. "I am King Fredris of Olan. We quest not for glory or revenge, but for the people of Ashyer."

Vigo responded slowly, as if he were trying to decipher whether an accusation or threat had been made. "As do we, King Fredris."

Frost nodded. "There is strength in numbers. You have met Omegas. This is Ty, Cirrus, and Nightshade. My comrades call me Frost. Shall we join forces Vigo, house of Arthur?"

"Why don't we get to introduce ourselves with cool titles?" Ty muttered.

"Because we don't have time," Frost shot back just loud enough for Ty to hear. "Royal Thief isn't a title."

Vigo scanned the group, his eyes lingering noticeably longer on Nightshade. Then he introduced his companions. "This is Victoria the Black Knight, and General Krenn of Acamea."

The two groups nodded formally, then Omegas reminded them of the business at hand. "The conjunction is final. I invite you to join us in the orb; we can cross the barrier with ease and assault the fortress of the Dragon King together."

Vigo extended his hands to accept the proposal. Eight now, the questers formed a tight circle and Omegas released the orb. A glass sphere encased them and began to float. Omegas touched the top of the orb, which sent it flying straight up along the impossible spire toward the yellow world far above.

Frost noticed that each of the giant rocks bore crumbling ruins and realized they were fragments of ancient stone stairs. A monumental staircase had once bridged gaps between the floating stones.

Suddenly, the world turned upside down. There was a deafening *crack*. Everyone inside the sphere gasped at the sight of their own world above, a bullseye shaped ruin of Redim marking their departure point, as they flew down toward yellow clouds. Soon, the sun rose over Ashyer, temporarily blinding the party.

"This must be fun for a dragon," Ty said, clutching his stomach.

"Not so fun for us." Victoria deactivated her helmet to catch her breath.

Frost raised an eyebrow. "Neat trick."

Vigo frowned slightly, a gesture that caused Frost to make a mental note.

The orb broke through the top layer of clouds and descended into a yellow atmosphere. Below them, the top of a structure that at first glance could be mistaken for mountains resolved into perfect triangles—obviously not natural formations. In the center, an enormous spire dwarfed the other peaks.

"The Dragon King will reside there," exclaimed Omegas, pointing with four fingers. "That, my proud resistance fighters, is our destination."

"You know," Frost observed, "I haven't seen any dragons yet. I thought there would be a swarm. Doesn't it seem odd?"

Vigo concurred. "I find the actions of dragons as a whole very odd. Their absence makes me wonder if there is something foul going on; perhaps a trap."

"We shall have our answers presently," Omegas replied.

The orb slowed, and following the path of the floating rocks, curved gracefully toward a cavernous opening in the large spire.

Omegas said, "I believe this is the proper entrance if we wish to request a formal audience."

The adventurers' sphere passed through large, roughly hewn arches into a passage long and wide enough to provide clearance for a squadron of flying dragons. The orb gradually proceeded at a cautious speed. Passengers gripped their weapons at the ready.

The passage ended at a grand arch opening into a vast chamber. Frost estimated the entire castle Olan would have fit through it with ease. At the far end of the room, an enormous dragon lounged on a golden platform.

Frost immediately recognized scorch marks around the eye sockets where fire had burst forth. *This Dragon King killed my father!* His hand tightened around the hilt of his sword. Cirrus gently squeezed Frost's arm. The sphere landed, and the small orb came to rest in Omegas' palm with a slight *clink*. The fighters spread out into battle positions. Nightshade positioned herself just behind the others. Ty cast her a confused look, but she just shook her head.

The dragon inhaled deeply. "So, you come to me. An old man, a wizard, a king, a thief, a knight who stinks of our dead flesh, one of my servants, an apprentice, and an angel." The dragon gazed unseeing at Nightshade for a long moment. When she did not cringe, the Dragon King said, "Belladonna the Fallen One, it has been a long time."

Nightshade's companions each stole a quick glance at her. She looked terrified and replied, "Not long enough, yet never too soon."

"The members of my court are here to greet you," continued the dragon.

Deep, inhuman laughter echoed off the cavern walls. Everywhere the eight companions looked, dragons stretched their heads out of openings along the perimeter of the gigantic room, too many to count.

"You have brought me the forbidden weapons, I see. Permit me to thank you. But something tells me you have not come here to surrender them. Do you, if I may be presumptuous, *freedom fighters* think you can slay me and my entire court? How do you intend to accomplish such an epic feat? Fear not, I will not strike first. It is a novel pleasure to speak to humans. I feel a tinge of curiosity again. How will I die? Indulge me."

Frost lifted his dragon-slayer, wisps of fog trailing the icy blade, and stepped forward. "I will slay you. Perhaps one of your court will succeed in killing me after you are dead and cold, but my father will rest in peace knowing you are no longer able to draw a breath."

"Revenge then?" The giant dragon raised his voice as if addressing his court. "This is how you repay my mercy?"

"I wounded you, liar. And you fled!" Frost yelled, his fury driving him closer to the Dragon King. "You showed no mercy on the battlefield."

The dragon laughed. "Ignorant fool. Do you believe your blade is the only forbidden weapon Xan forged?"

Frost stopped in his tracks.

The dragon continued, "A blade to destroy dragons is indeed a forbidden weapon, but your father Xan breached our pact nineteen years ago. As an immortal, he was never to have a child, but he did so, and here you stand. I went to your father's castle nineteen years ago to destroy you, him, your entire family, but I showed mercy on a fragile baby. Look what my mercy has wrought. A forbidden boy, grown into a killer wielding a forbidden blade. I will not show you mercy again, Fredris. You will not leave here alive, unless …"

They all waited as the dragon pondered his next words. Unable to bear the silence, Ty shouted, "Unless what, you big ugly bastard?"

Omegas cringed and stepped away from Ty, unconsciously avoiding the fiery response that the young thief's disrespectful outburst might well provoke from the Dragon King.

The dragon craned his long neck, his massive head wagging back and forth, nostrils twitching for individual scents, probing the adventurers with senses only dragons possess—taking stock of his enemy.

"One of you possesses, Spellfire … interesting."

Shocked at this disclosure, Omegas looked around at his companions.

The dragon chuckled. "You are all of you so foolish. You hide secrets from each other, and none of you know what is truly happening here and on Ashyer."

Flustered, Omegas stepped forward. "Omegas, head of the Order of Wizards—"

"—I know who you are, wizard," the dragon growled. "Omega, an ancient word of a dead language spoken by your distant ancestors. Will you be the last of your kind, Omegas? Very well, ask, and I will tell you truths that will darken your heart."

Omegas grappled for composure. "Dragon King, what do you mean about our ignorance of what is truly happening here and on Ashyer? Enlighten us, so we may die fully apprised."

The dragon sighed, a trace of smoke escaping his mouth. "As I thought. It makes no difference." He swiveled his head slightly toward Vigo. "Perhaps … *time before memory* then. My world was at war with itself. Two races battled for many millennia—the dragons and the ones you call angels. Her race," he rumbled, tossing his chin toward Nightshade. "I know of the common belief that you are all descended from angels, but this is not true. Both men and immortals have always existed on Ashyer since before we arrived. Their bloodlines have always intermingled. There were Giants as well on Ashyer, and many other creatures that have nothing to do with your strange beliefs—but the angels were born here, the world of dragons." The king yawned, exposing the blood red flesh inside his jowls.

"We were weary of war," he continued. "We wanted to end the fighting, but there was no end in sight until, one day, more than a thousand years ago, my world suffered the Day of Great Cataclysm. It came from the sky and killed many dragons and angels. It brought together two worlds, mine and yours. The Day of Great Cataclysm destroyed landmasses and our worlds began to circle each other.

"Soon, we discovered that the worlds aligned once every solar year, and that a crossing between the worlds was possible. The giant rocks showed us the way, the debris of Ashyer's true moon, otherwise destroyed on the Day of Great Cataclysm.

"Dragons crossed to the kingdom of Redim and were welcomed by the residents. Dragons and humans began to trade goods. Humans revealed magic, which was unknown to the dragons. In turn, the dragon kingdom fought alongside humans against their enemies. Human magic helped dragons end the war with the angels. Within a few short years, we wiped our world clean of them. A few angels fled to Ashyer. With the help of humans, we hunted them down."

The dragon turned his head, fixing his charred, unseeing eyes upon Nightshade. "Belladonna objected to the entire conflict—both sides of it. She abandoned her own people to their fate. Belladonna, you hid yourself well. We never could find you; we assumed you were dead. It is clear to me now, you lessened yourself to blend in with humankind."

Ty turned to look at Nightshade—her eyes cast down, her cheeks flushed, her expression a mix of emotions hard to interpret, perhaps anger, perhaps shame and regret.

The Dragon King resumed, "With the war over, we decided to return to our own world and live in peace. But the humans had other designs. The following year, when the bridge appeared, they crossed over to our world to ask us to intervene in the conflicts that had arisen on Ashyer. Redim wanted to rule all of Ashyer, but the other great kingdoms did not comply. Ashyer was consumed with war; Redim was losing. Dragons returned to observe the war and witnessed great suffering everywhere.

"Since it was our initial intervention that allowed Redim to grow so powerful in the first place, we proffered a treaty before the immortals who led the great kingdoms. It was decided then that one immortal leader from Ashyer would join with the dragons on our world, and together we would maintain a balance of power on your world.

"Peace was maintained for only a short time a thousand years ago. Then, a conjunction occurred, and we came to check on the lasting peace. Crystals powered massive airships carrying armies that slaughtered millions of people. The dragons surveyed your world and found few immortals had survived; fewer than a million humans lived to draw breath.

"That was when we forged a new covenant with the leaders remaining on your world. Humans, it seems, are always ruled by someone or something, so we proposed putting ourselves in charge—for your own good, you understand. The few surviving immortals agreed. Airships were destroyed along with many other massive weapons. In time, humans grew to fear dragons. They offered us annual tithes to stave off destruction. After many centuries, when the past was forgotten, humans perceived us as terrible taskmasters from the sky, just as you do today. No one remembers that long ago, their ancestors decided that this master and subject arrangement was the best way to prevent another war that could very well destroy Ashyer."

The Dragon King paused, allowing time for his brief history to sink into the minds of the questers come to destroy him. After a heavy silence, he continued, "Your arrival is a very brave act; most likely your last brave act. My dragons have grown uneasy with taking annual tribute and become contemptuous. Many dragons believe we owe nothing to Ashyer, or Redim, and that it is time to end our ancient agreement. I disagree. No dragons alive today were alive during the angel wars. They don't understand how much we owe the long-dead wizards of Redim. Many dragons have become cruel. Some lurk upon your world and never return here. I have heard rumors of a valley of yellow mist in the mountains of the Middle Kingdom where some of my dragons gather treasure and indulge themselves. I have a solution to this unfortunate situation. One of you must join me in ruling your world once more, the way our ancestors found peace so long ago, combined with laws to quash unsanctioned magic use. With an alliance between dragons and humans in place, the kingdoms of Ashyer can unify. Progress for all will result." The air about the rebels rustled as the Dragon King inhaled. "What say you brave fools?"

"I knew dragons were full of fire," Ty muttered, "but I didn't know they were so full of hot air."

Frost lifted his sword, regarding the sheen of blue steel, remembering his father standing defiantly on the bloodstained battlefield. He saw again the bloody hordes—eviscerated goblins and dead men. He remembered Cirrus' admonition—"The dragons are greedy and will always want more." He recalled the city of Olan in flames and wondered, *Could the King be telling half-truths? Is this the beginning of a new war and not the end?* "None of us—" he began to say when Vigo stepped forward.

"I will join you. I will rule Ashyer at your side for the good of all."

The group drifted apart leaving Vigo standing alone.

Victoria spoke with a broken voice, "Vigo, no. They killed your family."

"Or was it my family's actions that got them blown up?" Vigo shot back, his eyes exploding white with Spellfire.

Dragon King's jaws parted as if he were grinning, his teeth exposed like daggers.

The dragon was after Vigo the entire time, Frost thought. *Vigo has the Spellfire, whatever it is, and now the dragon has it.*

Frost retreated back to the others and whispered, "It's time to go."

The Dragon King chuckled. "I'm afraid you are too late, for the conjunction is ending. You are all trapped here with us for a year—or you would have been, if we allowed you to live. Vigo!" the dragon roared, "what shall we do with these usurpers?"

Vigo's raised staff began to glow along its length. A strange flapping sound came from above. Suddenly, Nightshade descended upon Vigo. For the first time, the questers beheld her true form—wings of black, metallic feathers stretching almost as wide as dragon wings, dwarfing her bright, luminous body. With incredible speed she seized Vigo and threw him at the wall with such great force he fell unconscious, extinguishing the Spellfire.

The Dragon King's tail crashed down on Nightshade before she could square off against him. She fell to the ground at the feet of the others. Her wings slowly withdrew, swaddling her body like a cocoon. Only then did her companions realize that her black scale armor had actually been her wings, wrapped tightly around her.

Ty rushed forward and lifted her. Frost leveled his sword at the Dragon King. Omegas stepped in front of Frost and addressed his former apprentice, Cirrus. "Remember the laboratory!" Then, to the others, he shouted, "The rest of you, go now!" Omegas cast up an enchantment shield a bare instant before the dragons filled the chamber with fire.

"This way!" Krenn yelled, tearing space-time with his blade, opening a portal to the tower of Redim. "Quickly! Run!"

Ty lifted Nightshade and dashed for the escape, Frost close behind. Victoria, tears in her eyes, stood next to Krenn in a moment of hesitation, then dove through the portal.

Only Cirrus lingered. "Omegas!" he shouted.

"Go now!" Omegas struggled to maintain the integrity of the invisible shield against the onslaught of steady Dragonshade. Cirrus leapt through the portal. Krenn followed, glancing behind to see that Vigo had regained consciousness and Omegas was being incinerated. He passed through the portal on an ebbing wave that thrashed him wildly. He landed on the heap of adventurers, all bleeding badly from the space jump journey. Overhead, the floating rocks had drifted apart. The conjunction was ended.

Cirrus stood slowly. "We must save Omegas!"

Krenn grabbed his arm. "Omegas is gone. Unfortunately, the traitor Vigo lives. The enemy cannot follow, for the alignment is no more."

Cirrus collapsed on ancient stones and began to weep. Frost put a hand on his shoulder, finally understanding—Omegas was Cirrus' father. He gave Cirrus' shoulder a squeeze; Cirrus grasped Frost's hand.

Nightshade came around and asked, "We're still alive?"

"Most of us," Ty replied.

She looked at the party members one by one, noticed Cirrus weeping, and understood.

"How did we escape?" she asked.

Ty just stared at her before speaking. "Why didn't you tell me you were an angel?"

Cirrus cut short Nightshade's opportunity to answer. "We have to go, now," he declared.

From below, thunder of approaching footfalls warned of an assault by many goblins.

Cirrus touched the rune at the base of his staff and the *Azure Sphinx* drifted toward them, hovering close to the top of the tower, the ramp lowered. Six haggard companions boarded the ship, and it sped away into the clouds.

8. The first battle

Frost had to reorient himself when he woke from a troubled dream about his father— he saw a dusty room in Acamea castle, far, far from home. In his dream, he had been in Olan castle, his home destroyed by vengeful dragons. It had been days—perhaps a week, he couldn't tell—since the confrontation with the Dragon King. After their escape from the ruins of Redim, the adventurers flew to Acamea, where General Krenn gave them leave to stay and rest for as long as they needed.

The first few days in Acamea passed in a slow blur of weariness. Krenn had addressed the people, Frost remembered, proclaiming that they will be free of the dragons at last. At the mention of someone named Sir Roland, Krenn's people cheered.

Old rooms of the castle were cleaned out; the old banners were raised; but Frost was too tired, his heart too heavy, to pay attention to such details.

He sat up in a giant bed and studied the room that, for the time being, was home. Though it had been cleaned, dust remained on most surfaces. He wondered if his room was a symbol of the entire world—*would everything they brought back to life be covered in dust? Probably so,* he mused.

Speaking with Victoria and Krenn, two companions Frost judged as honest and good hearted as his mates Ty and Cirrus, he asked them how Vigo could be so different. "I understand the lure of vengeance," he told them. "But I don't understand how that can drive a man to do terrible things. I thought there was more to Vigo than hunger for power. It makes him incredibly dangerous."

No one, to Frost's knowledge, had asked Nightshade about her true form. She seemed quite content that everyone treated her as they had before they learned her story, everyone except Ty. Frost was unsure what had transpired. Once fast companions, after meeting the Dragon King they were not often seen together. Frost resolved to speak with Ty about it.

Cirrus went into deep meditation after arriving in Acamea. He had appeared at supper the night before to inform them they would gather in the throne room on the morrow for a meeting to discuss their next course of action.

Frost jumped out of bed, dressed and hurried to the meeting in the throne room. He could already hear voices. Guards lined the halls—one posted at every other pillar.

The Captain of the Guard bowed. "Good morning, Your Majesty."

"Just Frost. Frost will do fine. I am not your king," Frost looked the well-armed guard up and down. He wore a ceremonial red blouse and black trousers trimmed in gold. "Why are you all stationed here?"

The guard, his voice unsure, replied, "I think ... that the General thinks ... you and your lot are pretty much the most important people in the world right now. I am stationed here to protect you."

Frost smiled and began to walk away. "Protection? Have you ever fought a dragon, Captain??"

The guard couldn't think of a response that wouldn't make him sound foolish, so he remained tight-lipped and hoped that no dragons would show up.

The large double door to the throne room stood open with a guard at either jamb. Frost nodded smartly. A few long tables in the throne room were littered with scrolls, but the rest of the furniture had been pushed out to the walls. Frost's companions sat at a square table in the center of the room eating breakfast while skimming over tomes and maps. The empty chair at the head of the table was his. There was a new face at the table that Frost did not recognize.

"Good morning, everyone," said Frost. All heads popped up and looked at him. "Good to see you all again." He addressed the stranger. "I don't believe we've met, Sir. Since you break bread with my friends, I must assume you are of good character."

The man pushed his chair back with noisy nervousness and stood. "Lord, I am Cidric, a historian of sorts. Your comrade Victoria remembered me from a conversation we had at the Inn before you traveled to the moon. She has invited me to help you with your research." Cidric adjusted his spectacles and straightened a blue hat that reminded Frost of a mushroom top, before noisily resuming his seat.

"Well met, Cidric. I am Frost, um, Fredris Olan."

"Yes," Cidric smiled broadly, "You are King of Olan. It is an honor to meet you, Lord."

"An honor?" Frost shook his head. "I seek not to be honored… which brings me to this empty chair. Reserved for me at the head of the table?"

Cirrus jumped up. "Frost, someone must take charge of the revolution. We have one year to prepare for war with Vigo and the Dragon King. We have chosen you to be that leader. I know you didn't ask to be leader, and you may have doubts about your readiness to lead, but it is our belief that you will make a fine commander. Please, join us. Sit—at the seat of Honor, where you belong."

Frost shook his head in resignation and sat.

Ty and Nightshade sat next to each other; no obvious tension between them, which greatly relieved Frost. Cirrus and Cidric sat together engrossed in excited, scholarly conversation. Victoria sat quietly next to Krenn. She had been quiet for days after returning, often standing on her balcony at night contemplatively staring at the waning yellow moon weeping—as if she expected something lost to return from above—pale moonlight illuminating her beautiful golden hair hanging loose to her shoulders. It was clear there was more in her heart than the mere loss of a traveling companion.

"Seven is a good number," Krenn said to Frost, drawing him back from reverie.

"The odds of seven of us vanquishing the dragon army are slim." Frost picked at his food but ate nothing.

"We will find a way to triumph. We must," Krenn said. The General's attempt at a reassuring smile did little to convince Frost that the revolt he was voted to lead could succeed. Krenn was charismatic, a formidable man for his age.

"Festive," said Frost, gesturing at the General's new hairstyle.

"Yes," replied Krenn. He'd woven his dark, curly hair into tiny tresses. "We need to look our best for the people. They think we will be killed by dragons any day now, so we must dress and act unafraid, like we know what we are doing. If my people see me in a ragged state, it will lower their morale. If I look bold and intimidating, it reassures them that perhaps victory is not an empty dream."

"What do you believe, General? Is victory an empty dream?" Frost asked, one eyebrow raised. "Or is it possible?"

"Once you hear what these two have been talking about, you won't have to ask." Krenn gestured to Cirrus and Cidric.

In response to Frost's inquisitive look, Cirrus said, "Finish your meal, Frost. If my guess is right, it will be a long day."

After a few quick bites to take the edge off his hunger, Frost could wait no longer. "When are we returning to Olan to free our people from the goblin filth?"

Nightshade shouted, "Thank you! I've been asking them that for days."

Ty thumped his goblet on the table in agreement.

Cirrus raised his hands. "Wait, as I have told you already Nightshade, we must first insure the safety of this city. Then we will take the *Azure Sphinx* to Olan. A messenger from the dragons should arrive here this very day. By evening we will have taken a great step to make the city safe."

Frost spoke up again. "Every day we wait inflicts more suffering on our people. We must be done here and move."

Cirrus spoke calmly. "I know you are anxious to help our people. So am I. But I am afraid I will have to try your patience even more. On our journey home, we must visit the mountain that Omegas called The Laboratory for a short while. It may hold the key to our overall victory."

Frost was about to protest, but Cirrus raised his hand again. "We have outfitted the *Sphinx* with ballistae, so we have weapons to fight dragons. I am not worried about the distant shade of dying dragons over mountains; we will blow them out of the sky if they try to attack us again."

Frost took a moment to calm himself. "Why the laboratory? What do you think we'll find there?"

Cidric the scholar interjected, "With the help of your extensive library, I have confirmed Cirrus' suspicion that the mountain is in fact the laboratory of Lorid the Sorcerer. The magical power held in that place should be incredible."

Frost was confused. "Lorid? Wait, what extensive library?"

Ty cleared his throat and said, "I never liked that Vigo fellow. So, when he was occupied in the dragon's castle, I borrowed the contents of his pockets." Chuckles erupted around the table; Victoria even gave a sad smile. Ty grinned, relishing the approval, and continued, "The only thing I thought I found was a writing device. I was going to throw it away, but then, what with the dragons attacking, I just shoved it in my sack. The other day I was going through my things and Victoria saw it."

Victoria took up the tale with much less enthusiasm. "When I was living with Vigo, he created a magical room. The door is drawn into existence with that pen or wand. In that room are all of his books from the old keep." She gestured toward a square hole in the floor near the throne. Frost rose and approached the hole, a ladder extending down into a lit room. Curious, he slowly closed the trap door. With a click, the portal became only faint lines in the dust on the stone.

"My gods," Frost said in astonishment.

Ty smiled. "Pretty amazing, isn't it? Would be invaluable for a thief with the city guard hot on his tail."

Frost turned to the table with a horrified grimace that changed the jolly mood of the table to somber silence. "Any wizard powerful enough to make such an item could easily defeat the entire world. He wouldn't even need the help of dragons."

After a moment, Cirrus gestured to Frost. "Come back to the table. We have much to discuss, much to plan."

Frost dutifully returned to the head of the table.

Cirrus addressed them all. "Any wizard powerful enough to make such an item must have great power, more power than is possible for a mortal man. In days past, great wizards used small crystals called power crystals, as does the airship. I believe Vigo must have a power crystal somewhere in his body, which is why he burns with Spellfire. Legends say that the most powerful wizards had Spellfire as a result of implanting crystals in their body. The telltale sign of the internal location is a strange glow, but in the dragon's throne room I was unable to perceive its location because he was covered."

A childhood memory flashed in Victoria's mind. She was tracking a strange boy through the woods when she saw him fly into the air. The memory contained more clues, but she could not summon them from the depths of time.

"We'll chop Vigo to pieces then," Krenn said seriously, "and recover the crystal."

Frost cleared his head with a shake. "All right then, that just leaves an army of dragons." He sighed. "Tell me, who is the sorcerer Lorid?"

"From all I've learned," Cidric explained, "Lorid was the greatest wizard in all of history. He vanished after the Cataclysm. Legend has it, wizardry was not enough for him. He invented a new form of magic called sorcery and proclaimed himself Lorid the Sorcerer. After that, he disappeared into the upper Middle Kingdom. He was last seen over a thousand years ago, just prior to the arrival of the dragons and their traveling moon. The magic he wanted to experiment with at the time involved time and space.

Some believe that Lorid forged the blade that General Krenn now wields, though I doubt it personally."

Frost looked around the table. The information seemed new to everyone except Cirrus. "The upper Middle Kingdom," Frost pieced it together, "the place we detected strong magic on our way to Redim."

Cirrus nodded. "Yes. The laboratory is there."

Nightshade spoke. "You really think he was powerful enough to bring my world to yours?"

Cidric appeared startled and confused by the question. Frost was relieved that Nightshade's true nature had not been revealed to others beyond their immediate party.

Cirrus answered Nightshade's question, "It is possible that, intentionally or otherwise, Lorid was the key to the Cataclysm that brought our worlds together, yes."

Frost leaned in close. "So, what do we have at our disposal for this plan to defeat the dragons? I have the blade my father made for slaying dragons, and my steel bow. What about the rest of you?"

Ty chimed in, "I got wicked darts! And a portable room ..."

"And I wield the Blade of Time and Space," Krenn said with grim purpose.

Victoria cleared her throat. "My armor is made from the metal I extracted from dragon scales. It also does this." She stood and pressed the first button on the neckpiece. Armor encased her. There were some gasps of awe around the table. Victoria pressed a second button and her helmet and swords emerged.

Ty broke the stunned silence. "That is some fun stuff! Can you make me a suit like that? I'll gladly borrow enough money to pay for it!"

Victoria retracted the armor and returned to her seat. "Vigo took some of my dragon metal for himself. He created his staff and cloak from them. I should mention, he was the one to enchant my armor, so it is possible he might undo the enchantment."

Cirrus stood. "I have my staff." He held up the blue metal staff festooned with enigmatic runes. "I do not know the scope of its power yet, but I am a full storm wizard now. I can strike dead with lightning just about any creature. Also, it summons the *Azure Sphinx*."

Cirrus reached into a pouch on his belt and produced two power crystals. "Omegas gave me these before we left the ship. He gave me something for you as well, Nightshade." Cirrus walked over to a strong wooden chest that looked out of place among the clutter and opened it with a wave of his hand. "The contents are yours, though I am forbidden to touch them ... as I am a mere mortal."

Nightshade peered into the open container and discovered something she thought had been lost to time. Using both hands, she lifted out golden plate armor. There were silver wings engraved on the chest. She spoke softly to Cirrus. "The armor of the Angel Queen ... thank you."

Cirrus nodded. "It was on the *Sphinx*, but for Omegas, the moment to present it to you never arrived. Now it is yours, unsoiled by mortal hands." Cirrus addressed the table. "We may find many relics over the coming year we thought were lost to time."

After a brief silence, Cidric said, "I have only the knowledge that rattles in my head. I am not a great warrior, nor do I have any magical talent. I am just a scholar, but if you would have me along, I can cook an excellent stew. Some of the best recipes in history rattle around in this head too."

Everyone laughed, even Victoria. The little man clearly charmed her.

Cirrus broke in. "My new friend, your knowledge may prove to be our greatest weapon."

T he group seemed in a good mood as they talked. Frost leaned back in his chair and waited for conversations to ease before asking, "How are we going to make this city safe tonight? What are we going to do about the dragon horde in the desert west of here?"

Cirrus flashed a cruel smile. "Tonight, we kill them all."

A round of "Here! Here!" erupted around the table.

Frost waited for the revelry to quiet. "Sounds good, but—"

Cirrus leapt from his chair and threw up his hand, silencing Frost. The adventurers listened as one to the clang of metal footfalls echoing in the hallway. Krenn slowly rose and readied his blade. Then a figure clad in shabby metal armor appeared, a human skull adorning the creature's crude helmet.

In a rasping voice, the foul figure addressed them. "I am the messenger of the dragons from the Sea of Sorrows. I have received your request for an audience and have come to inform you—"

Krenn tore a portal and appeared behind the figure in an instant, interrupting the creature mid-pronouncement, his blade to its throat. Krenn knocked the skull-helmet off, revealing a lizard-like visage beneath.

Cirrus settled back into his seat—a deliberate signal of disrespect—and said to the creature, "You will return to your vile masters and inform them that this city is free. We no longer serve their wretched kind."

The creature wriggled uncomfortably. Nightshade stood, blades extended on her arms. "Let's just roast him now," she said.

Victoria activated her suit and swords. "Sounds like a tasty treat to me. I'll bet he tastes like snake."

The creature stopped moving. "Harm me and every dragon will attack this city within the day!" it screamed.

Krenn spoke quietly into its ear, "And how many would that be? Two, maybe three? Nothing to us."

"We are ten dragons strong! And if you know what is good for you, you'll surrender now and let me go," the creature hissed.

Cirrus again stood. "We will let you go, but not to signal our surrender. You will tell these craven wyrms that this territory is protected by powerful warlords now. If they wish to keep it, they must come and get it." A rune on Cirrus' forehead started to glow. "Tell them! Powerful warriors and a grand wizard as well."

"Wizardry! You will pay for these crimes!" the creature wailed.

Cirrus gave a nod to Krenn and said, "Make us pay then."

Krenn slashed a portal in front of the lizard that opened to a mountain in the desert and pushed the screaming creature through. The creature landed hard on sand-swept rocks and began screaming before the portal closed.

"That should do it." Krenn smiled grimly.

"Ten dragons," Frost muttered, contemplating his sword doubtfully. *It would work just fine if the dragons lined up for us to slay one by one. Not likely, though.*

"Frost, they will never even reach the city walls," Cirrus said encouragingly. "We have thought this one through."

"Guard!" Cirrus cried. One of the guards posted at the throne-room door stepped forward. "Tell them to move the *Sphinx* to the designated landing."

The guard whirled and stomped out, the thump of his footsteps quickly receding down the hall.

Cirrus turned to the group, "By your leave, Frost, we shall walk through the city with our weapons out to show the people that we mean to succeed. At the spot in the outlands where Acamea pays tribute to the dragons, the *Sphinx* will be waiting. I will take the ship to a strategic point and conceal it. When the dragons come into view, I will bring the *Sphinx* behind them. You and General Krenn will launch our first attack from a great distance. If any dragons manage to reach the clearing, we will fight until all are dead."

Frost studied his sword for a moment, then looked up in astonishment as Cirrus' plan became clear in his mind. "You mean for General Krenn to create portals for my blade—dragon slaying from a safe distance!"

Cirrus grinned. "Exactly! Not a bad plan, eh?"

Krenn smiled. "If the dragons become confused, some may try to retreat."

"In which case, the *Sphinx* has ballistae now," Ty laughed, "and she'll be waiting for those cowards."

Nightshade shook her head. "*She* again. The airship doesn't resemble a woman, but I guess now that it's armed to the teeth, at least she'll act like one."

With weapons in hand or slung over shoulders, the revolutionaries left the throne room, guards following double file. When they reached the castle entry, more guards joined the escort.

"A show of force. I see," Frost said quietly to the General, who grinned with satisfaction.

The guards marched down the main street past the statue of Sir Roland. The column did look impressive, Frost thought, as throngs of people gathered either side of the street to watch the parade. The number of onlookers swelled until most of the city had assembled to behold the spectacle. Krenn raised his sword in a fearsome salute. The crowd started to cheer. As excitement caught on, the entire city roared its pride and encouragement.

When they had nearly reached the outer wall, a girl of about fourteen came running up to Cidric, books tucked under her arms. One look was enough for Frost to know that she was Cidric's daughter. The girl marched beside her father. At the front gate, guards separated into two lines. Heavily armed companions walked between the guards who returned Krenn's salute. The Guards of the Throne stopped at the city wall, and after a nod from Krenn, they closed the imposing metal gate separating the adventurers from the guards and city.

Raucous cheers faded as Frost led his warriors and wizards across the outlands towards the field of tribute.

When they were well clear of the castle gates, Frost joined Cidric. "This must be your daughter?"

Cidric looked nervous. "Um, yes. Her name is Miraph. I, um, I didn't want her to stay in the city without me, but she has um, some talent. She could be helpful."

Cirrus chimed in. "That book under your arm, Miraph, I recognize it. You must have magical talent?"

She held up the book. "Yes. I've mastered all the spells in this book and was hoping to learn more."

Cirrus appeared stunned for a moment. "All the spells in *that* book?" He looked more closely at the single rune on the cover. "This is the Book of the Shadow—one of the most difficult books to master, and one of the most dangerous. If I understand correctly, wizardry is forbidden in these lands."

"It was," Krenn interjected.

Unfazed by the exchange, Frost asked Miraph, "You realize what we are about to do, the danger?"

"I do, and I think I can help you. If you are going to use portals to slay dragons, I can help stabilize them using my magic," Miraph said proudly.

Frost fixated on Miraph's hair. Something about it was not quite right—wavy and white with black spots here and there—but when he tried focus on the spots, they disappeared.

"My hair?" Miraph asked. "Yes, it is strange. My spots are actually stripes, and someday I will be able—"

Cidric cut her off, gently but firmly. "That is enough for now, Miraph. We must prepare."

"Many of us are not quite what we seem," Nightshade said. "No use hiding anymore." The sound like great banners unfurling caused Ty to jump aside as Nightshade spread her shiny black wings—almost as wide as those of a mid-sized dragon—and took flight. With her wings spread wide, her Angel Queen armor glowed with a fiery golden light.

"This ought to encourage them to fly this way!" Nightshade shouted.

Ty muttered to Frost, "I don't like this."

Frost reassured him with a confident nod. "I think she can handle herself. She must be pretty tough to put up with you. Worry about your own skin. You're no angel, my friend."

Ty appeared more serious than usual. "I guess so ... what good are darts against dragons?"

"Never underestimate the smallest weapons, for that may be your biggest mistake," Miraph replied, her eyes still fixed fondly on Nightshade.

"You're not an angel, are you?" Ty asked, taken aback by the sage wisdom coming from a young teen.

A little crestfallen, Miraph answered, "Nothing so wonderful."

"Never underestimate the smallest things," Ty reminded her. They smiled together.

Moored in the clearing ahead of the warriors, the *Azure Sphinx* generated propeller wind that bent grasses, some swaying violently for at least a hundred yards aft, like a wake behind a sailing ship. Nightshade circled over the clearing, her silhouette against the sky like some giant bird of prey.

Cidric and Miraph, already witness to one marvel—a flying angel—were awed by the mystical ancient airship.

Before boarding, Cirrus called to the others, "Victoria and I wish the rest of you luck. May we all meet back here, safe and victorious!"

Victoria followed him up the ramp, her hair blowing wildly. Frost gave a terse wave.

Frost noticed Ty gazing up past the *Sphinx* at Nightshade. He said to his friend, "You love her, don't you?"

As if he had been caught red-handed at mischief, Ty mumbled sheepishly, "I do."

Frost gazed for a moment at the magnificent angel soaring above and quipped, "Those wings look a bit sharp, hope you don't get cut in the wrong spot."

Ty punched Frost in the shoulder. "Come on, Your Majesty. We've got dragons to kill."

Frost watched the *Sphinx* speed west, its foredeck equipped with ten giant ballistae, a massive iron crossbow bolt cocked and ready to fire from each one. As the ship grew smaller, storm clouds started to spiral out. It banked south and soon vanished into the dense wizard storm Cirrus cast. The storm began to slow and then hovered on the horizon, its unnatural clouds moored to the warship cloaked inside.

he stage is set, Frost said to himself. *Now all we need are dragons.* He peered westward. His stomach tightened when he spotted several black dots on the horizon. *How many are there? It is too soon to tell.* Frost shouted, "All right, everyone, this is it! The dragons are on their way."

Nightshade called down from above, "There are only nine. We may have to track down the last one."

"Let's focus on these nine first," Krenn shouted, waving his sword. "I need them to be closer before I can attempt a portal. Ready your blade, Frost."

With a satisfying *shink*, Frost drew the blue-steel dragonslayer from its sheath, readying it with both hands.

Krenn stood just in front of Frost, his blade raised for a first strike.

Ty watched Nightshade. The angel hovered about twenty yards directly above the group, her fists clenched. Her presence would assure to capture the dragons' focus, and guarantee surprise.

Cidric gripped Miraph's shoulder, the wizened lines of his normally kind and jolly face stretched taut with concern.

Miraph merely smiled, thinking how silence before a battle excited her.

Suddenly Krenn yelled, "Now!" He tore open a portal directly above that revealed only sky. Far in the distance, in the flight path of the first dragon, the exit portal ripped open. Frost did not hesitate. He thrust the dragonslayer into the portal just as dragon scales started to pass across the small tear in space.

The cold steel blade pierced the underbelly of the beast miles away.

Frost was yanked violently up toward the opening. "Help!" he yelled, unable to let go of the blade or wrench it free of the portal and the dragon thrashing in a death throe.

Krenn threw his strong arms around Frost's waist, pulling both Frost and the blade back from the opening. They landed on the ground hard. The lead dragon on the distant horizon spiraled dead toward the ground.

"My gods," Krenn muttered. "Nearly lost the blade. That would've been the end of it."

"We didn't nearly lose the blade!" Frost snapped back. "My grip would have held tight to my dying breath. We nearly lost me!"

The General tilted his head slightly downward. "My apologies, Your Majesty."

Frost shook his head. "No, no apologies necessary, my friend. Just a little jarred by dangling from a dying dragon." Frost crouched and said, "This isn't going to work. I'm just not strong enough to fight the force of flight."

Over Frost's shoulder, the others saw the first dragon plummet into a great cloud of dirt as it slammed into the distant desert to the west.

"Their momentum will pull Frost right through, unless we anchor him," Ty said. "Otherwise, looks pretty darn effective."

"I can help!" Miraph yelled, running forward. "Open the next one, trust me!"

Frost regarded Miraph with uncertainty. "Trust you?"

Krenn raised his blade and nodded to Miraph who cast a spell. Then, she touched Frost gently. Frost's body became dense and strong, a mountain rooted in bedrock that no force could move. With renewed resolve, he signaled Krenn to tear into space again.

The General made another tear, and Frost struck hard with arms like steel, stiff and hard to bend, but he was not pulled when his blade ripped a gash in the underbelly of the second distant dragon. A huge beast, the dragon fell toward the portal as it closed. The vortex sliced through its scales when it closed, covering the warriors on the ground with dragon gore.

Frost unceremoniously shrugged a hunk of dragon meat off of the top of his head and yelled, "Again, quickly!"

Krenn opened another portal, achieving the same result. A third dragon went down spraying flesh and ichor through the closing portal.

"This is getting messy," Ty grumbled, his cheeks splatted with drops of dragon blood despite his distance from the closed vortex.

The six remaining dragons slowed and circled in the distance, confused by the loss of their fellows. All the while, the storm silently slid in to block their escape.

"Find a target and use your sword!" Frost yelled to Krenn.

Krenn observed for a moment, gauging where the next dragon would pass, then he ripped open space time. Frost thrust his sword powerfully and another dragon fell from the sky. The remaining five dragons started breathing fire wildly at the ground, miles away from their true enemies.

"They don't know where we are!" Nightshade yelled. "Keep going!"

Krenn tore open another portal and Frost brought down another dragon, but this time he and his companions near the opening were blown back by dragonfire.

Ty and Cidric rushed forward to extinguish the flames raining down upon their downed companions. None appeared seriously injured, but Miraph had not seen the wave of fire while casting her spell and had been knocked back with its full force. She lay unconscious but breathing.

"Two coming this way, two retreating!" Nightshade yelled down to Frost. He looked to the west. Two dragons were bearing down on them at full speed while the other two retreated into the storm.

Suddenly, huge explosions flashed inside the clouds, creating a firestorm. The concussive sounds reached them after an eerie pause; a racket worse than thunder. Dragon gore rained to the ground from the burning storm. Then, the *Azure Sphinx* burst from the clouds at full speed, riding the shockwave toward one of two dragons still capable of doing damage. The beast slowed and hovered, craning its head back and forth from the angel to the airship, uncertain which enemy to attack first.

The *Sphinx* fired a volley of six large, iron bolts at the dragon. Maneuvering expertly, the dragon banked and whirled, dodging four of the projectiles, while another bounced harmlessly off its hide. The sixth arrow, however, sank deep between soft scales on its lower neck. The dragon exploded into chunks of scorched flesh and scales a safe distance between both the ship and the angel.

The last dragon decided to take its chances with the fighters on the ground and resumed its flight toward them. With a mighty whoosh, Nightshade sped to meet the dragon, catching the enemy off-guard. Unable to react in time, the dragon wrestled as Nightshade grabbed it around the neck. The two titans tumbled from the sky, spinning over and over in a jumble of wings and tail and limbs.

Ty sprinted toward them when they hit the ground with the tremendous crunch of breaking bones. He feared the worst, thinking even an angel could not survive such a fall.

Fortunately, the dragon survived the fall sparing the fighters on the ground from being consumed in its death conflagration. The beast thrashed in pain beside Nightshade, who lay immobilized. The dragon laboriously raised a twisted foreleg. Ty saw what it meant to do with its mighty talons poised to pierce the golden-armored form sprawled unconscious on the grass.

Ty leapt and yelled, "Hey, Ugly!"

The dragon's long-jawed head tilted birdlike in Ty's direction just as a steel dart pierced its cat's eye retina. The dragon snapped up the steely claws to cover the puncture, saving Nightshade from being shredded.

Frost stepped through a portal near the dragon and quickly assessed the situation—Nightshade lay motionless, Ty at her side; fiery plasma leaked from the dragon's punctured eye. The warrior king charged straight at the dragon. His powerful blade sank deep into the beast's belly. With a long moan that made Frost's temples throb, the dragon rolled over. Instead of erupting into an all-consuming explosion, its belly began to implode.

The *Sphinx* passed overhead and landed in the clearing. Ty knelt at Nightshade's side—her wings mangled and splintered, they slowly wrapped themselves around her body. Her face was badly cut in many places, a sticky clear fluid seeping from the wounds. Ty caressed her cheek. "Nightshade," he moaned, "what has happened to you?"

The angel's eyes opened. "I will heal," she whispered, "My blood is not red like yours, Ty. My blood is clear."

Ty held up two fingers wet with clear, prismatic fluid shimmering, sparkling, riveting. "It's beautiful," he muttered.

"It is true then," Nightshade said in a husky voice.

"What is true?" Ty asked, mesmerized.

"My ancestors said that the sight of our blood could enchant a fool." She laughed and began to cough. Ty looked into her eyes and flashed a smile marred by worry.

Frost hefted his sword out of the dragon's withering body and helped Ty carry Nightshade back to the clearing. Miraph was on her feet again, assisted by Cidric and Krenn. The ramp of the ship opened and two soot-covered figures appeared—Victoria and Cirrus.

"Close call up there?" Frost asked Cirrus.

"Nothing we couldn't handle. Will she be all right?" he asked, pointing to Nightshade.

"She says she will recover," Ty said without much confidence.

"We have healers onboard," Cirrus said. "Honestly, I don't know if they can help an angel, or if angels even need help healing, but we must all board. There were only nine dragons, leaving untold numbers alive to attack us again."

"There is still one in the desert," said Frost. "We must go and finish our work."

"Can't have a rogue dragon with a vendetta flitting around," Ty nodded.

With the eight companions onboard, the *Sphinx* flew a direct course to the western desert. On the bridge, Frost peered through the lens at the broken teeth of desert hills. Nightshade sat up and leaned against Ty. Cidric and Miraph watched with stunned pleasure at the desert whipping past below the airship.

Krenn, Victoria, and Cirrus all snapped out of a deep conversation about battle tactics when Frost yelled, "There it is!"

Just inside the mouth of a mountain cave lay a dragon curled up. A lizard messenger, dwarfed by its master, stood watch.

"It appears they're waiting for us," Frost shouted.

"Perhaps we should hold the *Sphinx* back and teleport to the cave," suggested Cirrus.

Nightshade spoke in a weak whisper. "You think it wants to talk? How much talking did the one that broke my wings do? Kill the beast! If you want to talk, speak with the miserable lizard servant."

Frost pulled his sword. "We kill it, like we did the others," he said.

Krenn did not hesitate to tear open a portal on the bridge, one so well placed that only dragon scales were visible through the hole.

Frost leapt through and plunged his sword into the dragon.

Krenn and Victoria followed him through the portal, with Cirrus straggling behind.

The other four watched through the lens as the dragon died, twitching violently, its bulk barely shifting from the spot where it had lain.

Frost strode up onto the back of the dead beast and called down to the lizard man, "You wanted to talk I presume?"

The servant hissed and circled, finding no way out but through Frost's companions who flanked the creature. "My master was sure you would talk with him," said the lizard. "He wished to surrender."

Frost smiled. "Instead, I'm talking upon his dead carcass. I accept your surrender. You will lead us to the chamber where you have taken the riches of the people who live here, or you will suffer for your master's crimes."

The creature bowed, quite accustomed to obeying orders, and led them deep inside the mountain to chambers littered with treasure, coins and jewels strewn about without attention to value or organization. They found the most recent haul from the time of the moon in a large cavern. The dragons had obviously been stealing from their own yellow world, as the adventurers discovered crates from all corners of Ashyer. Many of the heaps contained food and dead or dying livestock.

Krenn stared down at a familiar treasure chest bearing the markings of his city. He wheeled upon the lizard messenger. "You're coming with us. Your penance will be decided by the people of the land."

Krenn slashed open a portal leading to the statue of Sir Roland and pushed the lizard man through along with the treasure chest. Krenn bellowed to townspeople, "We have defeated the dragons!"

The throng filling Roland Square cheered when they recognized their Lord. Then a respectful hush fell over the crowd when Krenn spoke again.

"This is a dragon henchman. I leave his fate in your hands. He can be put to work or put to death. That is for you to decide. Guards, hold him." Guards stepped forth from the pressing crowd. "Now, I will be opening this portal many times and sending many goods through. Our city will eat well again, and we shall be the richest in all of Redim." Unrestrained cheers followed Krenn's proclamation.

The General raised his voice to shout over the clamor of the excited crowd. "When the dragon moon returns in one year, there will be a great battle." This lowered the crowd noise to hushed whispers. "I will be away, trying to prevent it from becoming a war. Use the time that remains to build fortifications and to train, lest you be caught off guard when the time for battle arrives! But today, and tonight, celebrate, for we are victorious!" The people cheered wildly. Even the lizard-man seemed heartened by the thought of ultimately defeating the dragon overlords, forgetting for one moment his uncertain fate.

9. A closed door

Krenn and his companions spent hours sending supplies, weapons, and all manner of treasure through multiple portals to Acamea. On the final trip, Krenn addressed his people, hiding his exhaustion, "There may be a disastrous war approaching, remember my words; and do not venture into the desert. The search for more treasure is a fool's errand. You now have all you need and mustn't draw unwanted attention to yourselves in this time of preparation. Farewell!"

Krenn stepped through the last portal, and it closed behind.

Victoria laughed, "What unwanted attention? You know no creature will dare venture to this mountain."

"The desert is a creature none of them understand...and so is greed," Krenn answered.

Victoria nodded her head in understanding, the smile vanished from her face. She thought of Vigo, *was it greed that caused his betrayal?*

"Our work here is finished for now General," Frost said. "Are you sure you wish to continue with us? You trust your people to heed the warning?"

"I will follow you. Your cause is just, and I wish to prevent a war." Krenn answered wearily and tore reality one last time to connect them to the bridge of the airship. It seemed the blade had almost sapped him of all strength.

Once they were all aboard, the *Azure Sphinx* sped away from the desert sands and turned northwest. Miraph pressed her face against the glass to watch the world sweep by. Her father conversed with Cirrus and Frost.

Victoria sat beside Ty and Nightshade. "How are you?" she asked the angel.

Nightshade opened her eyes, the gaze seemed somehow less human—both frightening and enchanting. "You are very conflicted about Vigo. He was the only companion you had for countless years…and you hope to persuade him back to sanity, to love?"

Victoria was shocked into stunned silence.

"She does that." Ty apologized.

Nightshade continued, "His thoughts that day in the Hall of the Dragon King were twisted between revenge and righteous rage. The path of madness he has followed seems self-justified, and therefore does not appear as madness to him. The man you knew is gone; he has chosen a new path." She paused. "I am sorry. It is what was in his mind. Both of my wings are broken, and it may be some time before I can fly again. That was the foremost concern in your mind, thank you."

Victoria looked troubled. "I'm truly sorry Miss Nightshade, for when you fly it is a wonderful sight."

Less than an hour later, all eight companions were in sleeping quarters as the airship raced northwest above the ocean toward the Middle Sea.

Exhausted as he was, Frost could not surrender to much-needed sleep. He obsessed about Olan City. *Will there be anyone left alive by the time we return? Am I a terrible ruler to abandon my people in their most desperate hour?* Over, and over the thoughts nagged him until he decided to give up and return to the bridge. Ascending the stairs and opening the door, he found Ty standing at the main table on the bridge.

"Who needs sleep?" Ty greeted him, dark circles under his own eyes.

"I keep thinking–"

"About Olan," Ty finished the statement. "So do I. My friends, the League of Thieves, they were in the tunnels last I knew. They're probably all dead."

Frost joined his longtime friend. "We will do what we can for the people who live still. One thing is certain—after we return, the only goblins that will remain in Olan, will be dead ones."

"It's going to take months to get rid of the stench," Ty said. Both, driven by sheer exhaustion, began to laugh giddily, as if boys once again.

"No laughing on the *Sphinx*," a stern voice issued behind them.

They turned to see Krenn had joined them. He had a smile on his face that belied the tone of his voice. "By all means laugh, my new young friends. You are right. When we reach your kingdom, we will slaughter the goblins like animals, and your people will be free. I cannot wait to join in battle." Krenn laughed.

Ty and Frost laughed along, but with a bit of uneasiness at the bloodthirsty nature of Krenn's mirth. A man who rejoiced in killing that much was a little scary. *He is a general; isn't that what they're good at?* Frost thought. *He is one of the greatest warriors our world has known, isn't he? Thank the heavens he's on our side.*

Cirrus joined them. "We are near the laboratory, gentlemen. I know you are eager to get this over with, so I will endeavor to make it as quick as possible. I still believe that the key to winning the war with the dragons lies there. At the very least, we will certainly find some answers."

Within the hour, the ship landed along the southern coast of the upper Middle Kingdom, and the eight companions hiked carefully toward the non-mountain. Soon, they saw something strange—at the base of their magic mountain was a large charred spot with a circle in the center.

"That must be the entrance," Cirrus postulated.

"Dragonshade," Cidric said. Reflexively, they all looked to the sky. But the marks were old and cold.

As they reached the circle at the base of the mountain, Cirrus began examining marks, and Ty inspected the edges of the round entryway, drawing on his expertise of locked doors.

"This damage is aged," Cirrus confirmed. "It seems dragons tried to gain access and failed—several times. The lowest layer of burning might be centuries old."

"We are going to enter a fortress that dragons have failed to breach in hundreds of years?" Frost asked dubiously.

"Not any time soon," Ty said, and they all looked at him. "The door has no damage on it, so it cannot be destroyed—the dragons tried that. Nor does it bear dust, so it must be magically protected and sealed. Look at the indentations all around it." Ty pointed to five large holes encircling the center. "These are the keyholes to this door. Once all five keys are inserted, the entrance must activate. I can find no hinges, nor mechanisms, so it cannot be circumvented."

"How do you know?" Krenn asked.

"Let's just say, I'm good with doors," Ty said with a smirk. "We need to find the keys, but these look like indentations the size of swords. Could the keys be weapons?"

"Yes!" Cidric startled them all as he ran forward to touch the door. "I know what the keys are! You are right, Master Ty. They are swords." He rustled in his large sack of books and found one. After locating the page he wanted, he quickly scanned some lines, then paraphrased to the rest, "Five swords there were, one for each kingdom. Some were old, and some were forged with great new magic to fight the wars." He looked up, "I believe we already have one of the keys … General."

They all looked to Krenn, who produced the Blade of Time and Space, held it up to one of the spots on the door, which began to glow. He started to move the sword toward its spot when Cirrus stopped him. "Wait General!"

Krenn withdrew the sword and re-sheathed it.

Cirrus explained, "The sword will likely not be removable unless we complete the set, and we need that blade."

"It has come in handy," Ty agreed. "Hell, it's the cornerstone of our offense."

Cirrus turned to Cidric. "What are these other blades?"

Cidric again quickly perused the book. "I can tell you what they are, and where they were intended to be, but not where they currently are of course. Let's see ..." He pushed his spectacles up his nose. "We have the Blade of Time and Space, the prize of the lower Middle Kingdom. Then there's the Blade of Kings of the upper Middle Kingdom, that can only be wielded by a king of noble birth. Next, is the Blade of the Forest, prize of Olan with dual abilities ... whatever that means. Then the Blade of the Inferno, prize of Anden, a blade with such intense heat it can cut stone. And finally ... oh."

"Oh?" Ty said, "What's wrong?"

Cidric closed the book and looked at Ty. "The last blade, I know where it is." This statement startled them. "The last blade is the prize of Redim. Its powers are vast and deadly even to the wielder. It was one of the objects I studied about at the academy. It is called the Darkblade, and it is currently in the hands of an insane immortal who calls himself Godslayer. You see, one of the properties of the black katana is instant death to anyone who has any long blood. The insane man who possesses it now has decided that it is his quest to rid the world of all people of long blood, believing them to be false gods. At last report, he was living in the cursed valley to the east of our city, General Krenn."

They all pondered the door and at the mountain for a few moments, absorbing these new revelations.

Miraph spotted something in the rocks to their right and investigated. She found what looked like a wash-basin on a pedestal.

"What is this?" she asked, touching it.

The basin began to glow, and the translucent figure of a girl appeared floating in its center. The figure began to speak. "A question. For centuries I have awaited a question. I am the information node of the complex that is contained within."

"A little talking ghost girl!" Miraph exclaimed as the others came to see. To the figure she asked, "What are you?"

"I am an interface node," the image said.

"What is your name?" Miraph continued as if she understood completely.

"Number twenty-one of complex eighty …"

"I'll call you Ghost Girl," Miraph cut her off.

"Very well."

Miraph was excited by her discovery. "Why are you in a bowl?"

"My designers decided that it would be more esthetically pleasing if I appeared to be standing on the surface of the water," the talking girl told her.

How long ago was that? Miraph wondered out loud.

"Yes," Cirrus stepped up beside Miraph, "how long ago were you enchanted and who was your maker?"

"I am not an enchantment. I was made many thousands of years ago—long enough that my memory has begun to fail. As for my creators, they were humans, but their names have also been lost."

Cidric was intrigued. "You mean you are not magic, but some kind of mechanical device?"

"I have no moving parts, but that would be a simple way to describe me," the Ghost Girl answered.

Frost stood behind the basin. "If you have been here for thousands of years, you should be able to tell us about this door and mountain."

"Yes."

Exasperated, Frost said, "Then by all means, please tell us."

"The door was created after the new planet was drawn toward this world. The other factions of this world believed that a facility that could harness the power of a volcano must be closed forever unless the entire world decided otherwise. The facility was discovered and repurposed by a creature called Lorid."

Cirrus squinted his eyes slightly and looked sideways at the image. "Creature?"

"I do not know how else to describe a human who does not age."

"So there were no immortals in the time when you were created?" Cidric asked.

"No."

Cidric was intrigued. "When did they first appear on Ashyer?"

"I do not know as my range of observation is limited, also there are large sections of time when I was dormant."

Miraph asked, "Can you be moved? Can we take you with us?"

"Yes; however, I am unsure if I will function correctly away from the facility. I do not know my range, but you may do with me as you please."

Frost lifted the basin. "You will come with us then. You know too much, and there are dragons near to this door."

"You are correct. The dragons have attempted to open the door for centuries, and for centuries they have failed."

Frost smiled. "We guessed as much." To the others he shouted, "Let's get back on the *Sphinx* and head to Olan." Casting a sideways glance at Cirrus he added tersely, "*Then* we can gather the other blades."

Cirrus looked hurt. "Frost, I too want my home to be restored. After we have liberated the city, I believe I may know where the Blade of the Forest is hidden."

Frost appeared chastened. "Sorry, Cirrus. I'm just eager to free our people."

"As you should be, my King," Cirrus said as he helped Frost carry the basin up the airship ramp.

10. The Battle of Olan

The *Azure Sphinx* hovered a few miles off the coast of Olan. As night arrived, and the shrinking yellow moon rose in the west, Frost peered westward through the giant lens at the chaos of his city.

"We kill them all," Frost said with gritted teeth. "Every quarter of the city is in flames, people hide from the goblins in every street. Those foul monsters are…they're eating people. No prisoners, no mercy, no quarter. We kill them all!"

Standing near Frost, Cidric spoke. "A little mercy could make way to cooperation. How will history remember this day?"

Frost looked at the humble man for a moment, contemplating. Then, his eyes flashed with anger again and he said, "I will be the king who killed every one of the foul, murdering filth that infested our city. You are the historian; write it any way you choose."

Ty peered through the lens. "They have one of those giant goblins guarding the city square. That drooling sack of manure must be fifteen feet tall."

"Bigger target," Krenn grinned.

"There will be our first strike." Frost turned back to the lens. "Then, we separate and clean out the city while rousing any willing fighters from their homes. I will kill the giant creature with the dragonslayer." He gave Cirrus a quizzical look. "If it kills dragons, I assume it will freeze goblins just as effectively?"

Cirrus nodded confidently.

"Ty, you have goblin-lethal darts?"

Ty nodded.

"Victoria and Krenn, I assume you can handle anything that mangy pack might throw at you?"

Victoria gave a little thumbs-up, and Krenn showed his white teeth in a menacing grin that sent a shiver through more than one of his companions.

Victoria activated her armor. The shiny-black plates clicked together all over her body, and blades shot out of each gloved hand.

"I love that," Ty said admiringly, "it never gets old. Seriously, I need one of those suits."

Frost continued his instructions. "Cirrus and Miraph, stick with Cidric. Nightshade will defend you from any close encounters in the square but use spells to eliminate goblins or help the people. Perhaps a storm to quench the flames?"

"Indeed," Cirrus agreed.

Frost addressed the crew. "After we land, take the ship up but not out of visual distance. The *Sphinx* is a powerful weapon that will distract and baffle small minds."

"Hey," Miraph said, as if taking Frost's remark about "small minds" personally.

"You know what I mean," Frost flashed her an amused grin. "Are we in agreement?"

Everyone responded in the affirmative.

"Then let's do this!" Frost pointed dramatically at the city through the window.

"He's going to be *that* kind of King then?" Nightshade asked Ty, who merely chuckled.

Frost turned around. "Let's just go do it." Nightshade saluted, and Frost laughed with an edge of anxiety.

The *Azure Sphinx* swept over the burning city and hovered directly above the giant goblin in the city's withered center square. The ramp opened, and Frost appeared with his sword drawn, blue steel twinkling in the firelight. With a battle-cry he jumped, sword clutched in both hands over his head. The slow-minded foe had not a moment to react to the bizarre scene unfolding above him. The blade sliced its massive head in two like a melon. Frost landed, bloody sword in hand, and the giant goblin toppled behind him with a ground-shaking *thud*.

The other companions floated magically to the ground, weapons drawn. Terrified goblins fled the square in all directions.

Miraph stepped forward. "One moment, Frost." She cast a strange spell, creating a portal three times her height beside her, and a glowing white horse stepped out. "Use him to pursue and raise the alarm."

Frost grinned and mounted the fiercely glowing horse. He charged down one of the larger streets waving his sword and yelling, "To arms! To arms! The King has returned! Rise up Olan! To arms!"

Cirrus raised his staff, "I will conjure the storm. Miraph, I assume you can provide light for our task?"

Miraph nodded. A storm began swirling above them, and rain fell. Then, giant orbs of light sprang from Miraph's hand, flew over the city, and gave light to darkened streets. The sounds of terrified goblin screams echoed from all quarters.

Krenn flashed an eager look at Ty and Victoria. "Time to hunt, my friends!" He pulled his blade and was gone in a blue blur.

Victoria and Ty exchanged glances, nodded, and ran separate ways, their weapons at the ready.

Nightshade gave her arms a twitch, and blades appeared all over her body just as a group of fleeing goblins came their way. The goblins froze when they saw the airship hovering over the square. Nightshade sprang at them. Their horrified screams were cut short. Goblin heads and limbs flew in all directions.

One goblin managed to circle around behind Nightshade with a crude axe and struck her in the back. It did not penetrate her tough exterior, but it did aggravate her existing wounds. She yelped in pain.

A wave of energy flowed through Miraph at the sound. She had felt it before, but never this powerful. She knew what was going to happen and let go. Her body twitched, and hair began to grow from every part of her body. Her arms became forelegs and grew razor claws. Now a white tiger with dark black stripes, she leaped on the goblin from thirty feet away with only one thought in her feline mind—kill.

The angel and the tiger easily bested dozens of goblins who had fled to the square in a frenzied retreat.

From a side street, a motley horde of goblins rushed in at full speed. On their heels were Ty and some of his ragged but hearty-looking old friends, all throwing darts and felling the ranks.

Nightshade and Miraph met the horde head-on and chewed through them. Miraph suffered stabs and slashes from desperate goblins, but none of the wounds were deep.

"Don't target the woman with blades or the tiger!" Ty yelled to his roguish buddies. "They're on our side … at least the woman is. Probably the tiger."

When the horde lay dead, Ty and his friends met Nightshade and the tiger in the midst of the reeking, piled corpses.

"That worked well!" Ty was ecstatic. He looked at the tiger. "Miraph?"

The tiger nodded its head.

"I knew it! You are full of surprises. Hey, can we drive more large groups into the tiger's den?"

Nightshade smiled deviously. "Bring them on!"

After two smaller groups were trapped and dispatched, the four began to hear a growing rumble. The largest horde yet was coming their way from the main street on the south side.

Cidric, who was clutching a shovel for defense and holding back alongside the wizard, said to Cirrus, "Perhaps a channel for them to be contained?"

Cirrus smiled. "I think I understand." He shouted to Nightshade and Miraph, "Wait for my signal on this one!"

They nodded and stood on-guard. A terrible stench wafted into the square before a stampeding horde, at least two hundred strong, charged into the trap, axes and swords drawn but in full retreat.

Cirrus raised his arms and shouted an incantation. Two walls of electricity appeared on either side of the enemy, preventing flanking or escape.

"Now!" Cirrus shouted.

With that signal, the battle was engaged.

Whenever pieces of goblin were tossed into the air, they were vaporized by the electric field. The stench was terrible, and the noise deafening.

A few goblins managed to get through the ambush, only to be summarily laid low by Cirrus' staff. Cidric even gamely jumped in and knocked a goblin's head sideways with his shovel.

As the ranks of goblins thinned, the fighters in the square caught glimpses of the carnage being wreaked on the back end of the dwindling horde. Death on the goblins' heels came courtesy of Krenn, Victoria, and Frost, along with a mustered force of about thirty men armed with everything from swords and spears, pitchforks and planks.

Soon, the last goblin fell, shown no quarter or mercy. Cirrus dispelled the electric walls.

"I think that's the bulk of them," Frost said as he dismounted the astral horse. The blood-splattered mount stepped back through a shimmering portal, which then vanished, along with the steed.

Frost the King raised his sword in salute to all the gathered warriors. "Good work everyone! Olan is free!"

The proclamation was greeted by cheers from the fighters, and the chorus was joined by people who now peered forth from doors and windows all around the square.

A short, ragged man approached Frost, "Your Majesty, Ty asked me to find you. He asks that you come to the tavern."

To the people Frost shouted, "Citizens of Olan, continue to search the streets and rouse the people." Then he turned to his friends. "Let's go see what Ty has for us this time."

The seven companions trudged through the half-ruined city until they came to a building that was largely undamaged. Frost remembered what Nightshade had told them the night they met— the goblins set up their headquarters at Dragon Snot, the tavern.

Apprehensively, he looked up. Perched atop the tavern was a dragon. Tiles slid off, knocked loose by the beast's twitching tail, and shattered on the cobblestone street. In its front right talon, it held Ty.

Frost wondered if forgetting the strategic importance of Dragon Snot Tavern was going to cost him the life of his dearest friend.

"So, *King*, you have returned. You were a coward to flee, but now I will make you pay for your absence," the dragon said in a guttural voice.

"If it's me you want, take me. Spare this citizen," Frost said.

"You think me a fool, Fredris? This is Ty, your friend. You may have destroyed my army of slaves, but I will make sure you do not live to see your kingdom rebuilt."

"I'm not worth it!" Ty yelled. "But if you must talk to this ugly loudmouth, by all means, *keep talking*."

Nightshade started to move forward, but Frost stopped her. "What can I do to persuade you otherwise?" Frost yelled up to the dragon.

"You wish to dicker with me? Look at what you have done! What could you possibly say that could ... ?" The dragon began to sway a little.

"I will say anything you want. I will promise anything you want," Frost replied as the dragon's wings began to droop. "As long as you keep talking so the poison can take effect."

"Poi ... poison?" The dragon's eyes flicked to look down from drooping eyelids at Ty, it's not-so-docile prey. Ty was smiling as he lifted up the slackening claws, one by one, and wriggled out from the talons. The dragon dreamily regarded its now-empty palm. Several darts punctured the spaces between scales. The wounds were not deep enough to release fire or emit pain.

Ty slid down the eves of the roof to the street and ran clear. The dragon's head lazily swung back toward Frost as its eyes began to close. "Curse you …"

The dragon rolled off the roof, crushing the building next to the tavern.

It lay sleeping in the ruins, its breathing deep and rough, as Frost picked his way through the wreckage. "No. Curse you." With that, he plunged the blade in, and it breathed no more.

Frost turned to see all seven of his companions waiting. They looked tired and bloodied. "Who needs a drink?" He shouted.

Krenn sheathed his sword. "If you're buying, I'm drinking."

Frost entered the tavern and immediately walked back out. The look on his face extinguished any small feelings of revelry that had arisen in the group. "The reality of goblin subjugation awaits us inside. Prepare yourselves."

Victoria extended her blades.

Frost held up his hand. "This task will not require weapons…but we must face it." The others exchanged bewildered looks, except for Nightshade. She walked forward and put her hand on Frost's shoulder. Tears were starting to run freely from his eyes.

"We are with you, Frost. I think I understand," Nightshade said.

All thoughts of celebration drained away as the victors entered the tavern.

Inside, they beheld a scene of horror. A goblin tavern now, blood coated the walls, most of the floor was covered with filth, and the worst—roasting spits erected at the back of the room. On each spit was a roasted human corpse. Some were very small.

Ty gasped. "Ivan and his family. They owned the tavern." He began to weep.

Frost nodded slowly. "We will restore this tavern to show the people that we can recover from the horrors of the past week. We will bury the victims in the graveyard this night. I will hold official court here in defiance of despair."

Somberly, some fighting back gag reflexes or shedding silent tears, they all agreed and began to work in solemn silence.

After Frost and Krenn removed the bodies of the family from the roasting spits, Ty covered them in cloth and the others helped carry them out in a procession led by Cirrus. Many citizens came to watch as they marched to the graveyard. Some followed in their grim wake.

Frost remained in the tavern with Krenn to continue working. When the funeral procession arrived at the graveyard, some of the men who had followed Frost into battle gathered shovels and other makeshift tools to dig holes. With over a dozen pitching in, and the ground soft from Cirrus' storm, the burial was quickly done.

A sizable crowd had gathered to watch. The companions took a moment in silence to reflect, then turned to the crowd.

Cirrus stepped forward and spoke. "We have reclaimed the city this night, and tomorrow the King, Fredris, son of Xan, will hold court at the tavern. Spread the word, and rest easy, our enemies are gone. Now is a time for mourning and restoration."

The crowd slowly dispersed as the companions made their way back to the tavern. There was no cheering, only a calm, resolute manner to the people.

As they walked, an old man approached Cirrus and said, "We are with you, brother. The Order of Wizards are all here in the city."

Cirrus nodded. "Come to the tavern tomorrow. I am sure the King will need your aid." The man bowed and walked away.

Miraph walked up beside Cirrus. "If there were wizards in the city, why did they not fight to prevent this? Surely they have enough magic to repel one dragon and the goblins."

Cirrus did not meet her gaze as his brow furrowed. "Once a coward, always a coward. I'm sure their entire lot stayed well-hidden during the occupation. They only came here because Omegas ordered them to come, but his intent was for them to help the people. We have seen how helpful they were." He cast a backward glance toward the graveyard, then said to Miraph, "You have a rare, brave heart, little one. I fear most people are more like those cowards, deep down."

As they turned up the final street, Victoria asked, "During the battle in the square, who summoned the tiger?"

Before Miraph could speak, Ty broke in. "Miraph summoned the tiger. Good bit of magic, huh?"

Victoria beamed at her. "Excellent magic! It was an exquisite tiger and a great fighter."

Miraph regarded Ty wonderingly. "Thank you, I think." She had a questioning look, but Ty merely winked, and shook his head. Cidric appeared relieved.

The mourners returned to the tavern to find the floors clean and the roasting spits gone. With the added help, and magic, the remains of the horror were swept away within an hour.

Krenn and Cirrus moved two large tables together near the back of the main gathering room. A chair was placed on the makeshift dais for Frost's court on the morrow. With the help of Victoria and Nightshade, Ty produced several barrels of unspoiled ale and clean tankards.

Their work done, Ty popped the cork from the bunghole of a barrel. "Now it is time for that drink." He filled tankards and Victoria distributed them. The companions, exhausted and grieving, accepted the ale gladly.

"You've always wanted to run a tavern, haven't you Ty?" Frost asked as they all took to benches around a side table.

"Yes, sure, but—" Ty started.

Frost interrupted him. "If there are no living family members to claim this property, I hereby proclaim that the Dragon Snot be yours. Try to forget the horrors we beheld when we first arrived.

We need a base of operations here in the city, and I doubt the castle will be just a daylong clean-up job."

"Some people might complain," Ty said. "I might complain."

"Let them. I'm the King, remember."

Nightshade smiled. "So *that's* the kind of king he's going to be."

The gathered friends smiled at this quip and continued to drink. After one last round, they barred the door and shuttered the windows. They retired to the upstairs rooms where the tavernkeeper and his unfortunate family had lived.

By the light of the small fire in the upstairs hearth, Nightshade, still awake, looked up and met Cirrus' gaze.

"What?" She whispered.

"You're blushing." He gestured with his eyes to her lap where Ty's head lay cradled. "It's not polite to watch someone's dreams."

The corner of her mouth lifted in a crooked smile. "You'll never know."

Cirrus shook his head, smiling ruefully. "I probably don't want to know." He rolled over and shut his eyes.

omeone was gently shaking Frost. His eyes focused on Victoria, who was kneeling beside his cot; morning had come. "The people are here," she said. He could hear the commotion of people gathered outside—half of Olan, by the sound of it. His companions were rousing themselves.

Ty stood at a glass-paned door that opened onto a balcony, the curtain drawn just enough to peek out. He whistled. "You've drawn quite a crowd."

"Perhaps you should address them," Cirrus suggested. "You could step out onto the balcony and say something."

Frost stood up, all his muscles stiff and sore, and pulled on his tunic and breeches over his undergarments. Yawning, he said, "No time like the present. Let's do this."

Ty pulled back the curtain and opened the door for him. As he walked past Cirrus, the wizard muttered an incantation and lightly touched Frost's throat, whispering, "Just speak normally."

When Frost stepped onto the balcony, a cheer arose from the huge crowd outside.

Frost nodded and waited a few moments for the cheering to die down. When it seemed like it would continue elsewise, he raised his hands, gesturing for his people's attention. To his own surprise, when he did finally speak, his voice projected so loudly it drowned out all remaining crowd noise.

"PEOPLE OF OLAN." His voice echoed from the far walls of the city and in the surrounding hills.

Modulating his voice as though he were talking to a person standing directly in front of him and not to a vast, sprawling crowd, he continued. "We have taken back our city!"

Many cheers met this. He continued, hushing the revelry, "I have come before you to help rebuild. The castle will be the last of our concerns. First, we must bury the dead and clean our city. There must be no acts of violence, no attempts to profit from others' losses or misfortunes. Such behavior will not be brooked and will be punished with severity. Any of the city guards that still live will report below for specific assignments. We must help each other to make our city live again. Also, we must prepare for war."

The crowd became very silent.

"With the next coming of the dragon-infested Moon, we will make our stand. We have seen the end of our oppression! The dragons will be defeated!"

There was a huge roar of approval from the crowd. Frost waved and left the balcony in the most regal manner he could muster. Ty closed the door behind him.

Frost turned to his friends, appearing relieved. "We will hold court downstairs for some official business. I am not very experienced at this, so I guess I'll need help. General Krenn, I would like you to sit by my side as a visiting dignitary from Redim ... if that's all right?"

Krenn nodded assent.

"Thank you. Miraph and Cidric, these upstairs rooms were unsullied by the goblins, but they could use some good cleaning and freshening. Can you two get them whipped into more appropriate shape? I think this will be our home for some time."

They nodded in acknowledgment.

"Ty, since you have been appointed the new owner of the Dragon Snot Tavern, perhaps you and Nightshade can start learning the ropes today? I think there will be great need for ale... On the house today, if you don't mind."

"First day of business and he's putting me out of it," Ty quipped.

"Put it on the royal tab. You will be compensated out of the Treasury."

Ty smiled at his own joke, but his smile melted as pictures of the dead flashed unbidden into his head. Whenever he looked at the far end of the tavern downstairs, he could almost see the bodies, the spits ... first chance, he would do some major remodeling.

Frost continued, "Victoria, if you will accept the honor, I would proclaim you First Knight of the King's Court."

She bowed. "My King, I would be honored to serve you, and hereby pledge my undying fealty."

Frost smiled in spite of himself. "I don't anticipate any death today, but times are strange. Oh, and please leave your helmet off unless needed. I want people to see a woman in charge of knights. Times are changing, and we will be the force behind that change."

Victoria nodded, activating her armor sans helmet.

Lastly, Frost turned to Cirrus. "Cirrus, my teacher, mentor, and friend. I'm afraid I must ask you to run the court, interview, and introduce, as well as advise. You may be the last person in the kingdom who really knows what they are doing."

"Of course," Cirrus nodded with a look of understanding.

Resigned, Frost said, "All right. Let's do this."

Royal court began in earnest. The first group to come before the king was the city guard as commanded. They complied with Frost's orders and set off to patrol. A small number of guards were assigned to the castle area where the city treasure lay, and new barracks needed to be built. Then came an endless stream of grateful well-wishers. Cirrus formed them into groups and bid them keep any gifts. He was usually successful, but on the few occasions he was unable to persuade them, Frost accepted the gift humbly.

The parade of people continued for hours. The only difference came mid-afternoon when the wizards arrived.

Frost stood, "Omegas ordered you to the city to defend. How did your magic go astray?"

The wizards clustered together and mumbled excuses.

Frost sat, still looking down on the old men, "You have new orders. Make plans to defend the city from a Spellfire Wizard and dragons. Also, choose an empty building and move the school here, within the walls."

They looked grumpy at this but did not object.

As they began to shuffle toward the door, Frost added, "One more thing—leave a complete set of spell books for a new pupil of Cirrus."

They looked even more put-upon by this, but again did not object. Frost thought, *Of any group, they might pose the biggest problem in the city.*

As the sun set, the crowd thinned to only a few. Finally, one last person came to thank the king.

"You'll want to listen closely to this one," Cirrus said as an old woman entered carrying something wrapped in cloth.

The old woman unwrapped an empty scabbard almost as tall as herself. It was green tinged and had black leather straps fastened to it in six places. "This has been in my family for generations. It was given to us by the people of the woods to hand down, until one emerge to save the world. As I did not have any children, nieces, or nephews, I thought I had failed the duty entrusted to my family line, but the time has come. I present you with, let's see, what were the exact words? Oh yes, I present the Key to the Forest to One worthy to wield the Forest Blade." She tried to hoist the scabbard up to a shocked Frost.

Frost jumped down from the table and took her burden. "Thank you. Have you been waiting all day?"

She looked on the edge of exhaustion. "Yes, my King, but it was important."

"It is indeed of the utmost importance, but you look as if you might expire from exertion." He looked to Cirrus. "I don't trust the old men, but the apprentices on the ship have been true and loyal."

"Say no more," Cirrus said as he touched the rune on his staff to summon the *Sphinx*. He carefully took the old woman's hand. "Come with me, I will make sure you are healed."

The childless woman fixed him with a tender smile and patted his hand. "There's no healing for age, young man."

"See," Cirrus muttered back over his shoulder to Frost. "Young Man."

The airship landed on the street in front of the tavern and the woman gaped at it in wonder.

Frost smiled. "We salute you and your ancestors for fulfilling your oath. Rest in our care tonight, amongst the clouds."

Cirrus led her onto the airship and returned alone. The boarding ramp folded upward and the ship sped away like an unearthly dragonfly, making the sign of the Dragon Snot Tavern rattle on its chains.

Frost examined the object in his hands. *The blade that is meant for the scabbard must be huge,* he thought.

Cirrus observed that the arrival of the airship had scattered the last of the onlookers.

"Sorry, Ty," Frost said, "No customers tonight."

Ty looked ready to drop. "That's fine. Im done." He threw the last of the cleaned tankards in a bin and flopped onto a bench.

"I hope you still have energy, Frost," Cirrus said. "The artifact has been presented. You and I should visit the secret place as soon as it is full dark."

"I thought as much," Frost said. "Ty, when I get back, we will have a talk with your friends in private. I understand they are mostly nocturnal anyway. It could be a few hours before Cirrus and I return, so you should be able to roust them by then."

Ty had closed his eyes. "Yep. I'm on it. No chance this guy is going to fall asleep ... no sir."

All eight companions were gathered together in the main room of the tavern now, so Frost took the opportunity to say, "Thank you, all of you. Last night was a great victory tinged with enormous sorrow, and I would not be standing here without all of you." Indeed, he mused, scanning the room, he did not know how events would have turned out had a single one of them been absent. Would fate continue to be so kind?

11. The Forest Blade of Olan

F rost watched as Cirrus presented the new spell books to Miraph. She was overcome with joy and began leafing through them right away.

"You shall study under my guidance to begin with," Cirrus told her. "That is not to say you need it, but there are some dangerous things that can go awry. You are a gifted spellcaster, and I would not want to see you accidentally blown up."

Miraph laughed but agreed.

Victoria sat next to Frost. "Are you sure you wouldn't like me to come with you? You may need your knight for unknown dangers."

Frost was sure he had to keep the lake a secret. He was conscious of Victoria's need to be part of the group, but he knew the task was only for him. "Thank you, Victoria, but I must do this alone. Cirrus will bring me to the entrance, but I must be the one to claim the blade of the kingdom."

"I understand. But if there is trouble, you make that wizard call the ship and I will be there in an instant."

Frost was a bit embarrassed by her show of loyalty. Despite his proclamation in the Court, he still harbored suspicions about her true heart. Now, he felt confused and a little ashamed of his mistrust. *Perhaps the world is not so black-and-white?* Frost extended his hand and placed it on Victoria's wrist. "It's a promise, Victoria. I know I can count on you. Make sure the others are safe while I'm away."

She arched an eyebrow. "With General Krenn and an angel, I do not think we are the ones in more danger. Be well, my friend."

Frost finished his ale and followed Cirrus out the front door. Without speaking, they nodded to each other and began walking northward along the streets of Olan. When they reached the city wall, the guard bowed and moved aside. They walked silently in the dark toward the northern bank of the bay. There, they made their way into the thickest part of the old forest, and Frost took the lead.

"There was a legend," Cirrus began quietly, "of a lake where the water was mysteriously calm even during a strong storm. It was called Dryad Lake and was said to be the heart of the forest. You would be challenged by the spirits of the wood if you dared to trespass. If one proved to be lacking, you were never heard from again."

"You think I swam in that lake?"

"From the stories you and Ty have told, I'm almost sure of it; and because you were able to swim in the lake, you have already passed the test. I dismissed the tale of the lake as mere legend. Now it will be a guide. There should be an entrance to an underground grotto on the shore."

Frost did not know how to broach it delicately, so he asked bluntly, "Will the woods judge you fit to follow?"

"I will not enter. I would not be judged fit because I have doubt in my heart. That is why you and Ty were allowed to swim—you were innocent."

"It's just over this rise," Frost said as they crested a small hill. The trees grew oddly close to the banks of a still lake with a mirror surface. It was completely unchanged from when Frost was a boy.

"Breathtaking," Cirrus said. "Come this way around." Cirrus started walking at a distance from the lake toward the opposite side. "Do you see that very large tree on the opposite bank?"

Frost gazed across the water. "Yes. We called that the owl tree, because we were sure there was an old owl living in the trunk of it. We stayed well away from it, lest we disturb the great bird."

"There is indeed something in the tree, and you were right to stay away, but now you must approach." They rounded the lake and came within twenty yards of the great tree.

Cirrus stopped. "I go no further. Take the artifact to the tree ... and just be yourself."

Frost was unsure, but he produced the scabbard and moved toward the massive sentinel. As he approached, a figure separated itself from the trunk.

The shape was that of a woman, but its form was composed of bark and leaves. It seemed to be silently regarding him. Then it spoke, "Welcome back, boy. You have become a man, and your heart is now heavy with sadness and pain."

"You must be a Dryad?" Frost asked.

"That is what your kind called me in ages past, and it will suffice. You bring an artifact, so you mean to enter your new home?"

"My new home?" Frost was surprised by the words.

"One who enters the grotto below the lake, is forever bonded. It will be part of you, and you a part of it."

"But I can leave if I wish?" Frost was a bit frightened.

"Of course, but at least once every year, you must return to refresh your strength. I think, however, you will desire the comfort of your new home more and more as time goes by; and at the end of your life, you will grow here and join the trees under the water."

"Trees underwater?" Frost was confused.

"You are armed. You must leave all your possessions and clothing behind when you first descend. Even as a boy swimming naked in the waters above, you felt the call. Make your choice, man-boy. Become one with the forest or leave here with your pet spell-mage."

Frost thought the term *pet spell-mage* was pretty funny and chuckled.

"That is more like it," the Dryad said. "Be at peace. Leave your sadness outside and join with the forest."

Frost smiled and began stripping. Cirrus saw from afar and started shifting on his feet uncomfortably. Frost waved reassuringly.

"Bring the artifact," the Dryad said as a staircase of knots and roots appeared inside the tree trunk. Frost picked up the scabbard and followed her into darkness.

At the bottom of the stairs, Frost beheld an incredible sight. Before him was a cavernous chamber of many sections with a transparent ceiling. He was paralyzed with wonder as he gaped at the lake suspended above his head.

"Is it really the bottom of the lake, or some illusion?" Frost asked.

"It truly is the lake. The barrier is formed of a clear crystal. Even the silt obeys our command here—we have instructed it to stay off the surface, so we may observe the waters."

"Incredible," Frost said as he slowly walked into an empty under-lake room. He watched as schools of fish swam by overhead. "How can I see them in such detail at this late hour?"

"The crystalline surface has a subtle luminescence."

Frost walked further into the room and stopped. He realized that there were several rooms, each the same shape as the first and linked with circular openings in the walls at equal distances. All rooms appeared identical.

"There's something at the center of the lake for me," Frost said. He walked with instinctual purpose, winding his way to the center of the lake, only to arrive at a sealed circle with the symbol of a sword pressed into it. "There," Frost said, "the Blade of the Forest is in that room."

"Very good," the Dryad said. "You cannot enter. You are called, but you lack the blood of the forest."

"Whom shall I seek that carries the blood of the forest?"

"You seek me, and I, you," the Dryad answered.

Before Frost could open his mouth to ask about the riddle, several lights approached from other doorways. He spun around to see many tiny fairies flying toward the Dryad and perching on her body. As more arrived, the Dryad began to glow, and the fairies started to merge into her as if the Dryad was absorbing them. When the last of the fairies landed, the Dryad began to glow so brightly that, far above, Cirrus could see the glow through the water of the lake.

"We shall bond together as one," the Dryad told Frost. "You and I will become one, and you will be of the forest."

Frost was alarmed as the Dryad began to glide toward him, but calming thoughts emanated from her, and he felt the warmth of her love. He gave himself over as the Dryad wrapped its branches around him in a loving embrace. He began to glow with her. He could feel himself changing. His skin tightened and became hard, yet still flexible. His eyesight changed, and he could see even the smallest detail of the empty room even in the dimming light.

Then, the voice of the Dryad spoke in his head, "We shall never be parted. You are now part of the forest, and your powers will only grow as you hone them. Look at the door and make it obey your desire."

Frost stared at the sealed entryway and thought, *Open!* To his astonishment, not only did the material that was blocking his way move down and away, but it seemed as if he felt an acknowledgment of his command from the soil itself.

The voice of the Dryad spoke again in his head. "You heard the earth speak; you cannot understand its language yet."

In the center of the revealed room beyond, a table of stone protruded from the ground and on the slab lay a twisted piece of metal.

As Frost entered the room, silence fell. It was as if the entire forest was watching him. He reached out and grasped the base of the metal. In an instant, it re-forged in his hand becoming a large sword of green hew. It looked exactly as he had imagined, *but*, he realized, *it did so by my mental command.*

The Dryad inside spoke. "You understand correctly. The blade will obey your thoughts. Your mind is an extension of your weapon in the forest. In ages past, it was commonly wielded, and was most effective, as two blades."

The image of the crest of Olan came to him and the blade obeyed. The large, unwieldy sword split into two smaller swords that could easily be held in each hand. As he spun them slowly, he felt great power all around, yearning to be summoned.

"As I told you," said the Dryad, "this is your home now. It will accommodate any of your desires."

For the first time since his transformation, Frost spoke out loud. "I understand." He was shocked at the timbre of his own voice—it had taken on some of the mystical tones of the Dryad. "There is a war coming, and I will fight for the forest and for Olan," Frost proclaimed to the creatures above and around, from the largest fish and tree to the smallest worms. He now understood that they were all connected, part of a larger living thing; and he was the weapon of that larger creature, defender of Ashyer.

The Dryad gave him one more command. "Lie on the table and gaze into the crystalline ceiling. You will be able to see far in time and space. Glimpse what our would-be destroyer has been planning on that other world."

Frost lay on the table, looked up at the rippling stars through the clear water and spoke one word as he closed his eyes. "Vigo."

12. Lord of the dragons

Vigo walked around the mountain of ancient books in the rough cavern dubbed "his royal dwelling." The cave might have been royal for a dragon, *but for a man,* Vigo thought, *it is a huge, filthy hole filled with piles of junk.* At least there were never before seen books. *Do the dragons laugh in distant caverns as I scramble up the piles looking for knowledge?* He wondered. *If only the books would arrange themselves for me.* As he thought it, his eyes burst into Spellfire, and the entire pile of books rose into the air, arranged themselves, and came to rest in an organized fashion.

"That's more like it!" Vigo exclaimed as he looked at his unintended work. "Now to find some books on the history of Ashyer." No sooner had he finished speaking, when several stacks of books levitated and moved to the front of the orderly stacks.

"Wonderful!" Vigo said and grabbed the first book.

Vigo spent days greedily consuming the knowledge from the tomes. The Dragon King had spoken truth—man invited the dragons to intervene, and it was man who needed to be controlled, lest he unleash terrible bloodshed.

The oldest crumbling book was a chronicle made in haste detailing great societies that destroyed themselves and the planet around them. It seemed to Vigo that self-annihilation was an insoluble part of mankind's nature. He knew then that, no matter how much blood was spilled, he must bring order to Ashyer for its own good. After that, perhaps he would take care of the dragons. They deserved his revenge, after all, and he would not need them after he restored order.

There were enough supplies in the main keep to last him a lifetime, though he had no plans of staying. As soon as the dragon's world conjoined with Ashyer next, they would attack in full force. When Vigo approached the dragons about strategy, the King directed him to a room where a crystal ball was stored. There he began to observe the world of Ashyer through its milky glass.

On the day that Frost acquired the Blade of the Forest and looked upward through the crystal lake, Vigo saw the most troubling things in the ball. All day he felt as if he were being observed. Watching the images in the ball he saw the dragons of Redim being slaughtered by Krenn and Frost, an airship flying across the world to a circular door with sword indentations etched in it, a battle in a city that ended with the slaying of a dragon, and finally, the ball revealed Frost lying naked on a stone table with two green swords next to him…and above the naked figure, Vigo saw himself looking into the ball.

A genuine feeling of panic seized Vigo. *How much had the boy-king seen? I must block the connection.* Spellfire burst from his eyes, and he grasped the ball. Concentrating hard on the image of himself in the sphere, he spoke a guttural curse, and the ball exploded.

13. Separate ways

Frost sat up suddenly as Vigo's face vanished, and the crystal ceiling made a loud *crack*. The lake was once again visible, and through the water, the night sky. Frost was alarmed to see a crack branching like a lightning bolt across the crystal above him.

The dryad spoke inside his head in a calm, measured tone, "When the wizard Vigo has been destroyed, the crystal shall be restored. Never have I seen a powerful wizard wield so much hate. He threatens the entire world."

Sounds of moaning came from the grotto all around him.

"What is that sound?" Frost asked as he slid off the stone table.

"Your predecessors. After time passes, you will come here to dwell with them. You will become a dryad with us, and you will not desire to leave ever again."

"What troubles them so?"

"They sense the danger."

The amorphous walls produced tree like dryads who encircled Frost.

"This has never happened before. They do not rest easy," the voice told Frost.

One of the dryads came forward carrying dark green, crystalline armor. Another produced a dark purple cape of silk.

"They offer their gifts to you, so you may destroy the one who has wounded this place. These are artifacts of great power from centuries past."

Frost accepted the gifts and donned them. He attached the scabbard to his back under the cape and sheathed the Blade of the Forest.

"Now go, you have much to do." The Dryad spoke not unkindly. "We will fight together."

When Frost emerged from the tree, Cirrus rose. He detected a subtle glow emanating from Frost's eyes. Those two deep-green orbs looked ominous in the dark.

Cirrus cleared his throat, "Everything go well, Frost?"

In a magically resonant voice, Frost responded, "We have much work to do, and yes, my friend, I am all right." He breathed in the forest air, feeling the tickle of energy all around him. It made him feel giddy, and before he could contain himself, he shouted, "Woo-hoo!"

Cirrus arched an eyebrow. "Woo-hoo?"

Frost fixed Cirrus with a near-manic gaze, wild energy darting in his eyes. "Yes my friend, this is very exciting! I smell victory for Ashyer!"

Cirrus regarded Frost somewhat warily, noting the new clothing and his changed skin tone. Mostly assured that this was still his former pupil and present King, he said, "Well then, Frost, we should get going, however, you will still need to carry the blue-steel blade."

Frost shrugged, picked up the blue blade as if it weighed nothing, and slung it on his back in a crisscross fashion with the Blade of the Forest. "So exciting!" He gushed. "Let us return right away!"

With great strides, Frost moved through the forest without making a sound. It was as if he knew where each branch and stone was without the aid of any light. Only a distant "Woo-hoo!" or "Come on, old man" enabled Cirrus to follow at great distance.

After several minutes, Frost stopped suddenly. Cirrus could hear him up ahead talking.

Upon arrival, Cirrus beheld Frost speaking to a large black bear. Incredibly, the bear seemed to be listening intently to what Frost had to say.

Amazing, Cirrus thought, *the forest has changed Frost forever. This new man, whom I barely recognize, can converse with nature itself! No wonder he feels so elated in the forest.*

Though anxious and impatient, Cirrus diligently waited, not wanting to interrupt a conversation with a bear.

Finally, the bear trotted off and Frost called, "Are you coming, my friend?"

"Right behind you," Cirrus shouted as Frost bounded off at an incredible and silent pace.

Frost only slowed when he could see the light of the city.

When Cirrus emerged from the dense northern forest, he found Frost lying on the ground and looking up at the stars, a strange twinkle in the green glow of his eyes.

Frost turned his head toward Cirrus. "What took you so long?" He sprang up and walked toward the city. "Come on old man, no time to waste!"

The tavern hall was dimly lit when they arrived, but the upstairs windows were dark. Far above in the sky, the *Azure Sphinx* held position.

Frost took a moment to admire the airship, "It really is beautiful."

Cirrus came alongside him. "Yes, I suppose it is. Are you sure you're all right?"

Frost's head swiveled toward Cirrus so quickly it made Cirrus jump. "Never better!" A wide grin spread across Frost's face. "Come on!" Frost pounded loudly on the door.

Cirrus shook his head. "Dryad magic. At least he's happy."

Inside, Ty sat at a table with many other people. All stood deferentially at the King's entrance.

As Frost and Cirrus came further into the light of the oil lamps and lanterns, there were audible gasps from some as they beheld his measure. Frost stood tall with dark crystal armor, swathed in a magnificent purple cape, but his eyes were unsettling as they glowed fiercely in the dim light. Green energy seemed to pulse with his heart. Like those of a wild beast, they did not give the sense of evil intent, only that a creature possessing such energy could be both extremely loyal and ferocious at the same time.

"Welcome everyone! At your ease, please resume your seats," Frost said with his new voice. "Cirrus, thank you so much my friend, but I will take care of this business myself."

Cirrus bowed and exchanged a furtive glance with Ty as he left the room.

The group of people at the table were visibly uneasy, their eyes darting around the room in case a quick escape route would prove prudent. They wondered what kind of "take care of" they were in for.

Frost sat down at the head of the table. "Hello, esteemed tavern-keeper of the Dragon Snot, finest tavern in all of Ashyer," he addressed Ty. "Thank you for assembling your friends."

"Of course," Ty seemed uneasy himself.

Frost peered at the people around the table with his piercing green-lit eyes. "I can smell fear."

The group moved back as one with this remark, leaning back in their chairs, the sounds of scraping as some chairs were scooted back on the floor.

"That is not good," Frost continued. "I need you all to be fearless."

He now had their rapt attention. "I know what you are. You were the league of thieves that troubled my father; no longer. Now, Ty will be your leader."

Frost sensed that someone wanted to speak against it, and he fixed his gaze on the older man with cool intent. "Do you have a problem with that?" Frost's eyes pulsed wildly. The man managed to shake his head.

Frost's good-natured smile returned. "Good. Ty will run your guild. I understand there will always be an element of crime in any city, but that does not mean it needs to be at odds with society. Ty will speak with me and give you your assignments from now on. We will have no murder in my city. Such a crime is beneath you and will be punished severely. Other than that, you will keep order amongst yourselves. After the coming war, I'm sure you will all become rich. Until then, you are to assist with the rebuilding of the city like everyone else. Without a city there can be no trade, and with no trade, you can gather no treasure; understand?"

Everyone nodded.

"Good. New people might start arriving in the city once commerce has returned. I leave it to you to deal with them if they are trying to move in on your territory." They all nodded more enthusiastically. "But that is not the most important job you will have. I need you. You are the ears of the city. You will report to Ty any rumors or strange activities. I'm sure some of you fancy yourselves adventurers, but before you go looking for riches in some newfound crypt, tell Ty. Dangers exist that you can scarcely imagine, and some might concern the entire city. You can get yourself killed all you want, but I don't want people disappearing without anyone knowing where they went, understand?" They all nodded. "Good. Questions?"

A long silence was broken by the older man. "What happened to your eyes?"

The group froze at this bluntness, expecting the worst. Frost threw back his head and laughed loudly. "Everything! Everything has happened to my eyes. I now see as a king of Olan."

There was nervous laughter from the assembled group, as the man held up his tankard. "Well then, long live the king!"

The night was nearly spent when Frost and Ty finally joined their already sleeping companions in the tidy rooms upstairs.

It was the smell of food floating up from below that roused Frost several hours later. The sun was fully risen, and his companions were talking loudly below. He was the last to wake, but he felt fully refreshed. He rose and walked toward the good smells and conversation.

When he appeared in the tavern, the conversation stopped. The companions who had not seen his transformation were transfixed by his new visage.

Ty broke the silence. "Get over here and eat something Frost. We have way too much food because your people continue to be overly generous."

Frost happily obliged.

Miraph regarded his eyes with unconcealed curiosity, "What happened to you Frost?"

Frost half-grinned with a mouth full of food, "Everything!" He swallowed the mouthful and laughed, feeling the joyful energy surging through his body. The others laughed uncomfortably.

Frost cleared his throat. "The short tale is, I have the Blade of the Forest now, and am connected to the land. This new relationship with nature has convinced me to stay here in Olan while you separate to find the other blades."

There were murmurs around the table.

"I know you all want me since, of course, I'm the best fighter here..." He said this broadly, indicating his boast was full of deliberate bluster. There were chuckles, and Frost continued with a wink, "But, Olan needs me. If I leave now, the people will see abandonment. They need guidance, and I am the only one whom all the factions in this city will listen to."

Cirrus nodded in agreement.

"So, this is what I propose—Nightshade, you will take the *Sphinx* to the yellow valley in the middle kingdom. Cidric, Miraph, and Cirrus will go with you. The Blade of Kings is in that valley."

"Only a king can lift the blade," Cirrus reminded Frost.

"I believe the former Queen did, and that is why the sword will be there. I am sorry you must face this, Nightshade," Frost gave a slight bow to her.

"I will be successful," Nightshade said lightly, though the worry-lines that creased her smooth, clear complexion betrayed her unease.

Frost turned to Krenn. "General, you will teleport with Ty and Victoria to the city of Anden. You have been there before, no?"

Krenn did not respond for a moment, his mind seemingly taken back to times far gone. Then he said, with a touch of wistfulness, "It is where I was born into this unlucky world. I remember some places there quite well, so I should be able to create a portal."

Frost nodded. "I thought as much. I also believe that the Blade of Inferno is still there. Anden would not and may not part with a treasure so great. That is why you will be with them, Ty. I think we will have to secretly borrow it. Please do what you can to avoid starting a second war, but remember, we must win a war against the dragons or there will be nothing left to fight for. When I obtained the Blade of the Forest, I was shown Vigo—he has used a crystal ball to spy on us. He knows of the door and possibly of the blades. We must enter the laboratory and find its secrets before he can return."

Observing how Frost now tore into the food piled before him like a ravenous bear, Ty said, "Man, you truly are a King now. At least you have the appetite of one."

Cidric lifted his tankard and declared, "No finer grub than what's served up at the Dragon Snot!" Miraph giggled at her father's remark, and they all smiled, except for Frost, whose mouth was now stuffed with food.

The friends prepared that morning and into the afternoon. When the sun was well into its downward journey, the companions said their farewells. The *Azure Sphinx* came to rest in front of the tavern, lowering its ramp. There were many onlookers as the group split up and some boarded the airship. After a final wave from Nightshade, the ramp closed, and the airship flew into the air.

Krenn pulled his blade. "Are we ready for this?"

Victoria and Ty nodded, and Krenn swung the blade creating a ragged-looking portal to a brick street. The three jumped through, but as they disappeared, there was a loud cracking noise and the portal vanished.

Frost was worried by the sound—it had not done that before.

Frost turned to the gathered crowd. "I will be here to help continue the restoration. Your King is with you."

There were a few cheers, but most of the people had come to see the airship and were shocked by the portal.

Frost turned again and returned to the empty tavern, a King alone, his palace the shabby upstairs rooms of an ale-hall. Yet he did not feel alone. He could sense the Dryad inside of him and, through her, all of Nature. No, he was not alone. Never again would he be.

14. The wait

Frost's footsteps crunched in the newly fallen snow as he made his way back to the tavern.

More than one advisor had suggested to him that perhaps the tavern should be renamed—"Dragon Snot" being perhaps not the most befitting name for a royal court. His reply had always been simple, "Naming is for the owner. Take it up with him when he returns."

Castle Road was completely blanketed in fresh, powdery drifts. Frost glanced back at the now completed tower as he walked. Its windows were closed tight against the first snow. He looked again to the tavern and thought back to that first week after his friends had set off on their adventures.

He had been full of enthusiasm and pitched in with the labors of the city, helping rebuild whenever possible. He thought the time of waiting would be short, and that he should make every effort to get Olan off to a good start before his companions returned. He enlisted roofers, carpenters, and artisans to repair and restore the dragon-damaged tavern. It probably looked better than it had when it was first built. He didn't think Ty would mind the remodeling—although he was not about to change the name without his friend's consent.

He had no problems with wizards or thieves that first week and was optimistic about his plan for stability.

full week passed before a troubling thought began to nag at his mind—his friends could all die in distant lands, and he would never know due to his isolation in Olan. Before the dragon attacks and the airship, he had never travelled any real distance. Loitering restlessly in the empty ale-hall late at night, he had to admit that before their adventures to the dragon moon and back, he himself had not really expected to see any other lands of Ashyer in his lifetime.

After a second week passed, his thoughts about his friends became obsessive. He had sent riders throughout the country of Olan to report back on the state of other villages, and they had all returned with the same dire news—Olan was the only city still standing. Even the watchtower on the Great Road at the crossing had been obliterated.

Feeling completely alone, Frost decided to try contacting his friends.

The wizards were building the new school within the city and were hard at work when he arrived. Frost waved at the nearest wizard. "Hello, old man! How's the new school coming?"

The response was silence and a glowering look as the man stopped what he was doing and stared at Frost. After a moment, Frost gave a half smile and asked, "Is there anyone else up there I can talk to?"

"What do you want?" A wizard appeared at the front door. "I am Axis, head of this order. Why do you trouble us?"

I thought Cirrus was the head of your order, Frost thought. He could see several wizards with discontent on their faces. Frost assumed a non-threatening stance. "Well, I was hoping to ask you for some help, but it seems there is something wrong. Can we talk about that?"

Axis advanced on Frost angrily. "Yes there is something wrong. First, you command us to make our school within the city; and if that is not insult enough, we have common people showing up to help build and expecting to become students."

The man was distasteful, but Frost needed help. "What is it that you want me to do for you, Master Axis?"

The wizard did not soften. "I want help building this accursed school, but from men who will take orders and expect no magical training. What I really want is the old school back! But that, I'm sure, is out of the question." Axis folded his arms.

Frost sighed. "I will send a detachment of guards to help, with strict instructions not to ask questions. As for your secrecy, I want you inside the city for now, not forever. While here, you can make the school hidden like the mountain was. You have vast magical skill; why don't you make an illusion? Vanish the building, or make it appear the same as any other? That way, only those who know can find you."

It seemed Axis had not thought of any of those things. His shoulders slumped. "Very well. Your proposals are acceptable. Now, King Fredris, why are you here?"

Frost still did not like the wizard's tone, but his need for their help outweighed his personal annoyance, "I need you to contact my companions—with a spell or crystal ball or something."

Axis laughed contemptuously. "Crystal ball? There is no such thing, and we have no one who can contact distant people without an existing charm. It is complicated, so I don't expect you to understand."

Frost was very tempted to test the Blade of the Forest on the man, and the Dryad in his head was in full agreement. Such crystal balls did indeed exist, but he calmed himself and said, "I'm sure you're right. Thank you for your time."

Later that day, Frost satisfied his displeasure by sending the most annoying volunteers to help with the school before dispatching a guard unit as promised.

The snow continued to fall, deeper and deeper as Frost made his way into the valley. The city lay covered in white. He looked to his right, pinpointing a dark spot where snow refused to pile, the only remains of the school. *How long ago had that been, the great conflict that culminated in the destruction of the school?* He mused, *It must have been at least two months ago, no, it all started before that …*

After his fruitless visit to the wizards, months passed without much trouble. To bide the time and take his mind off the unknown fate of his companions, Frost threw himself into the role of tavern-keeper. A strange sight it was, as the leaves began to turn—a king cooking food and pouring drinks for his subjects.

It happened one morning while he was frying up eggs for some farmers and listening with interest to their plans for winter. With the main fields destroyed in the dragon attack, they would have to ration food to survive the coming cold months. He offered that the throne would compensate the farmers for all their available food and guards would help with the harvest. A granary was to be constructed close to the ruin of the old castle to store and dispense the food, making sure that no one in Olan starved and that none hoarded more than their fair share.

The farmers seemed somewhat relieved and reassured and Frost was feeling quite content with himself as he scooped eggs onto plates, when a bloody man came in and collapsed on the floor.

The Dryad had been warning him, tickling his mind about a general unease in the city; but he had been suppressing the downbeat sensation, dismissing it as general anxiety—expected under the circumstances. Now, with this dramatic interruption, he was forced to confront the reality of the situation.

Frost rushed to the man on the floor and examined his wounds. He was the leader of the thieves in Ty's absence, the rogue who had spoken up on the eve of his companions' departure. For a moment Frost could not recall the man's name—a terrible realization considering this man and the rest of the Thieves' Guild were supposed to be keeping him informed. Then it came to him, "Kyr? Can you hear me? These wounds do not seem natural. What has happened?"

Semiconscious, Kyr struggled to speak. "Wizards …" he whispered.

Frost knew the wizards would end up being trouble, but he thought they would be trouble for him alone; but it seemed now that he would not be the exclusive recipient of their spite. "I will get a magical remedy, wait one minute."

The farmers tended to the thief while the King went upstairs to Cirrus' cache of potions. When he returned, the farmers were regarding the thief grimly, perhaps fearful that whatever ailed him might be catching. Kyr, whom they had managed to lift up onto a chair, looked like he stood on the very threshold of death's door.

Frost started administering drops of clear liquid from a small vial onto the wounds, which appeared to be claw-marks that sprouted suppurating boils. Immediately, the boils began to shrink and the cuts began to close. The last quarter of the liquid he poured down the thief's throat.

Color returned to Kyr's face.

"I knew you would help, my King," he said, his gruff voice regaining its healthy volume. "You are a good man. Ty always said you were."

One of the farmers, wiping his hands on a tablecloth distastefully, grumbled, "Those damn wizards. This is not the first victim to emerge from their quarter with marks like that."

Frost's eyes flashed a deep green pulse. "Their quarter? Not the first?" He fixed an inquisitive look on Kyr. "Explain this."

Kyr sat forward, "I'll tell you, but I think I need a drink to loosen my throat."

Frost tilted his head in a gesture to one of the farmers to fetch the thief a tankard.

After Kyr had taken a hearty swig that nearly drained the glass, he spoke. "The wizards have staked a quarter of the city for their own, like a gang. They have patrols to make sure only their kind of business is being conducted in their territory, and make themselves scarce whenever you cross their area, Your Majesty, because they fear you. I was following my orders and repairing the tunnels beneath the city when I was attacked. Apparently, the tunnel I was working on crossed their territory, and a wizard appeared in the tunnel ahead of me. He demanded that I collapse that section and leave. When I protested, he cast some spell. A strange, rat-like figure seemed to just materialize in the air in front of me. It began slashing at me with its claws, and then all I felt was pain. I could barely see straight. The only thing I could think of doing was to come to the Dragon Snot. My Lord, I'm sorry we haven't brought you fully into our confidence. We should have informed you of this before now."

Frost waved this away and sat back to think. "We must have peace in the city, but we might need the wizards for protection."

"If they keep this up, we'll need protection from those wizards!" Kyr rumbled. He tried to stand but cringed and collapsed back into the chair in pain.

"Don't overtax yourself," Frost cautioned. "The potion brought you back from the brink of death, but you'll need some more time to recover. Kyr, listen, I want you to operate this tavern in Ty's absence. As much as I enjoy cooking and serving out drinks, I must be more vigilant as a protector, it seems. I don't know how long the effects of the spell will linger, so you had better stay clear of the tunnels until you are better. Boris here can aid you for a while today." Frost gestured to a farmer, who nodded gravely.

Frost went around the bar and retrieved his swords and bow from below the counter, slinging them on his shoulder, and throwing on his cape. "I need to go to visit this wizard's quarter, it seems."

"Go with care, my King," Boris called after him.

Frost walked the familiar streets toward the school but was stopped by a wizard halfway there. "Ahh, my Lord. I was just coming to see you," the old man said with an air of indignation.

"Indeed?" Frost paused, pretending not to know what was going on.

"I'm afraid there has been a problem at the school with thievery. We caught a slimy little thief trying to grab some magical jewels about an hour ago. The jewels were trapped, and a spell blasted the thief. I am worried about the safety of the, um, man, as the spell could be fatal if not treated immediately."

Frost bit the inside of his cheek in anger but did not let his emotion show. "I am sure the thief has been attended to. Can I see the jewels?"

The wizard was obviously caught off-guard. "The, the Jewels?"

Frost smiled, "I would like to see the jewels in question and the magical markings of the trap. It may help me to solve the crime."

"Crime?"

Frost tilted his head to the side, finding it somehow cathartically amusing to run the wizard in circles and watch him get tied up in his own knots. "The attempted thievery of course. Also, summon Axis. Such unrest in the city must be dealt with as soon as possible."

The wizard blustered to himself and led Frost toward the school. When they arrived, the wizard showed Frost a statue that appeared to be in pristine condition.

"The eyes are, um, magical jewels. I will fetch Master Axis," the wizard said as he shuffled up a nearby staircase with rather more haste than the wizards were wont to display.

Frost looked at the statue through his Dryad-touched eyes and saw no indication of magic whatsoever.

Axis, the wizard who had laughed at Frost and dismissed him a month earlier, came down the stairs. "Yes my King, to what do we owe this ... honor?"

"Honor? I have been summoned by your subordinate to investigate a crime."

Frost waited for Axis to falter, but he looked steadily at Frost, his disdain barely concealed.

Frost plunged ahead. "This statue had a trap that injured a thief who tried to lift the jewels, or so I have been told. The area shows no sign of a sprung trap, nor any blood. Are you sure this is the object in question?"

Axis was tiring of Frost and answered through clenched teeth, "They must have cleaned and rearmed the statue, obviously."

Frost smiled. "You won't mind if I check the security …"

Before the wizard could protest, Frost roughly slapped his right hand onto the statue's left cheek. It wobbled slightly on its base. Then he slapped his left hand onto the other side of the statue's head, as if he were about to kiss it. "Interesting … the statue must know that I am the King, and of course it would not do anything to cross the King… a smart statue. Do you happen to have a tunnel under this area of the city? I think I know where the opening is."

Axis was infuriated. "What kind of trickery is this? Have you already spoken to the thief? Is he in your custody?"

Frost allowed his voice to take on the magical boom of the Dryad. "Custody? If you know that he was in the tunnel rebuilding, then you also know that one of your wizards attacked him with a diabolical spell!"

His eyes were lanterns of glowing-green fire as he fixed them menacingly on Axis. "You will allow the Guild to complete the task that I have set for them, and you will no longer interfere with this quarter of the city. I am the king of Olan, and every quarter of this city is mine to protect! If I hear even a whisper of wizard patrols that I did not command or request, you will find *yourself* in custody."

Axis' cold outward demeanor finally cracked and was visibly shaken. Never had he expected Frost to command such authority, and the king's knowledge of the wizard's activity was jarring. After a moment of twitching and attempting to find his voice, Axis merely bowed and meekly said, "Yes, your majesty."

Frost naively thought the encounter had solved the problem despite continued unease in the back of his mind. Reconstruction moved forward, and the guards began building a tower base on the hill next to a make-shift wall that protected the treasure of Olan. In the ensuing days, worries about the tensions between the thieves and wizards gradually faded, although he did regularly walk through the quarter where the wizard's school was for some peace of mind. Frost failed to realize that, in silence, the worst trouble can grow.

T rees began shedding their leaves, and still there was no word from any of his friends. Frost dispatched guards to aid in the harvest, and the rationing plan had been widely praised as excellent foresight by the king. It was then, when most of the guards were away in the fields, that the silently simmering trouble came to a boil.

That evening, the guards set up a harvest camp and were having a modest festival to celebrate a good day's work outside the walls. Walking the cobbled streets of the city toward the western wall to join the celebration, Frost heard shouting of a non-festive nature coming from *that* quarter. Thinking it would be a simple argument, he strode off toward the disturbance. When the disruption came into view, Frost realized how much animosity had been festering in the city for months.

Two groups were assembled, facing each other. In front of the school stood the entire clan of wizards, reinforced with all manner of strange creatures summoned to aid them in battle. On the opposite side of the square, virtually every member of the Thieves' Guild, joined by many citizens, all of them armed to the teeth, danced rhythmically in anticipation of battle.

Frost broke into a run as realization splashed over him that there was about to be a deadly skirmish in the square. *How had it come to this?* Running, he remembered how he had been less than friendly to the wizards. *Granted, they were sneaky cowards with a disrespectful attitude at best, but he had to be better.* Approaching the mob, he knew it was too late.

From the steps of the school, Axis yelled, "This is our territory, and we will destroy any who dare trespass!" The unearthly booming of his voice could only be an amplification spell placed on his throat.

Kyr, stepping out from among the motley throng of thieves, declared defiantly, "We all are of Olan, and we must stand as one! All the territory belongs to the King!"

Before pushing to the front of the crowd, Frost heard Axis yell, "Death to the King!"

Frost emerged into the empty center of the square.

"Has it come to this?" he did not need to shout as the square was hushed into silence by his appearance. He drew the Blade of the Forest and split it into two swords. "Any wizards who would be loyal and serve Olan and the good of all the people, come to me now."

Four of the younger wizards broke ranks and happily joined the thieves in friendship. Axis's stony face held a surety that the night would end in bloodshed.

With the voice of the Dryad Frost shouted, "Final warning! I do not wish for conflict within the city, but I will lay low all who are guilty of treason."

Axis smiled a greedy smile, "You can try, and I will stand on your dead body proclaiming myself as the rightful king! Attack!"

Immediately, spells lit up the sky. Knives flew. Flames erupted everywhere, followed by screams. The wizards summoned animals to fight at their side, but Frost turned them on their summoners with a Dryad command. He plunged the forest blades into the ground and vines tangled around the fighting wizards. The wizards responded by cutting and burning.

Axis began channeling energy directly from the school behind. Frost recognized the energy—it was Spellfire. The wizards were using a power crystal to fight the crown.

Frost knew what had to be done.

The loyal young wizards cast a magical barrier in front of Frost as he slowly advanced on Axis. The King raised both green swords into an "X" shape and lowered the blades toward the neck of the wizard. Spellfire blasted all around.

The barrier faltered and gave way. Frost swung his blades down and stopped them just as their razor-sharp edges touched opposite sides of Axis's neck. With a heavy heart, Frost pulled against the blades, his arms strong as the branches of a great tree fanning outward. The blades sliced through the wizard's neck, scythes through grass, and removed his head.

Next came a Spellfire explosion so enormous that out in the field, ranks of guards and farmers saw the white flames shoot into the sky. They mobilized quickly and headed for the city gates, although they would assuredly arrive too late. The Spellfire shot back into the school, and a second explosion lit the sky. All glass in the city shattered, and the school was blasted to black rubble. Many lay dead or dying—wizards, thieves, and ordinary citizens who were only standing up for their country and king. None left the square un-singed. All of Olan was horrified.

Frost reflected on the street fight as he regarded the blackened ruin where the wizards' school had stood. *The black stone must be cursed*, he thought. *Snow won't even collect on it.*

He picked up his pace, fighting back tears as he made his way to the tavern. He had issued a decree that none should touch the remains of the school until Cirrus could analyze them. Now, as snow buried the fields and the roads, he wondered if he would ever see his old teacher again.

The four wizards who joined him in battle that night had survived and proved to be loyal friends. If the worst had happened to his companions, they would make fine founders of a proper new wizard school. For the time being, they were housed with Frost and the guards in the tower, which had had been finished only a few weeks earlier.

The people of Olan had helped build the new structure on the hill. On the top floor, there were eight rooms, one for each companion, and a circular table in the center. Frost wondered if the effort was in vain. His friends had not returned, and seldom did he sit on the throne his people made.

Frost snapped out of his musings when he reached Dragon Snot tavern just as Kyr opened up for the day.

"Morning, Frost. Looks like winter is here with a vengeance." Kyr tapped the tavern's sign with a stick to knock loose overnight snow. "I don't think you'll want to be hanging out here today though … " Kyr nodded up at the tower.

Frost squinted, momentarily confused before looking in the direction of the stick in Kyr's hand.

In the distance, the *Azure Sphinx* came to rest at the top of the tower.

Barely containing his glee, Frost exclaimed, "Looks like I have some business elsewhere today!" Frost broke into a fast trot back to the tower, Kyr's robust laughter rumbling in his ears.

15. Reunited

hen Frost reached the tower, his boots heavy with wet snow, he kicked the stone arch before entering to knock off clinging ice. He could hear excited voices far above. *The guards and wizards must be greeting my overdue friends.*

Frost had regaled his retinue with tales of his missing companions as the days in Olan grew shorter—perhaps they merely humored their King, but they seemed never to grow tired of hearing about his adventures and his friends.

Frost bounded up the spiral stairs to the top floor where he found all the faces he had longed to behold for months. A weight lifted from his heart. He felt light enough to fly.

Ty crossed the room and embraced him. From his friend's enfolding bear hug, Frost took in the others more closely. They all looked gaunt and sad. Miraph looked as if she had grown up in the time she was gone. More than that, it seemed as if the joy of childhood was gone from her spirit. His gaze lingered on her. There was something wrong—a darkness from within that the Dryad sensed.

As Ty released him and he was able to again draw breath, he tore his eyes away from Miraph to regard the others. They all bore the scars of battles untold. Their clothes were ragged and scorched, and their skin sallow.

Frost smiled warmly. "Welcome back, my friends. You all look very weary. Please take some time to wash and rest. I have missed your company, and am very curious about what has happened, but I am content to see you all alive. Please, avail yourselves of your new rooms, and we shall tell our tales when you are rested."

The group separated to their respective rooms, except for Cirrus who tarried.

His old mentor looked worried. "Frost, what of the wizards? As we approached, I beheld a troubling sight even at a great distance."

His eyes cast down, Frost said, "I'm sorry, Cirrus … there is no hurry. Most of them are dead."

Cirrus drew in a shocked breath.

Frost looked up from the floor, meeting his friend's eyes. "I tried to reason with them, I really did. Four loyal wizards still live. Their rooms are on the floor below. You should speak to them first; they will present their side of the story."

Frost led Cirrus down the spiral stairs to the wizard's quarters. He introduced Cirrus to the wizards who had sided with their King against their mutinous headmaster, Axis, and then left them to converse so they did not feel they had to hold their tongue about any detail in his presence.

Presently Cirrus emerged, the sorrow that hung heavy on him making him look much older than his years. He truly did look like an old man now.

"I'm sorry Frost," he said. "It sounds like they were too tight in the clutches of greed and hungry for power. If you will accompany me, I would go look at the ruins now. Let the others rest; I cannot until I have visited the place."

Frost and Cirrus walked together through the snow to the blackened place. The sky would be darkening soon, and the tiny yellow world would appear on the horizon. The world of the dragons was getting closer with each passing day. Back in the early days of summer, it was small enough to be mistaken for a star. Now, the yellow world approached like inevitable doom.

The bone-chilling wind blew pelting snow into their faces. Cirrus did not react but stared straight ahead toward the ruin as they drew near.

He fixed his gaze on the blackened rubble and spoke loudly, "As the true Master of the Wizards, I command you to emerge!"

The rocks trembled and began to separate. From the center of the loosened rubble, a power crystal emanating black light floated up and drifted toward Cirrus. As it hovered over Cirrus' hand, it shed its blackness and began to glow bright once more. With this sudden transition, Frost noticed the blackened ruins become normal brick and stone again. Snow began to collect on the rock, no longer repelled by dark magic.

Cirrus put the crystal in his pocket and muttered, "Terrible power. We should destroy them all."

Early the next day, all eight companions assembled around the circular table. Kyr brought a feast in his horse-drawn sleigh which, with the help of two servants, he hand-delivered to the assemblage. Ty took the opportunity to quietly speak with the leader of the Thieves' Guild. Frost could not tell what they were conspiring in hushed tones about, but he noticed that at one point Kyr surreptitiously gestured toward Frost and Ty nodded.

Kyr departed, and Ty took his place at the table to the left of Frost. Taking a hearty swig of ale, Ty raised the tankard, "Thank you for saving my friends, and the whole city it seems."

The others appeared to be confused by this toast. Victoria asked what was on all their minds. "What has happened here?"

Looking around the table, Frost said, "It seems that curiosity is stronger than your desire for rest. I must admit, my curiosity is fierce. Therefore, as Kyr has been instructed to keep us supplied with food and drink, we shall tell our tales. I will tell you of the reconstruction—and sometimes deconstruction—of Olan. Then, I would hear why my dearest friends have been absent so long."

Frost drained the last dregs of ale in his tankard, wiped the foam from his mouth, and began. "So, here is what came to pass in Olan since you left …"

Frost unburdened his heart, telling them everything right up to his visit to the ruins with Cirrus the night before. With humility he bore the blame he felt was his due.

When he finished, he let a contemplative silence linger in the tower, as his tale sank in. He could barely contain his desire to hear their stories, and finally, he gave a nod to Nightshade. It was time to hear the Angel's tale.

16. Nightshade the Queen

ightshade watched the receding city below as the *Azure Sphinx* rose quickly into the sky. From this vantage, in the brutal light of day, she could see how much damage had been visited on Olan. It was her city—more so than any of the others, she thought. She had been living in the city for generations in one guise or another. None of the others could understand her larger view of history and time. With distance, the city resembled a detailed battle model. An appropriate metaphor, she thought, for her witness of time. She sees the world with longer vision, whereas men see things from the ground.

She shook her head to clear the thoughts. If she dwelt on such things too long, she would lose heart. Wasn't that the essence of *time before memory*? For centuries, she practiced the art of her people. She would consciously push the details of time from her mind in an effort to retain her sanity. There were other immortal creatures on Ashyer, but most of them went mad with time. She had never met an old vampire still sound of mind, and the possibly extinct race of immortal men? Did not all of them go crazy with the constraints of power and thereby plunge the world into unending war? Xan Olan was the only immortal man she ever respected. He seemed to grasp the art of her own people. For centuries she watched him with adoration for his calm and steady temperament. As for the fate of her own people, it was not by their own hand they were erased; it was likely by the claw and the tooth of dragons.

She was certain she would discover the ultimate fate of her people in the yellow valley.

Frost had seemed possessed with a certainty of knowledge when he returned from the "secret lake" and told her where she was to go. The lake was not secret to her. She had encountered the lake centuries before and held the memory as a warning. There was nothing malicious about the spot for any good inhabitant of Ashyer, but when she approached the beautiful lake, she heard a clear message in her head—*You who are not of this world are not welcome here. Be gone or be destroyed.* She did not linger, but she remembered.

"Are you all right, Nightshade?"

The voice brought Nightshade out of her reverie. Miraph was speaking to her. Nightshade realized she was still staring out of the window, but now only the cloud forest was visible.

She turned to Miraph. "I am well. I was just lost in thought."

"You look so sad. Do you miss him?" Miraph asked.

It took a moment for Nightshade to understand the question. *She must be asking about Ty*, Nightshade mused. The girl was mortal and thought of life from that narrow vision. To Miraph, it would seem only right for her to be missing Ty. Miraph could not understand the scope of lovers in the endless time of her existence. Ty understood and loved her, though he knew that their time together was but a breath in the life of an immortal. He embraced the ideal of living in the moment easier than most of her lovers had.

"I'm sorry," Miraph said, "I've made it worse."

Lost in thought again, Nightshade was staring blankly at Miraph.

Nightshade smiled. "Yes child, I miss him. My thoughts, however, are on our mission."

"Do you think there will be a battle?" Miraph asked with a little too much excitement.

Nightshade became worried. Would this fledgling wizard child, though very talented, become another casualty of the never-ending war?

"I do believe that," Nightshade said. "The dragons that inhabit the yellow valley will give over no prize easily."

Nightshade considered for a moment, looking around the clean bridge of the *Azure Sphinx*. On a side table sat the basin from outside the sealed laboratory door.

"Ghost girl?" Nightshade addressed the basin. The image of the young woman appeared, flickering and somewhat translucent. Nightshade drew closer. "The valley of yellow clouds just to the northeast of the laboratory is infested with dragons, is that right?"

"From all the data I have been able to gather, and based on observation, that would be a reasonable conclusion," Ghost Girl said.

"So, yes. Do you know roughly how many, and how often they leave the valley to scout the outlying terrain?"

The image flickered, not responding for several seconds. "I apologize for the delay. Being this far from the hub has limited some of my operating capacity. I do not have an accurate count, although I have observed at least twenty different dragons coming from that area. They send one or two dragons out on patrol daily."

Nightshade pondered this information, and when she did not speak again for a couple minutes, the image of Ghost Girl blinked out.

When Nightshade spoke again, it was to address the crew. "When we arrive at the sea between the middle kingdoms, I will fly our group to the valley myself. You will keep the *Sphinx* at a safe distance and hidden in the clouds."

Cirrus was sitting nearby, absently staring at nothing in the lens. When he heard this pronouncement, he furrowed his eyebrows in consternation. "The *Sphinx* is now armed to fight dragons. Are you sure?"

Nightshade nodded. "I think there might be more there than we can guess—not just dragons, but *answers*. I would like the opportunity to plum some of those secrets before we make our presence known."

Cidric spoke up. "Hopefully the sword is one of those secrets."

Nightshade smiled assuredly. "If Frost thinks the sword is there, then it is."

The *Azure Sphinx* flew through the pink-tinged clouds as the sun set. The four companions gazed out the darkening windows at the achingly beautiful sky. From their height, they could see stars winking into view above. No creature below would be able to see the sky that night, for a thick layer of clouds blew swiftly below the airship.

Startling all on the bridge, the image of Ghost Girl suddenly appeared above the basin and reported, "The laboratory is near."

Nightshade looked to the pilot of the ship, who nodded in agreement. She turned to her companions, "Are you ready for a much more uncomfortable and cold flight?"

They nodded, Miraph much more enthusiastically than the others. Observing his daughter's enthusiasm, Cidric shook his head with worry.

Nightshade pulled the wand-pen that conjured the library door from somewhere in the skin-tight folds of her wings and handed it to Cirrus. "Ty wanted the wizards to have access to the portable library. Hopefully it will aid us."

The four companions emerged onto the upper deck and were greeted by a biting cold wind. The moon illuminated the distant mountain peaks that pierced through the clouds in the north. Cidric lifted his daughter Miraph into his arms and was himself embraced by Nightshade. Cirrus put his arm around Nightshade's waist, and she held him tight with her other arm. With one motion, Nightshade threw her injured wings open. They stretched almost the entire span of the airship. Cirrus noticed clear blood starting to trickle from one of her wings. He opened his mouth to suggest that they should alter their plan, but it was too late. Nightshade jumped off the side of the ship.

She did not move her wings, but rather glided on the air currents using her passengers as counterweight. Cirrus looked up to see tears running out of the corners of her eyes. She was clenching her teeth against the constant pain of the flight. He wanted to cast a spell to aid her but was afraid that the sudden change would distract her and doom them all.

Nightshade was fighting hard against the pain. Cold air slashed like frozen blades, but she concentrated on the approaching mountains.

As they neared solid ground and Nightshade began to slow her approach, the precariously dangling passengers began to think they were safe. Relief was premature—as if summoned by their confidence, the silhouette of a dragon rose into the moonlight above the clouds. Its laughter was sadistic and hungry. Liquid fire dripped from its lips as its guttural howls seemed absolutely giddy with manic pleasure.

Miraph shouted, "What's wrong with it? Is it crazy?"

Nightshade yelled back, "It has gone mad with hunger! The valley is the final resting place of my kind, and the sight of an angel has driven it to ravenous lunacy."

The dragon was suddenly encased in fire that lit up the sky as it streamed toward them. For a moment, they hoped it had exploded. Then it flapped its wings once, spreading a wall of dragonfire across the clouds, blocking their advance.

Nightshade saw only one option for escape. With an obviously painful shift, she plummeted straight down into the clouds.

Cirrus took the opportunity to use his staff and create a giant lightning storm behind them.

Miraph looked around to see the electrified cloud mass burst into fire as the dragon plunged into the storm with deranged fervor. She could not help herself and began screaming. Cidric shifted his grasp to cover her mouth, but the motion unbalanced the group and they spiraled hopelessly toward the rocky peaks below the clouds.

Nightshade's wings were being shredded and folded inward. There was no recovery possible as they began to spin. Cirrus held his staff out, desperately timing their chaotic trajectory for just the right moment. When he saw a flat rocky surface, he blasted a lightning bolt out and held the spell. His staff became red hot as he used the electricity to stop the spinning and slow their descent, in hopes of surviving the crash landing.

His desperate calculation failed to account for the damage wrought to the rocky surface. As the lightning tether shortened, the build-up of electrical energy caused the stones to explode, sending the four companions tumbling in separate directions. The deranged dragon did not slow its approach and slammed into the obliterated rock face. It did not survive the impact and exploded with much greater force than Cirrus' spell. The already buffeted and injured companions were flung further apart from one another into the dark.

irrus regained consciousness and quickly sat up. In the distance, he could see the rock face covered in Dragonshade. The pain in his hand was excruciating. His staff was still clenched in his grasp. At first, he thought it was lucky he had not lost it, then, realization dawned. His hand was melted to the metal of the staff.

He stared at his hand, holding back panic. The staff was unharmed. *Good for the staff*, he thought, but his palm was most certainly annihilated on its surface.

How to detach? Panic swelling, he feared he might lose consciousness again.

Magic will be able to undo the damage, but how to concentrate?

His head spinning, he fixed his gaze on the storm raging above and calmed.

He concentrated on his hand. Slowly, he felt the pain receding. His eyes wandered, and he caught sight of the burning rock face. The fire made him think of the burning pain once again, and his concentration broke. The pain was enormous as unfocused magic flowed into the staff, spraying electricity in all directions. His hand was ripped from the metal with one final explosion of energy. He fell forward on top of his lifeless staff. Clutching his hand to his chest, he fell on his face and began to lose consciousness.

Must see, he thought, *can't bleed to death...must see.*

He lifted his hand to his eyes. The flesh and skin were gone on his fingers and palm. The edges were cauterized by the electric fire, so there was no blood. He beheld his own white bones exposed. The sight of his own skeletal hand was too much for him to handle. All went black.

After the blast, Cidric got to his feet as quickly as the pain would allow. He had lost his grip on Miraph in the second explosion. He wanted to call out to her but was afraid that other creatures would answer his call. A renewed doubt entered his mind. *What am I doing out here? A scholar has no place on a perilous journey.* Then, he felt shame, *I am not here for glory or riches, I am here to help save the world for Miraph.* Deep in his heart, however, he did not care if all other people on the planet died, as long as his daughter survived.

He shook off these thoughts and began searching the rocks. Scattered illumination came from the burning rock face in the distance as well as occasional blinding flashes from the storm above. Breathing fast, sweating despite the chill, he found himself exerting muscles he hadn't used so vigorously since he was a young man.

He was panicking. He stopped and made himself think, calculating his flight from the burning rocks, then approximating the point where they were separated by the second blast. He ran to that spot and found their first impact point in the dirt and scrub. He squinted his eyes, concentrating hard. In the chiaroscuro of dancing firelight and deep shadow, he could discern two departure points from the impact spot, where the scrub was bent and broken. The first one had been his own, which he had just re-traversed. *Well*, he thought, *this old bookworm would make a tracker proud.* He set off in the direction Miraph must have been thrown by the blast.

While he was pushing through some brush that had been nearly flattened back by the blast, a burst of electricity crackled from the other side of the rock face. He noted the direction and range for future reference. *That must have been Cirrus giving us a signal to follow*, he thought.

Then he saw a crumpled shape. She lay sprawled on her back, nested atop crushed branches. Unheeding his own pain, he dropped down beside her, tilting his head above her mouth. He felt breath on his cheek! She was unconscious but breathing regularly. He gingerly examined her for bleeding or signs of breaks and found none. There was no help coming, and they couldn't stay. Grunting, he lifted her, and set off toward where he'd seen the brief electric light-show.

Pain was the whole world; all other senses were gone. Nightshade forced air into her lungs. A slender thread of herself was clinging to and fighting for life, although most of her wanted to go the way of her people and let it end. *Yes*, she thought, *break the thread and leave, beyond existence, away from the pain.*

But wait, what was that a sound? It was not audible; it was another's mind in panic. *What were they panicked about? What did they see?*

Nightshade tried hard to shut out the world of pain and see through the eyes of the panicked companion. There was a flash of fire and a dragon speeding toward the rocks. Was she on those rocks? There was another explosion, and then even the pain was gone.

She floated in blackness, suspended somewhere neither existing nor gone—a place her ancestors called Voidspace.

Then the world of pain returned. Now she hurt even more. *How much pain can there be?*

There was panic in the minds of two others nearby. She reached out to one. She realized it was Cirrus, but he was in great pain too and it amplified hers, and she returned to Voidspace, alone with her thoughts. Everything went black again.

Was this going to be the end of her? How can she regenerate while exposed and so close to the valley? She had been grievously injured before, but she was always able to find a safe place to regenerate. She didn't even know where she was—she could be in the center of the dragon's burning corpse for all she knew. And the others, if they died, it would be her fault. Some guardian angel. She could not stay in the dark place, Voidspace, she had to go back.

A real sound greeted her return to consciousness, thunder? *That's right, Cirrus created a storm to mask their escape. How long would such a storm last, if the wizard never dismissed it? He had done something else too; what was it? He had used his staff to soften their fall. Had that brave act killed him?* She searched for his mind. Nothing.

Cidric was the only one she could touch, but in his mind, he believed that Cirrus was alive. The wizard had sent them a signal. Cidric also bore his daughter in his arms—lucky for him, Miraph was skinny as a twig, except when she turned into a tiger. So they had all survived. *How close to death am I?*

She pried her crispy eyelids open, and pieces of them crumbled away from her vision. *How bad is it?* She looked down at her body. In the dim firelight she could see the Queen's Armor, unscathed. Omegas' gift was the reason she still drew breath. She had to remember to tell Cirrus; he would be pleased. She turned her head. There were curious pools of liquid on either side of her. Was she in water? With horror, she realized the clear puddles on either side were her wings. They were pulverized, burned, and bleeding badly. Could she amputate? Then she would truly be the fallen one. She let go and floated back into the void as the pain overwhelmed her again.

When next she opened her eyes, it was to behold the interior of a cave. The pain in her wings was still very much present, but now muted. She carefully turned her head. She was lying on the rocky floor beside Cirrus. He had cloth wrapped around his hand in a disheveled manner, though she did not see any patches of blood.

Rolling her head the other way, she saw Cidric cradling his unconscious daughter, Miraph.

"How?" Nightshade managed.

Cidric looked up from her daughter's face. "Rest now. We are safe. Cirrus has masked our refuge and bound your wings in a protective spell. My dear Miraph will be fine. I am frightened, but we should be all right for now. Cirrus is resting. He will not summon the airship for fear of dragons locating our position. They are out in full force now, looking for us."

Nightshade looked back at Cirrus and noticed his staff leaning against the wall of the cave near his head. On the staff she saw the outline of his clenched hand, burned into the place where he had gripped it.

Wonderful start, she thought, as she faded into sleep.

A strange smell assaulted her senses when she woke many hours later.

Miraph sat beside her looking concerned. In her lap was a bowl with a steaming liquid, the source of the increasingly horrible smell.

Nightshade gave a weak smile. "If you're going to feed that to me, you are in for a fight."

Miraph looked sad but resigned. "I'm sorry." She proceeded to pry open Nightshade's mouth and dump the liquid down her throat.

Nightshade was too shocked to respond and began to slip into Voidspace again. If the clever and kind Miraph was willing to do such a thing to her, she must be grievously wounded. Before she drifted away, she remembered her glimpse of lightning reflecting in the pools of blood to either side of her.

Upon her next waking, the pain seemed much less. Nightshade opened her eyes a crack and saw Miraph staring at her with apprehension.

She opened her eyes all the way and tried to sound reassuring when she said, "If you had to do it, it must have been necessary. We will forgo the fighting this time."

Miraph smiled in relief. "Nightshade, how do you feel?"

"Not good, but we are alive. Are we?"

Miraph's eyes glanced furtively at Cirrus, who was leaning against the wall. "We are all alive, but I don't know how long we will have to be here. Your wings..."

Nightshade had been avoiding the question but turned to ascertain the answer. Her wings had been magically bound with the same disheveled cloth as Cirrus' hand. It was as if she were lying on a pile of wet rags. "Not good then."

Cirrus faced them. "I think Frost will be waiting for a long time. We may be closeted here for at least a month." He unwrapped his hand and showed her. "I do not think this injury will ever heal, but yours will. We need you to be at your full strength for the mission."

Nightshade turned her head back and stared at the ceiling. The ghostly skeletal hand of Cirrus was burned into her mind. Was all of this her doing? They should have walked. She was too eager and made a critical error. She scanned the minds of her companions, fearing their blame. In their minds she found only concern for each other and the mission. She smiled. "We will rest here as long as needed. Cidric, draw the door and organize the library. I'm sure we can teach Miraph while I heal."

Cidric came near Nightshade and beamed down at her. "Already open. Where do you think we crafted the healing potion?"

"Is there a recipe that doesn't taste so nasty?"

"I think it's made to taste bad so you don't over-use it," he said wryly.

She smiled up at the kindly old man as her eyes fluttered shut. "I'll just rest, then." Before she went back to the darkness, she muttered, "We will be victorious. We will stand true."

J t would prove to be well more than a month that passed while Nightshade healed. Cold crept into the air, but the friends kept a cooking fire burning in the hidden library for warmth. Cidric became an excellent tracker of the chewy lizards that wandered the deeper caverns. Though they were not a delicacy, bellies were always full.

With the wizard's assistance, Cidric also began mapping the tunnels and overlaid them on a map of the upper landscape. They decided there was a viable route under the mountains to the valley that would be preferable to the overland route. Their assumption was based partly on the caverns' extensive complexity and a particular phenomenon they noticed—the caves grew larger the deeper and further they went. Sometimes, the cavernous, black cathedrals were deeply unsettling. They heard strange noises from down in the deep and they decided they would not venture further until the group was ready to move as one.

Miraph managed to master fire magic, and wanted to move on to ice, but seeing Nightshade in such pain motivated her to study healing. The magic of healing proved to be the hardest of all the arts she had set herself to. *Much easier to destroy than create*, she thought. Healing magic needed a genuine desire to share one's life force with another. Concentration was crucial, for if the mind wandered in the slightest, the flow of life force could be reversed in a vampiric fashion. Miraph noted the difference in her meticulous mind.

The day to move came when Nightshade, a scant week after she had finally been able to wrap her wings around herself again, decided she was so bored that she was going to track a dragon that had circled close by. As soon as night fell, Nightshade began loading up equipment for a tracking expedition.

"That would be a fine thank you." Cirrus' voice came from behind her as she packed. "To go and get yourself killed after we helped you mend."

Her shoulders slumped, and she stopped packing. "I must do something. My body may be mended, but my mind is a disaster." She turned to Cirrus with tears in her eyes. "For so long I have been trapped in Voidspace with only my thoughts of failure. I must do something. I cannot risk ..."

Cirrus raised his hand and interrupted her. "We have been at your side and we intend to stay. Miraph has become a formidable wizard, possibly more-so than I. She has expedited your recovery with magic, and we are ready to finish the mission. If you are ready to move, as it seems you are, we will go the dark route under the mountains."

Nightshade looked deeper into the cave "You and Cidric really think it goes through?"

Cirrus nodded. "Just today we discovered our proof. Cidric and I were trying to spy out the source of some distant sounds—we have ascertained that they are most certainly not dragons, but large bipeds, and while we were trying to inch nearer for a closer look, the wind changed direction. From below, a strong draft of the yellow fog blew up into our faces. The presence of the fog means …"

"There is a way into the valley directly at the end of this cavern," Nightshade finished his thought.

"Indeed." Cirrus grinned and held his arms open. "It is good to have the old Nightshade back."

Nightshade embraced him. These mortals, she thought, were unlike any others she had encountered. Though she intentionally could not remember all the details of her entire existence, she was certain of some things through feelings that rose to the surface of her black liquid memory. She loved all of them.

Nightshade joined the others in the eerie library and took command once more. She laid out the route on the map that Cidric and Cirrus had made. Until they identified the source of the sounds below, stealth was of the utmost essence.

As they climbed the ladder out of the portal, Nightshade glanced back. "Shouldn't we douse the fire?"

Cirrus chuckled. "We discovered the strangest thing, though we should have inferred it—when we close the door and erase the entrance, the air is removed from the internal space and the fire is extinguished."

"And you find that funny why?" Nightshade raised a quizzical eyebrow.

"Because I was inside when my daughter decided to move the door one day," Cidric grumbled.

Miraph blushed. "Come now, father, you only passed out for a short while."

"What?" Nightshade was shocked.

Cidric shook his head. "It was not pleasant, so please remember that there is no air in the library when the door is—how would you say? Shut."

Cirrus nodded. "It is an amazing piece of magic. The library is actually in a different dimension, and the only reason we can breathe inside is due to the opening. It makes me wonder about portals and weather patterns."

Nightshade turned to face the deep dark of the cavern. "On that note, we are off."

The other three continued to chatter and chuckle for a while behind her as they descended into the darkness. Cirrus provided only the faintest light so they would not trip over stalagmites or fall into crevices.

After an hour of walking, the terrain became steeper, but there were obvious markings and handholds wherever Nightshade looked. Cidric and Cirrus had been meticulous in their mapping. Slowing their pace, the four emerged into a cavernous space that looked like a hive of tunnels and caves. The encasing chamber was enormous and had many entrances from other directions.

Whispering, Cidric leaned in for the others to hear, "This is where we spied from earlier. You can see why we thought we could identify the source of the sound from here. There seems to be a glow all around, very faint, perhaps in the rocks themselves."

Nightshade looked around. There was a glow that seemed to emanate from the walls of the cavern itself. How had she not noticed that right away? The sound she could hear was identified in her mind from a feeling that surfaced from the murk of her memory. She whispered in quiet awe, "The Giants."

"Giants!" Miraph could not contain her excitement, and her voice echoed off the cavern walls.

Nightshade clapped her hand over Miraph's mouth. "Yes, and they don't like unexpected visitors, but they can be quite helpful to polite guests." She began to lead the group down narrow ledges, avoiding the caves in the center.

When they reached the bottom, they realized that the hive of caves in the center of the cavern was actually a city. In front of them was a large opening that resembled grand city gates. The four approached the entryway and were stopped in their tracks by a creature that was at least ten feet tall and covered from head to toe in hair of varying colors. It emerged from inside the gateway and stood barring their path. Nightshade bowed deep and went to one knee, and the others followed suit.

Nightshade looked up and slowly spread her wings enough to be visible. "I am Belladonna the Queen, and I seek the wisdom of the village."

The giant's toothy maw spread into a wide grin that appeared to be one of genuine happiness. "Welcome Belladonna! It has been far too long since we sheltered an angel. You and your friends are indeed welcome!" The voice of the giant was kind, but loud enough to hurt.

Inside the underground city, they were led to the innermost chamber. The room resembled the exterior of the city—all the caves opened into this chamber. As they looked up and around, they realized the design enabled the residents to all gather in the center. Placed in the chamber was a worn, round rock with a flat top, around which stood three giants. Two of the "giants" would not be identifiable as such except for their strange furry hides of many colors and stone-like complexions, for they stood no taller than a tall man. The third, though, was at least twenty feet tall.

When the tallest giant saw them approaching, he dismissed the two short giants with a casual wave and greeted Nightshade with a smile that, though friendly, might send most people fleeing in terror.

"Welcome back, Belladonna. It has been many centuries since last we met, although I remember it fondly and well. Still, I know how you angels are with your selective memories, so I will introduce myself again."

The towering giant waved his hand, and four rocks rose out of the floor. "I am Bokk, and though I do not wish it, I am the leader of my people still. Please sit down."

Cirrus could not help himself; he had to ask, "You do not wish it?"

Bokk sat with a thump to a cross-legged position on the floor—a maneuver that sent vibrations through the ground under their feet—and rested his elbow on the table. "No. It is tiresome, and I have been doing it for over a thousand years. I told them I resigned hundreds of years ago, but they only laugh. It seems I have no choice in the matter as far as they are concerned."

Cirrus leaned forward on his staff. "Fascinating ... you do not seem overly concerned."

Bokk raised his long and tangled eyebrows in thought. "I think that it is ... because of the way we think." He grinned as if he had said something extremely funny. "We do not forget, nor do we go mad. We do not concern ourselves with the past as a burden. You men carry your past like an anchor until it drowns you with its weight. I have seen it, mortal or immortal. The angels merely forget by choice. We remember, but we find it merely a curiosity. We live in the present only. So I continue to be the leader of the city because I am not concerned. I am tired though. I think I slept last year."

Miraph looked dumbfounded. "You haven't slept since last year?"

Bokk laughed loudly, and the cavern rumbled, the ear-splitting sound echoing throughout the complex of caves.

Cidric flinched, fearing the giant's laughter would bring loose rock crashing on their heads.

"No," Bokk said, "I sleep every day. I mean, I think I slept all of last year. It is hard to remember because I was asleep."

Miraph laughed thinking it a joke, but then covered her mouth when she realized no one else was laughing.

Bokk broke into laughter again, though, and grinned down at her—even sitting, he was all of ten feet. "It is funny, young one; do not be afraid to laugh when something tickles you."

Cirrus spoke up. "Sir Bokk, I must say that the truth of the temperament of giants, from what we have observed thus far, is quite different from the collective belief of the men of Ashyer."

Bokk shook his shaggy head sagely, if somewhat sleepily. "Yes, we are aware of the superstitions of the overworld. They arose from the wars that men waged on us for our homes. You understand that even the most agreeable of creatures may become enraged and take fierce action if provoked or pushed too far."

Cirrus nodded with sure conviction. He understood all too well, thinking back on the vengeful wrath they had wreaked on the goblins that had overrun Olan.

Bokk turned his head back to Nightshade. "Speaking of being roused to action, Belladonna, I believe it is now time for you to take a side. Am I right?"

Nightshade stood and unwrapped her wings to reveal the armor beneath. "I have come to enter the valley and reclaim the Sword of Kings."

Bokk chuckled jovially. "Oh my Belladonna, after refusing to take sides in a hopeless war, you have decided to take the side of men. Your people did take the sword into the valley to make a stand, and it still lies there. The dragons long ago defeated your entire clan, I am sorry to say. They have infested the valley ever since."

Nightshade stared at the ground in contemplation. Then, raising her head to meet the giant's gaze, she asked, "Would you and your people aid us, Bokk?"

More laughter from Bokk echoed around the chamber.

"I had no idea giants laughed so much," Cidric muttered to his daughter. "It's a wonder any of these stones are still standing."

"I can't understand what you're saying," Miraph whispered back. "My ears are ringing."

"Angels, they forget so easy," Bokk replied to Nightshade's request. "Long ago I helped you escape through these very caves, and on that day, I promised our help to reclaim the sword and valley. We will honor that promise."

Cirrus exchanged looks with Cidric and Miraph, his eyebrows raised in surprise. "Somehow I wasn't expecting that."

Cidric appeared just as dumbfounded. Miraph was positively vibrating with excitement at the prospect of giants allying with them.

Bokk continued. "In fact, many of my own people have been clamoring for hundreds of years to destroy the dragons. They create that poisonous yellow air, and that valley was once our land. We grew such incredible things in the light of the sun. I caution you to prepare yourself, Belladonna. There are grizzly sights within the valley now."

With that, Bokk rose to his full incredible height and roared upward into the echoing chamber. Fur covered giants appeared in many of the holes.

"Fellows," Bokk addressed them, "We go to war! Today we take back our valley and fulfill our promise to the angels." There was an eerie, low growling sound that was amplified through all the tunnels. Their voices reverberating as one, the clan agreed.

After following Bokk down a huge passage, they saw the reason yellow air was able to penetrate the caverns. A large boulder was wedged at the end of the cave to block entrance. The sides of the great rock did not block the entire hole and were covered with spider webs. Through the small spaces, the stinking yellow fog streamed through. Bokk stopped at the boulder and turned to look back at his assembled force. One hundred of his people had joined them.

He looked down at Cirrus and Miraph. "The yellow air strengthens the dragons. If it were to be removed ... do you understand, wizards?"

Cirrus and Miraph smiled and nodded.

Bokk spun to Nightshade, "Once you have the sword, you can reveal yourself; but if they discover you before you are so armed, you may not survive. The sword should give you the ability to take their heads. Just be fast to avoid the explosions and do try to keep the fire away from our fur."

Nightshade nodded gravely.

Bokk turned to the boulder and touched it gently. The huge stone crumbled to dust, and a sour cloud of yellow air gusted in. Holding cloths to their noses, the companions went forward into the valley, Bokk at their side and one hundred giants at their backs.

It was as if they entered a yellow void. The air was so thick with the vapor that they could not see each other. Cirrus and Miraph found a small ledge to sit on and began chanting together. Cidric circled them guardedly with a short sword in his hand. He wasn't sure if he could actually use the weapon correctly, but against a dragon, what was the difference? He also kept alert for smaller threats—he knew all too well that dragons employed, or enslaved, servants like the goblins. Also, who knew what other travesties of nature this poisoned valley had produced? Centipedes as long as your arm, perhaps, or worse.

As the wizards' chant grew in strength, the yellow air began to swirl around them until a clear vortex formed. The wizards continued their chant, and the vortex spread outward. The magic built up by the chanting of the spell intensified, and features of the valley became discernible all around them as the yellow pall that had lain over everything for centuries was swept away.

Soon they could see a shape that seemed to be a fence around something in the middle of the valley.

As Nightshade strained to decipher what it was through the clearing air, she realized with sudden sickening recognition that it was no fence, but the bones of angels, strung up in a ring with their skeletal wings touching as if in some last horrid dance. In the center of the gruesome ring was a single skeleton with a white sword lying on it.

After several more minutes, the mountains that encircled the valley became visible. Dragons were perched on cliffs all around the valley, glowering down at the giants, whose huge forms were shielding the companions from view. Though they must be infuriated by seeing the purging of the air, they did not budge.

Finally, the voice of one dragon cut through the chanting. "Bokk! Why have you come here?"

Bokk gave the signal. "Run, Queen!"

Nightshade made an inhumanly fast dash toward the center of the valley. Bokk roared, and the giants began hurling giant boulders into the air. As the immense stones arced toward the dragons, the boulders grew in size. Before they could process what was happening, half of the dragons were crushed to death by rocks that had grown to proportions that matched their own size. Explosions blossomed to the sky, and the ground shook violently. The surviving dragons took to the air, breathing fire at the giants. Many of the furry rock-throwers caught fire and fell or ran.

Nightshade reached the grotesque display of angel bones, glancing up at the remains of her sisters as she passed. The dragons had stretched their bodies over the bones of other angels and made a mockery of their remains. Nightshade felt a terrible rage in her heart. She could feel the names of each of her sisters floating in her memory and could not control her anger. Her wings exploded open in fury. The black, feather-like blades glistened in the sunlight.

The dragons spotted her at once and dove toward the center of the valley, the sight of their age-old enemy overriding any concern for their own safety. Rocks continued to fly, but with the dragons airborne, it was nigh impossible to hit the banking, darting targets.

Nightshade reached the sword and paused only for a bare second to admire its beauty. It was a huge blade meant to be wielded with two hands. It appeared to be made of marble and edged with gold. The blade edges looked sharp to the extreme, but marble and gold? Such material could not withstand battle—but looks could be deceiving—this was a magic blade.

The rage flared anew as she heard the dragons approaching. She grabbed the hilt of the sword with one hand and lifted it easily. It was made of magical stone, and one who could wield it felt not the weight. Intuitively, she understood all of the blade's properties and how to use it. In her mind, she heard a voice issue a simple greeting, *My Queen.*

"My people, rise and attack!" she commanded her fallen sisters while brandishing the sword.

The skeletal angels began to move. They freed themselves and flew upward without the aid of visible wings. One by one they plunged into the dragons, piercing their hearts and evaporating in the ensuing explosions. Some of the skeletal figures were caught in the claws of the enraged dragons and crushed to dust.

Nightshade took to the air. It felt incredible to be able to fly again. She became a blur. Never had she attained such speed. Holding the sword with one hand, she struck again and again. Each swing removed the head of a dragon or sliced mortally into dragon scale. The rocks from below stopped flying as the giants watched the queen destroy all of the remaining dragons, save one.

The last dragon hovered before her and held up its front claws in a gesture of surrender. "Please, I yield. Spare me!"

Nightshade's response was quick. "Never in life." She smiled, raised the sword high, the white marble gleaming brightly, and all the remaining skeletal angels dove downward, slicing deep into the dragon. The resulting explosion scattered the ashes of her people to the winds.

Nightshade floated gently to the ground, coming to rest without disturbing so much as a stone in front of the stunned group. She scanned their faces for dissent. She still felt rage and wanted a challenge. Then her eyes met those of Miraph. The girl's eyes were a mix of pride and fear.

Nightshade thought, *Fear of me?* She looked at the blade.

In her head the blade spoke. *Through the ages I have been the tool of peacemakers and butchers alike. It is yours to decide how my power will be used.*

Nightshade folded her wings behind her, but not around her. She held the blade between her wings on her back and knelt in front of Miraph. "It is over. Perhaps I should have spared him? I don't know. The rage is gone now, and we are victorious. I have fought for my people, for the giants, and for the fate of the world. You have fought with me, and you have my thanks."

The surviving giants roared with jubilation, and began celebrating their return to the surface, some breaking into uncoordinated but hearty jigs that made the ground shake.

After a short conversation with the giants and declarations of alliance and of friendship, the four companions gathered their scant belongings from the cave. Emerging back into the daylight, Cirrus touched the rune to summon the *Azure Sphinx*.

"Krenn, Ty, and Victoria should have returned to the ship. I am surprised they did not come looking for us after all this time..." Cirrus mused.

The airship landed in the valley, the ramp opened, and the crew came running out. Exclaiming that they had seen the battle and were so glad to finally hear from someone, they explained that the others had not joined them. The ship had been docked in the south waiting without a word from anyone.

This news tempered their own success with a dreadful foreboding. A note of alarm in her voice, Nightshade said, "We need to fly to Anden. Something has gone wrong there as well. If the others are not back after all this time, I fear the worst."

The giants watched and raised their furry, boulder-crushing hands as the airship took to the air and turned southwest. On the main deck stood Belladonna the Queen. She looked down at the final resting place of her kind and raised one hand in farewell.

17. The Anden heist

rack! The sound stung in the ears of Ty, Victoria, and Krenn. The cobbled streets of Anden appeared for an instant. A second later, the trio found themselves lying on their backs in a wheat field, disoriented, staring up at the sky.

Feeling a temporary paralysis leave his mouth, Ty said, "Well, that was different." He managed to turn his head to see the others. They looked like they were suffering the same lingering petrification. "You two alive?"

General Krenn frowned. "That should not have happened. We were there."

Victoria sat up, rubbing her arms and legs to get blood circulating through them. "Indeed, for an instant, I saw a great city. It seems we are not welcome."

Krenn pulled himself up with an old man's groan. "I have never encountered anything powerful enough to repel my blade before."

"Yes you have," Victoria reminded him. "Vigo's magic. The crystal he holds."

Ty mussed his hair with his fingers in an attempt to steady himself. "Anden has a giant version of that crystal in their city, right?" Admiring the clear blue sky, he added, "At least the weather is pleasant out here."

He had barely finished his attempt at a witty quip when a shadow fell over them and something that was not a cloud passed overhead.

"Why do I say such things out loud?" Ty whispered as the three scrambled to hide in the tall wheat from the dragon.

Cautiously peering out from the stalks, they saw a huge city with a glowing magical dome around it. Light seemed to radiate from every building but was strongest in the center. The dragon either did not see the companions or it was not interested in them as it continued at great speed toward the city and let loose huge plumes of Dragonshade. The magical dome repelled the flames and ultimately the dragon itself when it rammed into the outer shell of teal-tinted light. The dragon crumpled as if it had flown into a solid mountain. It slid down the sloping side for several hundred feet, then it regained its focus and began to flap its wings again. It slowed its descent and found its legs to soften the impact. Touching the ground for only a moment, its talons raked furrows through a garden patch as it took to the air and flew away in a different direction.

Victoria observed, "That would be why we couldn't get in, I'd wager."

Krenn was studying the approach to the city. "We will be able to go to the city on foot. The dragon touched the ground and was not repelled. Whether they let us in or not is another issue, but the fields go all the way to the gates. I am curious, however..."

Ty was wondering the same thing. "Why are the fields still here? City under siege, that'd be the first thing they'd destroy, starve 'em out."

"Exactly," Krenn said. "There must be another weapon in the arsenal of Anden we have not yet seen. A weapon they use if the dragons attempt to burn the crops."

"A weapon they might be able to use on us if they choose," Victoria grumbled.

"Perhaps a night approach?" Ty suggested.

Krenn looked around. "I don't see any towers, so the weapon must be in the city. I suppose it depends on the reason we were repelled. If they meant to do it, they don't want us in there, but if it was just an unfortunate interaction of magics, then our safer course would be day travel because we would be protected from the dragons by the city. Given that there are no watchtowers, however, I don't think they use the weapon by choice; else the dragons would sneak in to burn the fields by night."

Victoria frowned in thought. "So, the weapon must fire—or whatever it does—only at dragons under certain conditions?"

Ty said impatiently, "So are we walking now or after dark? You've lost me in your loops."

Krenn stood. "We should go now. If we are repelled, we die or try again at night."

Victoria grinned. "Logical, but not preferable."

Ty was already walking between the rows of wheat. "Thought I'd start before you guys talked yourselves out of doing anything. The last thing I want to do is get stuck sitting around here for months. There's a road up here."

The three emerged from the field and stepped onto a brick road that led to an enormous gate in one of the many walls of the city. From a distance, Anden looked like it had been built as a hexagonal walled city with many towers inside. As they approached the walls, they realized the original city must have been built on a mountain and the rocks of the foundation had been used to build outward. The walls were uneven and multi-leveled. The original mountain was all but gone; its core now constituted the center of a natural palace where the crystal undoubtedly was housed.

As they neared the gate, they could apprehend how tall the city really was. From a distance, they had assumed the walls and gate to be the same size as most city walls and gates, but that was only an illusion of distance. The outer walls were as tall as the ancient tower of Redim in some spots. None of them had ever seen such a marvel of construction. The gateway, wondrous to behold, was crafted from solid gold inlaid with sapphires.

Krenn marveled. *This majestic wall had not existed when I was young, or had it? So much has happened since then.* He had heard it said that when you return to your childhood home after being long years away, everything seems smaller than it was in your memory. This was certainly not the case for him!

Standing at the entryway, which was tall and wide enough to allow a dragon to walk through, was one guard. He was attired in light clothing and did not appear to hold a weapon.

Krenn whispered from the side of his mouth to his companions. "This might be a problem."

Ty and Victoria both snickered, thinking Krenn was making light of the guard's unformidable appearance.

Krenn frowned and said, somewhat more loudly, "Don't be fools. *Look* at him. This might be a weapon free city."

The others suddenly understood the problem that would pose. If they were not allowed to carry their weapons, where would they put them? Krenn's blade was their transportation.

As they approached the guard, they noticed his physical similarities to Krenn. His skin tone, facial structure, even the way he wore his hair bespoke that they shared the same ancestry. Prudently, the General instructed them, "Allow me to do the talking."

When they were within a yard of the glowing light that marked the edge of the magical dome, they stopped. The guard stood just inside the protective radiance.

"Come in the gate," the guard said cheerfully. "You are no dragon and cannot be harmed by it."

The three companions held their collective breath and stepped through.

"Welcome home," the man said to Krenn.

Krenn shook the man's hand. "Forgive my ignorance of the protocol, but I have not been in the city since I was a small child and do not remember."

The man regarded Krenn with surprise. "You've never been back?"

Krenn shook his head.

"How far have you men come?" The guard asked.

Ty started to speak, probably to correct him that they were not all men, but Krenn quickly cut him off. "We come from the kingdom of Redim where we have escaped after a fierce battle."

The man looked shocked. "Redim? I heard it fell into the sea a hundred years ago."

Krenn smiled coldly. "It should have."

The man considered this and said, "What is your business in the kingdom of Anden?"

Krenn proceeded carefully. "We are on a mission that began with a great battle in Redim and have come to speak to the leaders of the city. We will ask for aid in this great task."

The man seemed amused. "Sounds important. Well, you can try and gain entrance to the palace and speak to the emperor, but he seldom sees anyone. Seldom does anyone seek his council ... perhaps the two are linked. No matter, you may try. This is a weapon free city, however, and I see you are all armed."

Ty began cursing himself for sending the portable library with the other party.

The man noticed Ty's frustration. "Worry not. We have an arrangement for visitors just for this occasion. We understand you need to be armed outside the city, and we do not wish to keep track of every weapon. Therefore, you will be magically marked with these red scarves." The man produced a red silk scarf for each of them. "Wear them at all times and no one will question your weapons. But draw any weapon, and you will be instantly repelled from the city." He offered the scarves, and Krenn accepted them.

Passing the other two scarves to his companions, Krenn nodded at the man. "Thank you for your help. Is there anyone we should look for to gain an audience with the emperor?"

The guard shook his head and said, "You are welcome, but I have no knowledge of anyone who can get into the palace ... perhaps ... no, the only people I know are servants. You might talk to them. The emperor loves to have lavish balls and employs many servants to organize the events. Perhaps one of them knows the way to get an audience. They gather near the servants' entrance on the opposite side of the city. Good luck, and welcome home."

The three, now clad with red scarves tied conspicuously to their belts, made their way into the city. As they walked, they drew the stares of many. Some appeared happy to see visitors, but most looked askance at their weapons, as if they were committing some embarrassing *faux pas*.

Ty tilted his head toward Victoria. "I don't think they like us."

"We would be better off if we were not marked," Victoria said.

Ty wondered aloud, "Do you think we would be ejected if we took them off?"

Krenn chuckled. "You two. You are still both fools, aren't you?"

"I think we've been insulted," Ty said.

"Why are we still fools then?" Victoria sounded slightly annoyed.

Krenn stopped and turned to them. "What happens if we draw our weapons, according to our friendly greeter and marker?"

"Ejected from the city," Victoria said impatiently.

"Whoosh! On our butts in a wheat field, like the first time," Ty added.

Krenn held up a finger and waved it at him. "And that happened when we teleported into the city with drawn blades, yes?" The others began to realize.

"Without these silly scarves," Victoria said.

Krenn nodded slowly and dramatically, as if his foolish young pupils were finally catching on. "The scarves are to mark us as outsiders only. The magic lies in the power crystal and the spells that bind the city. Any weapon drawn anywhere, by anyone, will most likely result in ejection. We should strap our blades to our backs in traveling style so we do not accidentally draw and be expelled."

Ty blushed as he shook his head. "Wow. You're right, we are fools. Hold on, how do we adjust our weapons without it being considered drawing?"

Krenn pondered this a moment. "A good question; I don't know. Perhaps we should just try to complete the mission and leave as soon as possible."

The three made their way down streets that took them toward the center of Anden. The entire day was spent before they attained the center of the city—it seemed as if it truly were bigger inside the walls than it was outside. Granted, this was a city of strong magic.

When they finally reached the palace, they circled around to the back and found the servants' plaza in a large alcove, shabby but clean. Near a wide entryway, many people were gathered with food and musical instruments.

Ty held up his hand to the other two. "My turn. Stay here, I can handle this." Before the others could object, he had slipped inconspicuously into the crowd of servants.

Krenn and Victoria moved into the shadows of a nearby alley to avoid attention.

After several tense minutes, Ty returned carrying bundles of cloth. He divided them up and tossed some to each of his companions. "Put these on. They are the uniforms of the servants. There is no way in to see Emperor Shalik. He never has official visitors, only invited guests. Apparently, there are rich nobles that have been waiting more than ten years to be invited to one of his parties."

Krenn looked aghast. "He has no formal meetings? How does he conduct trade and commerce?"

Victoria laughed. "I remember trying to get an audience with a certain general but was told he never saw anyone either."

Krenn began to stutter a retort but gave up. He chuckled and shook his head, defeated. "At least it wasn't because I was spending all my time throwing decadent parties," he said, without rancor.

The three donned the servant's uniforms over their clothes and joined the waiting group.

Finally, as the sun began to dip below the towering walls of the city, the servants' door opened and people began to file in. Ty, Victoria, and Krenn allowed themselves to be swept in with the throng.

For hours, the three companions followed orders and helped set up the elaborate ballroom. They had decided that the best way to meet the emperor would be to approach him when he was in his revels.

They were setting a table with some of the finest settings any of them had ever seen when a strange, echoing voice from the opposite side of the ballroom commanded sudden silence throughout the vast space.

"You do not belong. Who are you, and why have you snuck in with my servants to invade my palace?"

The three companions froze and slowly turned toward the voice. On the other side of the dance floor stood a tall and pale man clad in regal flowing clothes dyed a shimmering, almost otherworldly purple. There was no question that the man was both the emperor, and a vampire.

"Great," Ty said under his breath.

The emperor answered despite the distance. "What is great? That I have discovered you, or that you get to speak to me so soon?"

Krenn took a few steps forward, dropping the servant's act and resuming the bearing of a general. "That we get to speak to Emperor Shalik." He removed the servant uniform, and his companions followed suit. "I am General Krenn. I hail from Redim, and this is Victoria also of Redim."

The emperor floated across the dance floor in a blur and put his finger to Krenn's lips. "What do you want? I don't care who you are or where you come from. I have a party to arrange, so out with it."

Krenn took an involuntary step backward from the cold finger. "We, we have come to ask for the Blade of Inferno. We have need of it."

Shalik stared at him coldly with pupils that were ghastly yellow slits. "No one living knows of that object. How is it you have come by this knowledge?"

Krenn took a step backward and gestured toward his own blade, careful to do so in a way that was non-threatening. "I possess the Blade of Time and Space, one of the Five Swords of Power. We need all five … Your Highness. To defeat the dragons. Once and for all."

The emperor looked shocked for a moment to see the blue blade of legend, but he recovered his cold, nonchalant demeanor quickly. "No. There are no circumstances under which the Blade of Anden will leave the city."

Victoria stepped forward. "Your Majesty—"

The Emperor took to the air and the atmosphere of the room filled with menace. Shalik curled his lips back and two prominent white teeth appeared in his mouth. Before they realized they were being goaded, all three drew their weapons. The next moment they were lying in the field of wheat looking at the night sky.

Ty started to laugh. "We are all fools."

Krenn sighed. "So it seems."

"Lousy vampire tricked us," Victoria said angrily.

Krenn nodded, admiring the stars. "Indeed. What now?"

Ty was still laughing. "We steal it." He laughed more loudly, motioning for the others to laugh as well. Krenn and Victoria did their best to join him, producing some half-hearted chuckles. Ty stopped laughing abruptly and said loudly, "I'm kidding; let's get some sleep!"

Rather than preparing for sleep, though, Ty signaled for the others not to speak, putting a finger to his lips and then covering his ears. He then pointed to the city and made a funny gesture with his fingers to indicate fangs in his mouth. The others understood—the vampire emperor might be able to listen to them at even this distance; they could not know.

Victoria put her hands over his ears and nodded, then she mimicked the pointy teeth gesture and began laughing again.

Krenn shook his head and padded out a place to lie down in the soft wheat. In the field, under the starry sky, the laughter slowly died and soon there was only the steady breathing of three sleeping adventurers.

The companions were aroused by the first bright rays of the sun. Discovering how uncomfortable sleeping on crushed wheat stalks had actually been, they stretched and popped their backs.

"We should stow our weapons now," Krenn said.

"Easy for you," Ty said to Victoria. "Your armor and weapons conveniently double as a pretty pendant."

Victoria dangled the pendant on its chain around her neck. "It is rather pretty, isn't it? I guess Vigo had an artistic side, buried somewhere in that heart full of vengeance."

"We should continue to wear the red scarves until we find a place to hide in the city," Ty explained, "then, I will poke around and find us a route inside the palace. We won't be able to pose as servants again—they will be on the watch for us. We should only conduct our activity during the day, supposing what they say about vampires is true."

"It is true," Krenn said. "We had to destroy one in Redim. A nasty foe, it took out thirty-seven of my very best men, quick as a blast of Dragonshade."

"We shall endeavor not to get caught then," Ty said.

Victoria stood up. "We should get going right away. Do you think the guard will remember us?"

Krenn followed suit, Ty offering him a hand up, which he courteously took. "I am sure he will, and he will know we did not leave the city by foot since we still have the scarves. But I think honesty might be the best gambit for dealing with him."

"Let's just say we got in a fight at the pub," Ty suggested. "Pulling blades on the emperor might just get us banned from the city."

The others agreed with this cover story, and they set off again toward the gate.

They were met by the same guard, who grinned with amusement when he saw them approaching. Though he said nothing as they passed, they were sure he and his fellow guards would be having a laugh at their expense once they were out of sight.

"That went well," Ty said out of the side of his mouth as they strolled down the main street.

"Let's hope our luck holds," Victoria said, fingering her pendant.

Krenn continued to hold his head down, saying nothing.

The trio made their way toward the main palace and found an out-of-the-way inn on a side street near the servants' entrance. The inn was a dark and dirty establishment teeming with dirty people. It was obviously not one of the city's jewels, Ty thought, but would serve their purpose well.

As they climbed the unkempt stairs to their room, Ty cast a beaming look back at the other two. "Home sweet home!"

Victoria made a face that looked like she had just bit into something very sour. Krenn remained impassive. He seemed to have slipped into a general's mindset and made no acknowledgement of Ty's frivolity.

Ty put the key in the door and entered the grubby room first, his eyes darting all about—he was an experienced enough rogue to know it best always to thoroughly examine a room in such an establishment before making oneself comfortable.

When he was sure there were no lurkers, Ty said in a more serious tone, "You two lay low, keep those weapons stowed. I will start the next phase of our mission. Try to get some sleep, if the rats will let you. I think we will need to make our entrance at night."

Krenn, who had sat down in a wicker chair that appeared dubious to hold his muscled weight, opened his mouth to protest.

Ty put his hand up to allay the general's fears. "I know, I know. We will not proceed with the main objective until the sun rises."

While Victoria and Krenn made themselves as comfortable as was possible in a room where, no doubt, many unpleasant things had transpired, Ty left the inn to hunt down some leads.

Despite the dankness of the room, and the sound of rats chewing in the walls, Victoria managed to fall asleep after a short time. Krenn sat by the grease-smeared window and stared out of it for hours. He watched the progress of the sun and glanced uneasily at the palace from time to time.

When the sun began to set and tint the sky with orange light, Ty returned. Krenn heard the key click in the lock and he put his hand to his hilt out of habit.

Ty entered so quietly he could have been a ghost. He walked to the hammock where Victoria slept and shook her gently, whispering her name. He was alert to where her hands lay, on guard lest she wake suddenly and instinctively trigger her armor and weapons, sending her back out to the wheat. She mumbled something unintelligible, then her eyes snapped open.

"It's me, Ty," he quickly said as her muscles tensed to strike.

"Oh, Ty. Did you bring food?"

"Yes. There is some bread and cheese on the table. And I have found a way in, but it will be wet."

"When do we leave?" Krenn asked without emotion.

"We can wait until a few hours before sunrise. That should put us in range of our goal by first light."

Victoria sat up and untangled herself from the hammock. "Wet? Don't tell me we are going into the sewers."

Ty gave her a consoling smile. "Sorry. It's the only way."

Victoria looked up at the water-stained ceiling. "Wonderful."

Ty looked at Krenn. "So, what's eating you?"

Krenn cringed. "Eating is exactly what I'm worried about." He looked back out the window at the dark silhouette of the palace. "I saw their faces, my men. We assaulted a castle on a forested mountain, but the creature inside did not wait for us to breach the walls. It seemed he was driven mad by the prospect of so much blood and could not hold back from the feast. He rose from the battlements like a bat and fell on my men in a blur. At first, I thought there was some kind of dust storm blowing dirt on the battlefield, but then I realized, the strange mist in the air was the blood of my men. In seconds, the creature had ripped the throats of dozens and was dancing in a frenzy of excitement as the blood swirled around him … whirlwind of human blood." Krenn paused.

Neither Ty nor Victoria said anything. After collecting himself, Krenn resumed. "I took the chance to kill the vampire while it was in its ecstasy. I ran into the blood mist behind him and lopped off his head. The creature began to melt into a sick puddle of unmentionable filth, and I looked away. Around me lay dozens of my men … some of them trying to scream, and some … some were begging me to help them. To put them out of their misery. There was nothing else I could do. The carnage was appalling."

He turned his gaze from the window and focused on Ty. "I hope your plan works, Master Ty, for the alternative may be another appalling slaughter."

Ty sat in silence, absorbing the horror of Krenn's story. Then he pulled up a chair next to the general and joined him in watching the palace.

From the corner of his eye, Krenn observed the deep worry that now lined the normally carefree face of the young man. "You understand, then," Krenn said quietly.

Ty gave the subtlest nod. Words would be superfluous.

Victoria, who had slept most of the day, took the watch so Ty and Krenn could get some sleep. After several hours, she adjudged it was about the time Ty wanted to be awakened and roused her companions.

Ty rubbed his bleary eyes and looked out the window, craning to see the stars and ascertain the position of certain constellations in the sky. Satisfied, he said, "Good. A bit early."

"I'm sorry," Victoria said. "You could have slept longer?"

"No, no, it's good. Better a bit early than late for a date like this," Ty said.

They waited about three quarters of an hour, stretching and preparing themselves mentally for what lay ahead, then quietly slipped out of the inn and into the early morning shadows of the silent streets. It was the gloaming hour, neither night nor day. The time when magic is at its strongest. And, hopefully, not far from the time when certain creatures of the night retired to their soil-lined beds.

Ty led them down an alley away from the palace and pointed to a crumbling building on one side of the narrow passage. At the base of the building was an opening into darkness. The ground there had sunk in beside the building's foundation, leaving a hole just big enough for a person to squeeze through. No one had bothered to put a barricade around it, much less try to repair it, as this was obviously a neglected part of the city habited only by people that few would miss if they fell into a hole and disappeared. The sinkhole opened into the underground world of the sewers.

The three companions exchanged looks of resolve, then quietly lowered themselves into the opening.

The stench was incredible, and the passage was much narrower than Ty had hoped. Wading in knee-deep liquid through a dark tunnel that was barely higher than their heads, they had to make their way in utter darkness for a bit, until Ty deemed it safe to light the small lantern he'd bought in the marketplace that day. The flow of the disgusting liquid was constant and putrid. When the lantern illuminated the tunnel, actually seeing the filth they were smelling did not help. Victoria began to gag. She turned away from the others, embarrassed, and vomited.

When she had finished, Ty pulled some small balls of scented cotton from a pocket and passed them around. "Put these in your nostrils; it'll help some."

"Might have passed these out earlier," Victoria muttered darkly.

They pressed on against the current toward the palace. After an hour of wading, they began to see light filtering down through small cracks in the ceiling.

"We are inside now," Ty whispered. "We should come upon an open room soon. The palace has access to the sewers for maintenance."

It took nearly another half hour for them to reach the room, and when they stepped with relief from the contaminated stream onto a dry floor, Ty bent over and vomited.

"Watch where you aim," Victoria said, "that's the only dry floor down here."

When he was done retching, Ty wiped his mouth off with a cloth that he tossed back into the flow of sewage. "I was saving it up," he said self-consciously. "Glad Nightshade wasn't here to see that."

"The sun should be up by now," Krenn said, apparently more relieved by this thought than by being done with their sewer traverse.

"So much for being unobtrusive," Victoria said with a grimace. "They'll smell us even if they don't see us."

"We'll be fine, just stop wafting so much," Ty smiled dubiously. He doused the lantern and left it sitting on the floor.

They found a service stairway up from this basement level and quietly made their way into the lower levels of the palace. Surprisingly, they did not hear or see another soul. The palace felt empty, un-lived in.

After skulking a while, Ty produced a crudely-drawn map from his inner pocket and consulted it. He scratched his chin, turned in place a couple times orienting himself, and pointed down a nearby dark corridor. The three hugged the wall and silently crept down the hall. When they reached another junction, Ty pointed down a different corridor that seemed to slant downward toward a strange light. The three crept down the lowering grade.

When they had gone far enough, they saw where the strange light came from. At the end of the hall was a large bronze double door inset with glass panes, and the light shone from the room through the glass.

Ty silently approached the doorway, crouching below eye level of the panes. When he got to the doors, he cautiously lifted his head just enough to look over the lower frame into the room. Then he gestured for his companions to come forward.

They beheld a chamber of enormous size, lit from an object high above. Floating twenty feet above an altar in the center of the room was what could only be the power crystal. It was the size of a small cottage, and it rotated slowly on its invisible axis, defying gravity. It emitted a beam of light from both tips. The upper beam shot skyward out of sight, bright and strong. The lower beam shone dimly and tapered into a single point of focus that intersected with the Blade of the Inferno lying upon the altar.

"We have it," Ty whispered triumphantly. "Let's take it together. As soon as we touch it, we should be teleported out of the city."

Victoria and Krenn exchanged approving glances and nodded. It seemed an infallible plan.

"I assume you can get us through these doors?" Victoria said to Ty. He was already scanning them, feeling the edges.

"Good news and bad," he finally declared.

"Oh?" Krenn said.

"Good news. There are no locks on these doors. Bad news. That might mean magical traps."

"Opening them could blast us to pieces," Victoria muttered, "or turn us into frogs or something."

Ty nodded. "Yeah, something like that. Why don't you two back up. If anything happens, I'll bear the brunt of it." He paused and gave them a stare that brooked no question. "If this takes me out, you two get in there and proceed with the plan."

Victoria put her hand on Ty's shoulder, then gave in to her emotions and embraced him in a hug, new respect for the thief swelling. Krenn took his hand and gave it a single, bone-bending squeeze. Then they backed up several paces and Ty pushed the old doors—terribly heavy, made of solid bronze. Ty strained with all his might, and slowly they began to budge. After the doors were open a few inches and no ill effects were suffered, Krenn relented and came to his side to help push. Together they opened the doors enough to slip through.

Ty led the way to the altar, his eyes alert for any signs of traps in the floor. He felt through the soft leather soles of his boots for any slight give on a tile that might be a trigger.

They safely reached the altar. *Too easy?* Ty wondered. He gave his companions a nod, and they all reached for the sword, prepared to be surrounded by a field of wheat.

Instead, all three were frozen stiff as their hands came within an inch of the blade. None of them could move.

"Ty?" The muffled voice of Victoria came from her paralyzed mouth.

"Game's up," Ty replied, barely able to form the words with his numb tongue.

All three could feel the electric buzz of a spell coursing through their muscles, holding them in place.

They were soon discovered by guards, who seemed confused by an alarm they had never heard before. They spent no time wondering what to do with the intruders, however. After being disarmed, Ty, Victoria, and Krenn were thrown into a cell in the dungeon. The paralysis was wearing off, but it did not matter. They were chained to the wall awaiting nightfall, and the pleasure of the Emperor.

There was a single, small, barred window at the very top of one high wall of their cell. *Perhaps it was put there for no reason other than to taunt a prisoner with the passing of days beyond reach,* Ty thought. *Or, to harken the coming of night.*

The guards did not return all that day, bringing neither food nor water. When one of them needed to urinate, the chains fortunately had enough length that they could reach a rusted bucket in a near corner.

They could do nothing but watch the sun's rays make their slow climb up the far wall, until they disappeared, and they were cast into near-total darkness. Soon, some scant light from lanterns outside the palace shone in. The sun had set, and they prepared for the worst.

Ty could not help but notice that the general, one of the bravest men he'd ever met, was silently weeping. Chained and powerless, the proud warrior was about to confront that which had haunted him most of his long, long life.

Now they could hear the slow, steady click of footsteps coming down the dungeon hall. There was only one set. Only the emperor entered the cell. He sat in a wooden chair opposite them, the only piece of furniture in the room other than the bucket. The vampire fixed his preternatural eyes on his prisoners.

"Well?" Shalik implored in an exasperated tone. "Please explain yourselves."

"Are you going to eat us?" Ty asked in a near whimper.

The Emperor turned his mouth down in disgust. "Even if you didn't smell worse than the lowest sewer rat, I don't defile myself by feeding on people. Only animals do such things. I am the Emperor of Anden and will not lower myself to their level."

"Your Majesty," Krenn began, "we came for the blade."

"That much is obvious." The emperor smiled cruelly. "But instead, you will live the rest of your days in this cell … and you have given me another of the five blades for my collection. I do thank you for that."

He rose from the chair. "Talk is finished. You should feel privileged that I do not kill you all for trying to destroy my city. The blade would have vaporized you all had you touched it, you know. I have saved your lives, and now I must keep you safe for your own sake. I tried to make you leave, but it seems you do not have enough sense to avoid danger on your own."

Victoria opened her mouth to object, but the Emperor held up a hand to silence her.

"Enough talk. Enjoy your stay. The chains will be removed after we have seen to the long-term security of your new apartment."

With that, the Emperor left the cell. They heard the lock click back into place on the wooden door. The three companions hung their heads.

There was some small consolation—soon after the Emperor departed, a servant accompanied by two guards delivered food and water. The food was stale bread, and the water had more color to it than one would hope. Ty tested it first, alert for the tang that would indicate it was drugged. Satisfied that it was just very poor fare, the three consumed and drank ravenously.

The next day, a contingent of servants, again with two guards, arrived and transformed the bare cell into a room suitable for long-term imprisonment. They were at least going to be treated as official prisoners, and not as low-life criminals locked away to rot in their own filth. Three beds were provided, a table, and two more chairs. They were not, however, freed from their chains that day and could only stare at the beds on the far side of the room with longing.

The day after that, an iron gate was installed outside the cell's wooden door, double caging them in their prison. After these precautions, including new mortar slathered onto some loose stones, were completed, the three companions were released from their chains and allowed free movement across every foot of the 20-foot by 20-foot cell that was now their whole world.

The seasons in Anden were not as pronounced as they were in their homelands, so it was hard to tell how much time had passed. Accordingly, Krenn took to marking the days on one of his bedposts. With nothing else to pass the time, the three often argued over many things, from the idle to the grand—including, sometimes, who was to blame for their failed mission. When these arguments became too heated, they always managed to back off. Victoria was often the calming voice of reason between the headstrong general Krenn and the passionate young Ty. Above all else, they knew they had to survive. If they took to each other's throats down in the dungeon, any slim hope of ever escaping— much less retrieving the Blades—would vanish. And hope, however faint, was the only reason to get out of bed, to face another day in the cell.

The vampire emperor did not visit them again. Sound from the revels of his court sometimes filtered all the way down to their cell. Then, after Krenn's bed-marks had surpassed three months, something changed.

On the third day following the third month, there was an immense sound like an approaching cyclone above them that caused general commotion in the palace. The guards were frantic and distracted, but the three did not consider escape. Ty had, in fact, tried escape several times, only to be caught by some magical means.

As the sound grew, the companions all recognized what it was. Their emotions were a mix of elation and shame. The cyclonic vibrations stopped right above the palace and diminished as the *Azure Sphinx* landed. They were to be discovered as failures by their comrades.

Krenn, sitting at the table with his head in his hands, looked especially dejected.

Cheerfully, Ty said, "Well, at least we'll be out of this cell."

Krenn looked up. "That is far from certain."

"*They* were undoubtedly successful in their quest. This won't be pleasant," Victoria said without raising her face.

"We don't know that either," Ty said. "Why did it take them so long to come for us?"

An hour after sunset, they heard many footsteps coming down the corridor. Ty and Victoria stood to attention to meet whatever was coming, but Krenn remained slumped at the table. They heard the iron gate open, then a guard opened the inner door. The guard stepped aside and the Emperor himself entered, followed by Nightshade.

Ty gazed upon her with awe. She stood resplendent in her queen's armor. Her black wings were unfurled slightly as if she wore a fabulous cape, its forked high collar towering behind her head. He could tell immediately that the White Blade of Kings must be strapped to her back. After months of imprisonment, the glow of the blade was almost blinding.

She met Ty's gaze with a regal stare that was almost as blinding. Then she shook her head, and a smile played at the corner of her lips.

"Once a thief, always a thief?" she asked him.

Ty shrugged and tried to return the magnificent angel's smile. He was suddenly self-conscious of how grubby he must look, and how badly he must reek.

Nightshade looked reprovingly at Krenn. He too, stood up from the table when he saw Nightshade in her resplendent, queenly guise. "I would have expected more diplomacy from you, General. I have explained the situation to the Lord of Anden, our esteemed Emperor. He has agreed to release you, and to loan us the Inferno Blade."

The prisoners were speechless; they merely gaped in obvious shock.

The Emperor smiled with a touch of cruel amusement, like a farmer seeing just desserts meted out to a gang of naughty boys caught raiding his gardens. "Gentlemen, your quest is just. Your methods, however, leave much to be desired."

"We're not all gentlemen," Ty grumbled, but Victoria gave no indication she wished to correct the oversight.

"I was in error to hold you," the vampire continued, "but only out of ignorance of your—or, I should say—our situation. Had you begun by approaching me as diplomats rather than spies and thieves, I would not have held you. Luck is in your favor, though—you are allies of the Queen of the angels, who pilots the last airship in all of Ashyer. She has agreed to allow my mages to examine the vessel so that we may start building more again. Anden once built the finest airships the world has ever seen, and now we can recover that lost craft. You will be welcome in the palace for the next week with your companions while we examine the ship. Try not to steal anything."

The Emperor's brief grin flashed his fangs, and he left the room.

Ty took a hesitant step toward Nightshade. She shot forward and embraced him. "Come here, you idiot. Even now I love you." She then took a step back, her nose crinkling. "Though you smell terrible! Perhaps we should take the three of you to the bath houses."

"We?" Victoria asked. "Did the others survive your adventure as well?"

"And was your quest successful?" Krenn asked anxiously.

"Yes, we are all here. I will tell you the tale after removal of your stench allows you to be in the same room with other people," Nightshade said as she led them out of the cell.

Over the following week, the three newly-freed prisoners regained their strength and bearings. They heard the tale of the yellow valley, the Battle of Giants and Dragons, and of the Last Return of the angels to finish the conflict with the dragons who had desecrated their bones long ago.

On the seventh day, there was a grand reception in the palace ballroom where all seven companions were seated and honored as diplomats of state from Olan. At the reception, the Emperor presented Krenn with his blade in a declaration of peace. Then, using special gauntlets, he presented the seven with the Blade of the Inferno.

"Touch it not without these magical gauntlets, lest you be consumed by your own weapon," Shalik told them. "May you be victorious in your quest and free our world from the tyranny of the dragons forever."

There was uproarious applause from the court at this declaration. The Emperor looked at the court as if seeing them for the first time. "Do not think we will sit idly here in our bubble, my people." Murmurs greeted this. "We will start building airships right away, and we will be ready for a final battle, both at home and in Redim, if these brave heroes do not succeed in stopping the war. Let it not be said that Anden did not play its part when the final blow was struck. We have until the moon arrives, but we will be victorious. This world will be ours again!" The Emperor smiled as the crowd cheered him again.

Either way, you're not the one putting your neck on the line, Ty thought as he politely clapped.

After the reception, the companions were given leave to depart and finish their quest. Emperor Shalik advised them to acquire the last of the five blades with as much speed as they could muster. The *Azure Sphinx* rose into the clouds with the seven companions aboard. The city of Anden vanished beneath them, although they could still see the glow from its magical dome tinting the clouds for some time.

"We must apologize to you again for our failure," Victoria said to Nightshade.

Nightshade shook her head. "It was not a failure. Personally, I think that if you had not made fools of yourselves, the Emperor would not have been so willing to cooperate with us. You made him feel as if he had the upper hand, and we arrived to beg his assistance. I think that if you had done as he suggested, in his pompous way, he would have simply laughed off your diplomatic request. The only thing that held real sway on him, I think, was this ship."

"Should we follow his advice about the next blade?" Ty asked. "Frost told us to regroup before going after the Darkblade."

"Much as I hate to admit, the vampire's advice, I think, is sound," Cirrus chimed in. "We must not tarry any longer. If we cannot find a way to get the blade between the seven of us, I doubt Frost would be of much assistance."

They agreed to head east toward Redim, and the cursed Valley.

18. Darkblade

A t a great height, the *Azure Sphinx* shot across the sky toward the rising sun. The clouds looked like wispy white streams far below. The seven companions on the bridge could see the curve of the world. Fortunately, the airship's magic kept the air inside warm and breathable, otherwise they would not survive long at this height, for what little atmosphere there was would quickly freeze their lungs.

"Must we fly at such a height?" Ty said as he turned from the vertiginous view with a dizzy expression.

Nightshade laughed. "It is best to stay out of danger so that we may arrive without incident."

"You've changed," Ty said as he crossed the bridge to her.

"Oh, you noticed? It's my hair. I'm cutting it differently."

"Your sense of humor's intact," Ty said, brushing a hand through her long black locks. "I do like your hair."

She placed her hand on his and pressed it to her cheek. "Of course I've changed. No longer a vigilante skulking the streets of Olan. Now I'm Queen Belladonna. Yet, I am still myself, and I will love you while I can."

Ty did not look much eased by this declaration. A hint of sadness lingered in his eyes as he gazed into hers. "I wish things were different."

"That's why we fight," Victoria said from the other corner of the command center. "To make a difference. To change things for the better."

Ty nodded, but did not seem comforted. He withdrew his hand from Nightshade's cheek and turned to stare out the window again, steeling himself against the disorienting effect the view had on him.

Also gazing out of the window, Cidric did not seem to hear any of the conversation. "Incredible!" He exclaimed in wonder as he pressed his nose to the glass.

They all turned to look as the sun burst over the slightly rounded edge of Ashyer below. It cast a dazzling yellow light across the rolling lands, driving away the shadows of night. They were stunned into silence by the beauty.

Staring out across the rim of the world, Krenn broke the silence. "This is why we fight. This is ours. Not those overgrown, cinder-stuffed lizards from their cursed moon."

Land gave way to sea as they tore eastward. The rising sun became an explosion of light reflected on the water. Miraph joined her father and gazed out the window. The others retired to their rooms below while the *Azure Sphinx* cut its inexorable path toward Redim.

Mere hours later, the airship was fast approaching its destination as the companions gathered on the bridge once again. They watched the easternmost mountain range come into view.

"To the southern end of the range," Krenn directed the crew. "There lies the Cursed Valley."

The ship banked slightly to the right and they all beheld a strange formation in the craggy peaks. From a distance, it seemed as if an enormous giant had drilled a perfect circle into one of the mountains at the western edge of the range just east of Acamea.

"How did it come to be?" Miraph asked.

"Legends only tell of an ancient demon that dwelt in that valley," Krenn explained. "It is now home to the immortal creature known as Godslayer."

"How do we approach this entity?" Victoria asked as the *Sphinx* began to slow and circle in.

"We should land there, in the center," Cirrus said, pointing. "In the center stands a structure. Perhaps this Godslayer is but a man and not a legend?"

"We can do that, but I think we must proceed *very* carefully," Ty said.

"And that's coming from Ty," Victoria interjected, "so you know we'd better be extra cautious."

"We are almost certain that he possesses the Darkblade," Krenn concurred, "and if the description is true, most of us could be slain by it."

"I will watch the skies," Nightshade said, and she departed the bridge to take flight.

The airship slowly lowered toward a humble structure, a dot in the valley's expanse. It appeared only to be an ancient shack, its wood dried to petrification from untold decades of exposure.

Dust flew up and filled the valley as the ship landed. Nightshade gyred far above them, scanning the valley for signs of life. From the ground, she could have easily been mistaken for a circling vulture.

The others descended the ramp and headed toward the shack, shielding their eyes against the dust. They came to a halt when they were within shouting distance of the hut. There were no signs of life.

"Hello?" Ty shouted, "Anyone in there?"

Cirrus elbowed him in the side.

"What do you want me to say?" Ty protested. "'We're here for your weapon, come on out?'"

Cirrus could not help himself; the young rogue's characteristic light-heartedness made him chuckle and shake his head. He opened his mouth to make a clever retort but stopped when they all heard something approaching. They could not ascertain the direction, the sound echoed around the valley.

Nightshade landed behind them suddenly, causing a few of them to jump.

"He comes from the mountainside at great speed," she reported. "I could not tell what he looks like—he throws up a great cloud of dust—but he does not move like a normal creature."

As it drew nearer, the sound became a screaming wind crossed with a large, rolling wheel. They singled out the cloud of dust that was approaching and noted with alarm the velocity of its approach.

Victoria activated her full armor and blades, and the others drew weapons. Only Miraph stood fast.

The silence was deafening when the object stopped suddenly before the shack and a figure became visible in the dust.

The shape was man-like but had no visible flesh. There were floating tatters of black cloth that crawled and flowed around its form as if the fabric lived. In the right hand of the creature, its tip pointed at the barren ground, was the Darkblade. The metal emitted a palpable menace and fluctuated with the rhythm of Godslayer's breathing. They could not see the blade's true shape, for it was surrounded by a dark light, as if it was but a shadow of itself, expanding and contracting imperceptibly.

"Hello," Ty began weakly. "We are ... um, friends, from a distant land."

"I am Godslayer, Avatar of Power, and I will purge all false gods!" The creature's voice was a hissing buzz. "Each of you will be tested and judged!"

Godslayer raised the Darkblade in front of him, hilt clasped with both bony hands. Whenever the blade moved, it did not seem to traverse the space between, but merely reappeared in its next position. The dark shadow of the blade winked on and off as it moved.

The six who had readied themselves shifted as one for the fight. Miraph began walking toward the creature, her arms at her sides.

"Miraph, stop!" Cidric yelled. She put her hand up to stay her father and continued to walk.

"I am Miraph, and I contain no immortal blood. I have come to replace you. Allow me to touch the Darkblade and prove my worth." She extended her hand to the Godslayer.

The creature tilted his covered head to the side slightly, as if considering, and pointed the blade at her. Miraph continued forward, and very slowly lifted her hand to the blade. In an instant, the blade became solid. It was an obsidian-black steel katana, and marvelous to gaze upon.

Godslayer tilted his head the other direction, as if examining her. "Why would I need to be replaced? This makes no sense as my mission is not finished." The voice was now barely a hiss, "I must purge the world."

Miraph slid the palm of her hand up the blade. "Because you have failed. You have been corrupted by the mission and become a god yourself."

The creature stiffened but did not try to move away. "How do you know this? Who are you to judge me?"

"I am no one, but you are Godslayer. You have proclaimed yourself an Avatar and have therefore failed your mission. I will not prove it; you will prove it yourself. Touch the blade with your true flesh. The blade will judge you." She tightened her grip on the blade and waited.

Godslayer did not move for several tense seconds. Except for the continually flowing rags snaking around his body, he could have been a lifeless scarecrow. Then, with one swift and final movement, he shook the black rags off a near skeletal hand and touched the blade.

Instantly, the rags dropped to the ground, an inanimate pile. Miraph stood alone holding the Darkblade. A puff of ash, the remains of Godslayer, blew away on the breeze.

Silence stretched out as the others watched stunned. Miraph reached down to the rags, retrieved the scabbard, took the blade by its hilt, and sheathed it; but as she tried to turn to her companions, she was flung out of her body.

Miraph looked down at her body holding the blade, then she travelled into the blackness of the stars above at great speed. She saw other worlds, giant stars, and clouds of gasses with many colors as she flew past them faster than light. She tried to scream but found that she had no mouth or voice. Then, in the distance, there seemed to be a tear in the blackness. She sped uncontrollably through it and entered some other space. In the new blackness, there were no stars or clouds or worlds. There was only one thing in this entire universe, a large wooden throne with a figure sitting on it. She thought it might be a man, but his shape was not solid.

"I am not yet," the figure said.

Miraph did not understand, but she had no voice to respond.

"I will be. Only I can control the blade, but I am not yet … born."

The vision vanished, and the voice of her father was calling to her.

"Miraph, please, Miraph!" Cidric was brushing her hair out of her face. She was on the ground next to the rags and screaming strange, incoherent things. She opened her eyes, and Cidric gasped. Horror emanated from her pupils.

"He is not yet born. He waits on the chair at the end of the universe," she said.

The others gathered around and exchanged fearful looks. As they approached, she pulled the sheathed blade close to her chest in a protective gesture.

"We must carry her to the ship and return to Olan quickly," Cirrus commanded. "Take care not to touch the blade—not even the slightest tap."

They returned to the ship and began their journey across the known world to Olan.

All took turns sitting with Miraph and Cidric during the ensuing days. Miraph floated in and out of the trance state. When she was not too deep in the trance, she recalled as much as she could remember. It became clear to all of them—they needed to separate her from the Darkblade as soon as possible.

19. The lost laboratory

Frost sat back in his chair and stared at Miraph. He eyed the blade cradled in her arms and thought about trying to remove it after hearing her tale of woe.

"You must not," The Dryad warned in his mind. "The attempt would be fatal for both you and her."

Frost bit his lower lip in concentration, then addressed the entire group. "We will leave at once. It is imperative we bring all five blades to the door and hope that the curse is lifted when she releases it. I hoped to go in stealth, but the moon grows larger, and, Miraph must be released."

"Thank you, my King," Cidric said.

"Your King? You are all my friends—my equals at least, if not more than I."

"Nevertheless, only one may wear the crown," Cirrus chimed in. "And it is, as you have learned, a great burden as well as a privilege."

Frost abruptly stood. "We must go before another day passes. Bring only what you need. I will instruct my servants to load provisions on the ship tonight. We leave with the sunrise. Until then, get some sleep."

Their tales had consumed the day, and the sun was setting. With full bellies, the reunited friends retired to their separate quarters.

Next morning, the *Azure Sphinx* began its long flight east, leaving the city of Olan far below. All eight companions stood on the bridge and gazed toward the rising sun as the horizon line began to curve with their increasing height.

As the airship drew near the Middle Kingdom, Ghost Girl awoke. Her form appeared above the basin, "I have regained contact with the laboratory."

The companions on deck, having not spoken much for some while, were all startled by the interruption of silence.

Frost turned to the glowing figure on the basin. "Can you tell us if there are any dragons near the entrance?"

"Yes, I can tell you that information."

Frost waited and waited. Finally, he realized she was waiting for him to actually ask the question. He sighed. "Are there any dragons near the entrance?"

"No. I can detect no dragons in range."

Cirrus stepped up next to Frost. "That is not surprising. Remember, we—well, mostly Nightshade, her army of giants, and death angels—obliterated their nest."

Frost looked out the curved front window musing for a moment. "Land the ship. We must make haste and open the door. Land the ship right next to the thing."

The airship shuddered as it descended quickly, and all the companions except Miraph held onto solid objects for purchase. Cidric held fast to a table with one hand and his daughter with the other. The ground swelled into view as the ship approached the small strip of beach. Several of the friends cringed in anticipation of a crash as the airship braked to an abrupt halt. Ghost Girl's basin almost slid off the table, but Frost caught and steadied it.

"Everyone, let's go now!" Frost shouted as he turned and exited the bridge, his crystalline armor catching the rays of the morning sun.

The eight left the ship and found themselves standing before the rock face with the circular door. Frost strode forth and inserted the Forest Blade without hesitation.

Krenn tarried a moment longer, his own history so intimately intertwined with his sword. He muttered a few words beneath his breath, as if he were speaking to the blade—saying farewell, perhaps, should the blades not survive this usage. Then he stepped forth with determination and thrust the Blade of Time and Space into its slot.

Nightshade did the same with the Blade of Kings, far less sentimentally. She looked like she was stabbing the mountain as she pierced its slot.

With the heavy protective gauntlets, Ty lifted the Blade of the Inferno, standing on his tiptoes to reach its notch.

Then, finally, carefully, Cidric guided Miraph's arms to gingerly slide the Darkblade home.

As soon as the deed was done, Miraph collapsed with a sigh of relief and began to sob. Cidric held her, and she held him. Slowly, as she wept, her hair turned completely white. The others were at her side, concern in their hearts.

They all looked up as the huge circular door began to rotate slowly, generating a grinding noise as if a giant boulder was being dragged across a rubble surface. The eight companions watched as the blades slowly turned with the door and began to glow. As the door turned, it receded into the rock face and a spiral, grooved surface was revealed. When the door reached a depth of ten feet, it stopped and began to crack. The Dryad cried an alarm in Frost's mind.

"Get under cover!" Frost shouted to the others.

As they all scrambled away from the entrance, the door exploded outward, sending a volley of rocks and blades into the air.

When the dust cleared, a perfectly circular hole into darkness remained. The five blades lay scattered on the rock face. Frost began to rise slowly, only to be frozen with surprise by a familiar voice issuing from the door.

"Welcome to Volcanic Laboratory Two. This facility has been dormant and may have high toxicity levels in the air count. Please proceed with caution. Uplink with exterior terminal complete." The voice of Ghost Girl continued, "Frost, you and your companions should be safe. I have initiated ventilation."

Frost looked over his shoulder, then back at the door. "Does that mean there are no traps?"

"All security measures have been disabled. There are no traps," the disembodied voice replied.

Frost strode to the spot where the Darkblade lay. "We can't just leave it here." The others joined him and regarded the black sword as if it were a contagious corpse.

"I will wrap it up in cloth and place it in a box for storage," Cidric said. "I will stow it in the ship's hold. I suspect there are many treasures within we will wish to remove to a safer location. If that ghostly woman is correct, not only is it safe for *us* to enter here, but anyone else who wishes. The moon rises fully in a matter of days, and we must safeguard our secrets."

Krenn nodded. "It's a good plan. I shall gather some of the crew, have them bring crates and wrappings."

Nightshade swooped over to the Blade of Kings and retrieved it. She looked at Ty, then gestured to the door, "She may be lying, you know."

Ty raised an eyebrow. "Can't you tell? With your, um, your angel mind-reading?"

Nightshade shook her head. "Her voice is…human and *not* human. It is artificial. I cannot read her mind, nor sense her emotions."

Frost and the others recovered their respective blades. All had survived the blast. If anyone noticed Krenn put his cheek lovingly to the flat of his blade as if reunited with a long-lost companion, they did not comment.

Frost thought for a moment before speaking. "Krenn, hold off on bringing in the crew. Gather the men and supplies you need, but don't enter until we come back out. We must investigate first. Cidric and Miraph, you two stay here and guard the door. Miraph, if you are able to use your magic to signal us should any situation arise at this end."

"Why not?" Ty quipped as he strode toward the door, casually swinging the Blade of the Inferno like it was a baton. "We've come this far. Nothing like a dank, dark hole in the side of a mountain with mysterious voices to get the blood pumping."

"Watch where you're swinging that thing!" Cirrus chided him. "Do you want to burn us all to a crisp?" The wizard shook his head and followed the chastened rogue, holding up his own staff to provide light.

The tunnel walls were rock for only ten feet, then gave way to a polished metal surface. Ty stopped and put his hand on it. "I've never seen the like."

As far as the companions could see, the passage stretched on into the mountain. The sides and ceiling were made of a silvery metal, and the floor of an unknown, slightly flexible material.

"What do you make of this?" Cirrus asked the others as he stooped and pressed his hand into the soft, springy material of the floor.

"It's a floor," Nightshade said. "Shall we proceed?"

Ty grinned, utterly smitten by this forceful angel even when she was vexed and impetuous.

Victoria said, "One second." She activated one of her blades and thrust it into the floor. It came into contact with more metal, about an inch down. "The stuff is only a coating. The way is solid."

Frost, Ty, and Cirrus led the way down the widening passage under the mountain as Victoria and Nightshade brought up the rear. They noticed the air becoming warmer and soon heard a faint rumbling sound ahead. After continuing for many minutes, they saw an orange light issuing from an opening at the end of the straight corridor.

"Smells bad," Ty said as they all slowed.

"Rock fire," Cirrus remarked. "The voice said volcanic, so we must be inside a volcano, and the smell must be rock fire. I have never seen a volcano, but I have read of them. We must be cautious."

The five approached the opening and saw the lit chamber beyond. The circular room was enormous, easily a quarter mile in diameter. In the center floated a huge power crystal above a circular hole in the floor. Above it hung a strange apparatus with large lenses and metal arms. Along one whole side of the chamber stood rows of bookshelves stacked with books in varying states of decay and disarray. On the other side of the chamber, a huge sphere at least six feet across floated inside a slightly larger bubble. Another apparatus held lenses around the bubble. Scrolls and maps lay scattered all over the floor.

"Look at the ceiling!" Nightshade exclaimed as she entered the chamber.

They craned their necks. It took a few moments to decipher what their eyes beheld. At first glance, the ceiling above looked like the top of a giant cavern; but as one stared at it, the spell wavered. They could clearly see that there was no ceiling. The top of the mountain was an illusion. They were standing in a capped volcano where the power crystal apparently drew power directly from the churning lava below. The apparatus above the crystal seemed to be some kind of focusing device pointed up through the false ceiling.

"This is what we have been searching for," Cirrus said as he approached the crystal.

"By all the gods!" Frost yelled.

The others spun, instantly ready for battle. Frost was examining the sphere inside the bubble, and something had clearly shaken him badly.

The others joined him, and at once they understood—the sphere was a replica of Ashyer down to the finest detail, but closer inspection revealed it was far more than a spherical map. Frost moved one of the lenses to their current location on the world and adjusted it. Through the lens they could actually see a tiny airship from high above. Cirrus added another lens, and the ship appeared larger. They could now see the tiny propellers slowly turning, and several ant-like specks moving tiny square objects up the rock face.

"Krenn and some crew members," Cirrus said with wonder. "We are looking at them from … from outside the world. This must be one of the most powerful magical items ever created." He turned to the others. "Touch nothing! We must find a guide or journal of some sort before we proceed. Let us turn our attention to the books please." All followed his lead and began to rifle through the piles of dusty tomes.

Frost decided that it would probably take several days to explore the entire complex, so he sent Ty to fetch the others. Krenn and four of the stoutest crew members joined them with crates for objects to be removed. Cirrus directed them to carefully begin boxing some of the books. Frost commanded that a larger crate be constructed to encase the world-sphere for transport. He was not sure if it would be possible to move such a delicate thing, or if its power would be lost on removal from its base, but they could not leave it behind. In the wrong hands it would grant terrible power—the ability to spy on anyone, anywhere.

Eventually Cidric and Miraph joined them, marveling at the wonders inside the mountain. To the delight of the already dusty searchers, they brought food.

Together, they continued to page through the tomes on the shelves, searching for anything that looked like instructions pertinent to the chamber. After several days, most resorted to merely tossing books on the floor and scowling at the crystal with distain.

The situation seemed hopeless until Miraph suddenly slapped herself in the forehead. "Gods!" The others wearily turned. She smiled. "The answer is too easy! Ghost Girl?"

The figure of the ghostly girl winked into existence in a far corner of the room above a platter, of which none of the companions had taken notice.

"What is your request?" Ghost Girl asked.

"The last person to use this laboratory was named Lorid, was it not?" Miraph asked as she approached the figure.

"Lorid was the previous master of this facility," Ghost Girl affirmed.

"Where can we find his personal notes or journal?" Miraph asked.

"In me," Ghost Girl stated, in the same matter-of-fact tone she stated everything.

The others looked bewildered, but Miraph simply nodded. "*You* are the journal."

"Lorid's Journal is one small part of me," Ghost Girl said. "It is contained in my memory. I am to keep it sealed until someone with proper clearance requests it."

They exchanged quizzical looks. Then Cirrus asked, "Do, um, we have clearance?"

"Yes," Ghost Girl said.

Everyone waited. And they waited.

Finally, Frost broke the silence, "Oh, I know this. Ghost Girl, give us clearance to read Lorid's Journal."

"Better yet," Miraph broke in, "just read it to us."

"As you wish."

Cirrus pulled up a steel chair and sat. The others followed suit, gathering around the image of Ghost Girl, the platter above which she floated becoming like a stage, and they, all spectators at a puppet show.

Ty opened a pouch filled with dried meat and bread and passed it around. "Story time," he said with good humor, and the diminutive ghost began to recite the tale.

20. Lorid's journal

Ghost Girl began to recite Lorid's journal entries, calling them up perfectly, word for word, from her memory …

1. My name is Lorid, a wizard of the first order from the Kingdom of Romasia. I write this journal to document my quest for a higher order of magic, please see attached designs and formulae for my spells and creations, which I have included for posterity. My entire life, I have studied all the magical arts available in the five kingdoms and have become a master of all. I suspect there is a higher order of magic that goes beyond our current understanding of the magical scope. I am somewhat of an outcast for my strange beliefs and have recently exacerbated the suspicious nature of the Court by conducting explorations underground in the capital city of Romasia. I found evidence of a civilization that existed on Ashyer tens of thousands of years ago buried beneath layer after layer of ruins. On one occasion, I swear there was writing that used the word "Rome," which indicates, to me at least, our civilization had its root in the previous ones, however lost to time. That ancient civilization used mechanical apparatuses or machines to power their world, and I am convinced there must be other ruins hidden all over the world. I found small mechanisms that started to perform simple functions when I applied simple electrical spells to them. It was then that I realized magic combined with these mechanisms could create a new order of magic that I will call Sorcery, and I will become the world's first sorcerer.

2. I have been expelled from the city for suggesting that we are not the most powerful civilization that ever existed on Ashyer. The fools! I will prove them wrong. I have started traveling west toward the western edge of the middle sea. I am convinced there must be a hidden ruin there. For years, I have studied the myths of the smaller villages in the Kingdom and have discovered a myth from that area that speaks of a mountain that disappears during lightning storms. I have surmised that it must be a ruin from that forgotten age, as it seems to be linked to electricity. I am afraid that is all I have to go on, but I have a strong hunch about it. It will take many weeks to reach the location on foot. No one wants to help a wandering wizard, either out of fear or hate. Don't they understand that I am trying to improve the world we live in?

3. The villagers were quite welcoming when I came to inquire about the magical mountain. People there were happy to tell me everything they knew. It also happened that they needed the help of a wizard, as a giant had been rampaging nearby, and destroying the farms of the people. It was easy to dispatch the pitiful creature. It had been starving since it was separated from its tribe, which is why it had been raiding the farms. The giant had no information about the mountain, so I destroyed it with flame and ice. When I presented the head of the giant to the people of the village, they threw me a feast and told me many tales of the strange mountain. Apparently, at times it shakes and groans, suggesting to me that it might be what is called a volcano. This might make things harder, but I am determined. They also mentioned that a hunting party came close enough to the mountain once and saw an opening on the southern side. When I asked if it was a cave, they paused to consider and shook their heads. They said the opening was far too perfectly circular to be a natural cave. I am convinced that it must be what I have been looking for, and will set out in the morning loaded with enough provisions to last me for a month.

4. It is a laboratory, and an amazing find! I have taken control of what the ghostly image of a woman calls a "scientific research facility." She has enlightened me as to the age and intent of the facility. The ghostly woman claims to be something called a hologram; I have come to call her the Soul of the Laboratory. She says this facility was the ultimate in volcanic research twenty thousand years ago. The people who created it managed to close off the opening at the top to control the heat and pressure from below to generate power. I have learned that the floor I stand on is actually that cap, and I have so much to learn. To continue my research into sorcery, I will attempt to bring one of the large power crystals here and link it to the existing equipment. I have also discovered that the people who invented this facility were obsessed with the stars and were convinced there is life out there. Perhaps this is the next level I have been searching for? Is there greater magic to be harnessed in the cosmos?

With the next entry, the rapt listeners were shocked to hear Ghost Girl's voice change from her own to that of a man's. Her measured, impassive voice was replaced by one that was emotional and passionate. Presumably they were now hearing the voice of Lorid himself.

5. This will be my first entry spoken directly to the Soul of the Laboratory. She can record everything I say, and she has also scanned my earlier entries, notes, and drawings into her memory, which she calls "uploading." It is a far more effective assurance of longevity than parchment and paper, for she has been here twenty thousand years and presumably will be here twenty thousand more.

I have done it! I will not elaborate on the acquisition of the power crystal. Needless to say, I have it, and have connected it to the ancient cords and wires hidden in the floor. With the help of the hologram woman—the Laboratory's Soul—I have activated different systems of the facility and connected them to the crystal. The results have been promising thus far. The crystal reacts favorably with the old technology. Also, I have been experimenting with the old lenses to peer into the night sky. The Soul has shown me that the ceiling can be made transparent, so I can point the devices at the stars. There are wonderful and mystifying things out there, including another world very close to ours. Its surface, though, is completely obscured by orange and red clouds. I will investigate further.

6. Unbelievable! I linked the telescopes—the lenses are called telescopes—to the power crystal and can now even peer through breaks in the clouds on the distant world. There are life forms there! Imagine, life on a different world ... I cannot see them clearly yet, but I have been working hard to increase the capabilities of the device. Also, I have been making devices that are powered by smaller power crystals, one of which is a flying machine. I have only made one out of a barrel so far, but I managed to fly twenty feet in the air before the wood broke under the strain. I went to the village and asked them to start building a ship on the land according to my designs. They had many questions, but a small display of power and a few gold coins convinced them to proceed with the work. One other thing to note, I have found a strange device in a cluttered and forgotten corridor of the laboratory. It is a perfect sphere as great in diameter as I am tall, and it at times it glows. I will investigate this further.

7. I have no words to describe the wonder of the sphere. It is a perfect representation of our world, but much more. I have mounted powerful lenses around it so that I can observe it in more minute detail. In so doing, I have discovered that it is not just a representation, but an *actual smaller version of the world*. It is hard to describe. The object, which I have called the Sphere of Global Observation, presents what is happening right now. I used many lenses to observe the village nearby and witnessed the ongoing construction of the ship they are building for me. The sphere is encased inside an outer protective bubble. I wonder...if I could remove the outer bubble, could I turn the Sphere of

Global Observation into a sphere of global *intervention*? With such power I would be a god! Imagine, the power to create giant waves by dipping your finger into one of the miniature oceans, or the power to destroy an entire kingdom by merely squashing it under your thumb. I can share this discovery with no one. I am the only one to whom I would entrust such awesome power. I have continued my work on sorcery, specifically in regard to how magic can be used to influence the heavens. I am working on powers to move celestial objects. Perhaps I can bring one of the falling stars down to earth by my command—consider the destructive power of such a spell! I have also increased the power of the telescopes; and perhaps I am losing my mind, but I sincerely believe I glimpsed a woman looking up at me from the distant world. Her face haunts me in my dreams.

8. All attempts at removing the outer bubble from the sphere have failed, but perhaps mortals were not meant to have such power. No matter, the sphere is still a very useful device. I have aimed a lens onto the entry of this cavern and set a spell to alert me to movement, so no one can approach without my observation. Three nights ago, I attempted my first sorcerer's spell of the cosmos. I waited for hours, watching the heavens, and when I saw the telltale streak of light in the sky, I performed the spell to bring the object to me. I was surprised to learn that the object was only a burning rock! It was fortunate that I performed the spell well away from the laboratory because the devastation created by its landing was incredible. I could level a small city with such a spell. I must do some further calculations on what nights of the year the streaking stars are most likely to come, for I cannot stand and wait fruitlessly all night for a streak to appear. Most troubling to me, of late, have been my observations of the distant world. I have once again increased the power of the telescopes and have observed the horror of a great war on its surface and in its skies. I was not mad when I saw the woman, for there are many such women on the world. They are winged creatures of stunning beauty; indeed, they make me think of the ancient legends of angels. They constitute one side of the warring parties. Their foes

are hideous lizard-like creatures with wings vast as ships' sails. These behemoths can expel fire from their monstrous mouths, and they spontaneously combust when mortally wounded. They remind me of another legend of the human race—dragons, those monstrous wyrms from children's bedtime tales that fought ancient heroes of old. I fear for the survival of the "angels." I feel compelled to do something, but what can I do but watch as they are slaughtered? The people of the village have finished my ship, and I instructed them to wait for me in the village, although I doubt any of them are brave enough to approach the laboratory.

9. Success! I spent a week in the village enchanting the ship they built. I must say, they are wonderful craftsmen, and the ship is perfect and solid. After I finished my modifications and enchantments, I affixed the smaller power crystals onboard the vessel. The propellers began to turn immediately, and the ship rose slightly upward. At first the villagers were stunned and afraid, but as I showed them how useful the ship could be, they became delighted. I have trusted them to learn its functions and pilot it for the current time. The villagers have seen the benefit of such ships and wish to build more. I have given them leave to devote all their resources to the construction of more. I took the long journey to the city of Romasia to secure resources for the endeavor but was met with the same scorn and jeers. There was only one group interested in my ideas, and the Thieves' Guild should be a lucrative partner. Indeed, when the head of the Guild came with me to the village and observed our one working ship, he decided to pull the entire Guild into the project. A flying armada will be the most powerful force in Ashyer, and I can think of no better revenge on the aristocrats of Romasia than the city's thieves assaulting and sacking the city by air! One more development—I believe I can use the combined power of the volcanic laboratory and the large power crystal to generate a focusable beam of energy. The hologram has told me that such a beam would affect the power of "gravity" itself. I am unclear of what this mystical gravity is, but perhaps it can also be used in my sorcery?

10. Much has transpired since last I spoke my thoughts for posterity. The village has now constructed a fleet of ten airships—that's what they are calling them—and have deployed them over the Middle Sea for defense. I am afraid the need for defense is my fault. I attracted the attention of the royalty of Romasia when I tried to peddle my theories and have exacerbated the situation by performing experiments that can be seen from great distances. Let me explain ... I perfected the gravity beam with the large crystal and started testing it. When I test the stream, a huge ray of light is emitted from the peak of the false mountaintop. The beam is observable for many hundreds of miles. I was even shocked to see a small version of the beam rising from the surface of the sphere of observation and hit the inside of the bubble. The real beam does not end. Using the telescopes, I observed the beam traveling far into space. I think I have done enough experimentation to attempt my plan now. Using a reverse beam, by inverting the crystal, I will attempt to bring the distant world closer to ours. Perhaps the angels can flee to our world...and I can greet them as an ambassador of peace? I now have only to wait for the distant world to pass within the range where I can aim the beam.

11. Disaster! [*Unintelligible sobs and groans*] Disaster. So many things have happened, I don't know where to begin. Romasia launched a full assault on the village with mounted knights and wizards, fearing our growing power. We responded quickly with strikes from our airships, but the most devastating error was mine once again. I used the star-slinging spell to bring a flaming rock from the heavens down on their army, but this time the rock I pulled down was much larger. I watched as the entire horizon was lit in flame, and the army was consumed along with the airships and the village. I retreated into the laboratory unscathed to lament my terrible deed. It was then that the Soul hologram told me that the distant world was entering the targeting area. In my loneliness, I used the reverse beam and managed to hit the distant world. The ground began to shake

violently, and the skies turned red. The chaos was indescribable. I stood helpless to change things as fire engulfed the crystal, and the great beam continued to pull the distant world. Too close! Too close! This "gravity" force that the Soul once referenced seems to be the culprit; two large celestial bodies cannot pass so near without cataclysmic consequences. I ran from the laboratory and saw the devastation happening all around. Great mountains and geysers of spewing fire were being pulled from beneath the crust of Ashyer. I returned to the lab to observe the destruction through the lenses on the sphere—protected from bodily harm, but now a weak, powerless god who could only watch from afar and could not lift a hand to intervene. The oceans seemed to be boiling and covering all the beaches, their great waves eventually splashing against the roots of the new mountains that continued to thrust up into the red sky. Then I became aware that the lab was awash in sickly yellow light. I looked up through the illusory ceiling, and I saw the distant world looming large in the sky. It had become a huge yellow moon in the sky of Ashyer. Finally, the beam ceased; and with it, things regained a sort of new equilibrium. The tremors settled, fissures stopped tearing Ashyer's skin, and the turbulent waters died down. The crystal had shifted slightly, breaking the spell. If there are gods, they most assuredly intervened ... for I believe that if the beam had pulled the other world any closer, both worlds would have been obliterated. As it is, I believe our own moon has been cast out from the sky. I will gather supplies and set out to discover the full extent of the damage. Perhaps, though, I need not leave the lab. A day observing the Ashyer-Sphere will reveal more than I could ascertain traveling a year on foot.

12. Gone. My entire civilization is gone. At first, I looked for days in the sphere for signs of life, but I needed to see for myself. I found some wreckage of an airship and repaired it enough to take me to Romasia. When I arrived, what I saw in the sphere was confirmed. The entire peninsula was gone. Romasia and all traces of her are wiped clean from the world. As I investigated further, I realized that this entire side of the world

has been destroyed. The great southern kingdom is also gone. Only giant craggy mountains and deep oceans remain where sprawling cities full of people once thrived. I returned to the laboratory and continued watching the sphere in despair. One strange thing I saw gave me pause. For a moment, on the far kingdom of Aulia, in the city of Redim, I thought I glimpsed one of the flying lizards from the distant world which still lingers huge in our night sky. Have I brought them here? What have I done?

13. This New World I have wrought is terrible. I have not told anyone of my part in the new world's creation because it is terrible, terrible. The lizards—men have indeed taken to calling them dragons—have extended their war to Ashyer, and the angels have fled here. A traversable corridor of space forms over Redim nightly, but it seems to be wavering as the new moon—that is what people think it is—slowly recedes. Perhaps it will return to its distant position? Meanwhile, Ashyer has become terrible. War in Aulia, Anden, and Olan … forced upon them by dragons. I will attempt to help by creating the airships again. Perhaps that can help atone?

14. The dragon's world—a name unpronounceable with the human tongue—now circles in an orbit around the sun like ours, bringing us within cursed proximity once a year. I have learned that much through my observations during these cursed years since I brought their reign of terror down on the people of my planet. This will be my last entry, as I have been sealed into the laboratory and do not intend on trying to escape. I am responsible for all this death and do not deserve to live. I have spent the past few years trying to help the people of Ashyer fight against the dragons. Each year, the moon rises, and more dragons come. Only the first year did the angels come, but they have been hunted down and, as far as I can tell, no longer exist. I did all this to help them … instead, I sealed their doom and brought the dragons here to enslave us.

For a time, we had enough airships to wage a valiant fight. The dragons have no magic, and we used everything we could to destroy them. But in the end, they only brought more devastation. They started using their own bodies as bombs to destroy the airships. Now, like the angels, the airships are gone. During the last cycle of moonrise, the people of Ashyer surrendered to the dragons. We had no choice lest we be wiped off the planet. The dragons covet our magic but despise us. When the leaders of the remaining kingdoms discovered that the dragon moon had been ripped from its trajectory and pulled toward Ashyer, they started to investigate. It was Xan Olan who discovered my blunders. The three kingdoms decided to seal away the laboratory. They know I am too powerful to bring out against my will, so they hope I will grow old and perish inside this cold steel prison. I have decided this will be my tomb. They used the five ancient blades from the five ancient kingdoms to seal the door. Two of those kingdoms, I inadvertently wiped clean from the world. For that alone I deserve my fate, but I now see that my blind lust for power has created death on such a grand scale that I deserve much worse. I leave this journal as a warning. Ha! Only fourteen entries in all those years … all the way back to those early days when I was an ambitious young wizard who set out to be a Sorcerer. And not a single entry about friends, or love, or children. No, I spent most of my restless nights watching the lives of others unfold through the lenses. The tiny people on the sphere, their suffering, grief, fleeting moments of happiness, and their triumphs. Sometimes I found myself cheering them on, but I am only a watcher, not a god, and there is nothing I can do to help them. When I finish dictating this final entry, I will step into the fire beneath the crystal. I hope that our kind will persevere, and that there will be some future generation who can learn from my mistakes … and that beautiful woman I beheld on that distant world so many years ago … I hope she and her people are avenged.

21. Prelude to war

ncredible," Cirrus muttered, absently scratching a newly sprouting red beard with his half-skeletal hand.

"We must not repeat his mistakes," Krenn said as he stood up with a groan and stretched.

"They were biggies," Ty murmured. "All this was because of him."

"We will not repeat his mistakes," Frost proclaimed, a strange glow coming into his eyes. "We must repair them." The Dryad inside his head listened to his thoughts with great interest and urged Frost to speak his mind. In a more resonant voice he continued, "Cirrus, we will remove the remaining objects of value from this room, especially the sphere. Take the sphere to the tree; you know the one. She will allow you to enter and hide the device. After removing all that is of use, we will regroup here. This is where the final battle will be waged."

"Here?" Ty asked. "Don't you think we should go to Redim and assault Vigo there?"

"No." Frost looked at them all. "They will come here once we begin, and we will need to protect this place as long as possible."

"You want to push the moon away using the beam, don't you?" Nightshade asked.

"Exactly." Frost nodded. "This is the only thing that matters. Kill a hundred dragons, a hundred *Vigos*, and we still have the same problem … but push that world away, and we win the war."

"When Lorid used it, it created mass devastation," Cidric observed.

Cirrus spoke up. "The damage to this side of our world has already been done. There are no more kingdoms here to destroy."

"True, and the Dryad can connect with the giants to warn of impending disaster." Frost agreed.

"I think I can do it," Miraph's voice issued from a stack of books. She lifted a tome. "This is the Book of the Cosmos, and I have studied the spell Lorid described. I know I can use the sorcery." They observed her doubtfully. Hair now radiant with loss of all color like white tiger fur, she steadily met their gazes. "Don't you think we should use everything we can to defend our world?"

"I was hoping it would not come to that," Victoria spoke up almost shyly. "We can convince Vigo that he is on the wrong path and should join us against the dragons. The journal Lorid tells is enough to convince anyone."

"So you would think," Krenn muttered. "But I have seen men reject the evidence of their own eyes and the sound guidance of their reason because they confuse belief and fact. Otherwise-sane men have been led to their very dooms by raving prophets that you or I would clearly see as charlatans."

Frost saw the pained look on Victoria's face at the thought of Vigo being characterized as such a misguided dupe. He crossed the room and put a hand on her shoulder. "Victoria, I know how you feel. I know that if Ty turned against me, I would do everything I could to help him, so perhaps …"

A voice spoke in Frost's ear, startling him badly. He spun around only to realize the voice was speaking to everyone at the same time, as if the speaker was an inch from each ear.

"People of Ashyer, I am your Lord and Master, the wizard Vigo of the house of Arthur. I have been chosen as your ruler by our benevolent guardians, the dragons. When the moon rises next, I will return to you and begin a new era of peace and growth. As your new Lord and Emperor, I will make peace with the dragons and insure no further unwarranted destruction. I will bring to you the new laws of Ashyer as written by the Dragon King. Obey these laws, and you will have nothing to fear. There will be no more petty wars, no more poverty. We will all live in peace with the dragons to watch over us, and I will be a kind, but firm Master. I will expect all existing rulers to lay down their weapons and titles upon my return. I will make a grandiose future."

Troubled glances were exchanged, confirming that they all heard the same. Frost realized he was inadvertently squeezing Victoria's shoulder and withdrew his hand.

She wiped tears from her eyes. "It is not the same as the bond you have with Ty, or even with me. I spent years with Vigo, but I feel closer to all of you now. He has no friends and cares only for himself. The Vigo I loved is gone, perhaps he never really existed."

Frost nodded sadly. "A ruler such as he would be a terror so great, I fear this world could not endure it. We therefore have no choice. Cidric, can you study the operation of the machine that moves the moon please? Rather, have Ghost Girl teach you, since she will remember how it accomplishes the task."

Cidric nodded agreement. "Quite nice, that, actually. My eyes are not what they once were; the strain of small print taxes them terribly."

Frost said, "The rest of us will get to work transporting and preparing for battle."

The next several weeks elapsed in a flurry of activity, with the *Azure Sphinx* making continual runs at full speed between the laboratory and Olan. Cidric studied and experimented with the crystal while his daughter prepared the spells she would need to master if they were to save the world. Frost kept constant watch with the help of Ghost Girl—he finally thought to ask her what her real name was and received an incomprehensible series of letters and numbers in reply. He decided to continue calling her Ghost Girl. Between his own heightened senses and the monitoring by Ghost Girl, Frost was able to know if there were any dragons nearby. As the moon loomed ever larger, the laboratory was gradually emptied of all but non-essential items. They had successfully looted Lorid's tomb.

Cirrus returned with news that the sphere had been entrusted to the dryads in the hidden home under the lake. He had many questions about the curious place, but Frost avoided answering. Discerning the futility of his attempts, Cirrus turned his attention to Cidric, and the two collaborated on controlling the crystal device. The one item they had avoided became their last order of business, and it was Ty who arrived at a solution.

"So, I've been thinking," Ty started.

"Never a good sign," Nightshade said with a grin.

"Right," Ty agreed at once, eyebrows raised in surrender. "But the Darkblade, it's been sitting in the hold of the *Sphinx* this whole time, and no one wants to deal with it."

"Where could we store such a dangerous item?" Krenn asked. "No kingdom in its right mind would want that in their land. I'm glad it has left mine."

"Exactly," Ty answered. "We have that portable library. I think we should put it in there and send it to the place with the sphere."

"Suppose the wand that draws the library loses its power if Vigo dies?" Victoria asked.

"All the better—no more Darkblade, no more problems!" Ty smiled.

"I don't think it will be that easy," Frost said. "But your idea has merit, my friend. I forgot about that library."

"A good place then … to store things you want to forget," Ty smiled.

"The Blade is eternal." It was Miraph's voice, but flat and distant. "It has been, and always shall be. It was the beginning, and it will be our end. He waits." Her eyes were glazed and unfocused.

Cidric put his arms around her. "Miraph, come back to us please."

Her eyes cleared, and she looked around at them curiously. "What are you all looking at?"

No one answered, but there were pained expressions on many faces, and not a little lip biting.

Cirrus broke the moment. "Well, it is decided—Ty, proceed with your plan but make your way back as soon as possible; the moment approaches. As for the rest of you, please stand back. I need to reverse the crystal and align it now. I am unsure if it will work properly... there is the slight possibility we will all be vaporized."

"I'm off then!" Ty said and began to hurry out the corridor.

"I think I will make sure he gets there," Nightshade said. She followed Ty and was in turn followed by Victoria, Krenn, Cidric, and Miraph.

Frost stepped back a few steps. "Looks like it's just us chickens. Go ahead, Cirrus, I will try to intervene if something goes wrong."

Cirrus gave him a half smirk and leaned in toward the crystal. "Here we go."

The sound of the airship leaving gave Frost a start as he watched Cirrus intently casting spells. When he realized it was just the ship, he let out a slow breath of relief. Then the crystal started to thrum, and the whole room began to shake. Frost held his breath. He watched as Cirrus moved his hands boldly near the giant crystal without ever touching it, and slowly the immense menace began to upend. The thrumming became deafening for a few seconds, and Frost clinched his teeth with the pain. In one quick motion, the crystal flipped and settled into place upside down. The sound and rumbling stopped suddenly, and the room became much brighter.

"Camouflage systems have been damaged." The voice of Ghost Girl startled Frost again. "The mountain is now exposed."

Frost was not sure what that meant, but when he followed Cirrus' gaze upward, he understood. The brighter light was from the sun, because the false mountaintop was gone. Frost looked at Cirrus, who gave a shrug as if to say, "What are you going to do?"

Frost looked at his hands. "At least we were not vaporized."

Cirrus observed the sky grimly. "Not yet. Wait till tomorrow night and that may change." He strode to Frost and embraced him. "We will fight, and we may die, but I am proud of the man you have become, and so would your father be, were he here."

22. Worlds collide

The morning brought heavy fog that rolled in from the sea. Frost and Cirrus sat on the rocks lining the beach south of the laboratory. In the distance, they heard the approach of the *Azure Sphinx*. Cirrus' pipe crackled as he pulled slowly on the burning weed inside.

"So calm," Frost reflected as he looked southeastward, the direction of Redim.

"Most of life should be. I suspect after what will seem an eternity tonight, there will be calm. Only after the fiercest storms do you really appreciate it, the calm."

"I wish I had your confidence." Frost pondered for a moment. "I can't help feeling like something terrible will happen despite our preparations."

The sound of the great propellers became overpowering as the airship swept out of the fog and landed on the beach. The ramp lowered; both secretly wondered if all their friends would return and waited anxiously as the companions emerged.

Nightshade and Ty came down the ramp first. Nightshade was wearing the Queen's armor and looked resplendent and deadly at once. Ty appeared almost encumbered by a full set of darts slung inside his billowing cloak, and the Blade of the Inferno at his side. On his hand, he wore the gauntlet that allowed him to use the blade. Next came Cidric and Miraph. The elder looked worried but resolute. He wore a suit of light link-mail armor and a scholarly cap, in his hand a book.

Frost noticed his fingertips were stained with ink. *He must have been writing about these events. May his story have a happy ending.*

Miraph was dressed only in a light cloth tunic of white. Her arms were bare, and her hair matched, giving her the visage of a mythical goddess. Cirrus discerned a very "cat-like" look in her eyes. Last to descend the ramp were Victoria and General Krenn. The General was dressed in captain's guard with the colors of white and black painted on his full plate armor. At his side was the blue Blade of Time and Space. His dark skin shimmered in the morning light. Victoria had activated her full armor with helmet and looked the ominous Black Knight once again. The quality of the armor gave her an otherworldly look, like a visitor from another planet as strange and exotic as the Dragon Moon. At the top of the ramp, behind them stood the crew of the *Sphinx* at full attention, beaming awe and respect upon their heroes.

Frost once again admired the great airship but noticed an addition had been made to its front. A huge lance-like blade now protruded forward from the bow, and several more ballistae had been added.

"Looks like she has been fitted for full-out combat," Cirrus said as Frost rose.

"I am going to tell the crew to stay out of range unless the worst comes to pass," Frost relented. "I don't want them to die."

"They want to help, Frost," Cirrus said. "They have been with us for almost a year, fighting at our side. If we are fighting to the death, they wish to fight as well. Do not deprive them a chance to prove their bravery."

Frost pondered and approached the company. "Welcome, my friends!" He embraced all six of his companions. Then, he walked up the ramp to the crew of the *Sphinx*. "You wish to fight with us?"

They all gave their heartfelt assent with a bold yell.

"Then you shall. You will have your chance to prove your dedication to our world, and your bravery. When the battle begins, you will come at the dragons from the north. Come from behind a mountain peak … take them by surprise." He pointed up to the lance. "That. *That* is a last resort, do you understand?"

The crew nodded and bowed to their king. Frost came forward and embraced each crew member.

After Frost descended the ramp, the airship took to the air flying north to prepare the ambush. Frost returned to his friends. "So, what's new with you? Anything interesting happening today?" They all laughed and relaxed.

The eight sat on the rocks and broke bread together. They spoke of many different plans and wondered about the enemy's strategy. The talk served to calm them for a battle that defied preparation. They all agreed—there would be innumerable dragons to contend with, and a wizard of immense power.

While they discussed Vigo, Victoria kept drifting into childhood memories. She did not know why, but there was something she needed to remember. What was it? Was it important? She was sure it was the most important memory of her life, but she couldn't quite touch it. As the day's preparations commenced, she continued to be distant, considering. The others thought she was feeling bad about the coming betrayal of her old friend; but in her mind, Victoria was tugging on a string of memory that remained frustratingly just out of reach.

With the mountain now exposed as the bowl volcano it truly was, they changed their plan. Originally, they were hoping for some measure of secrecy in their deed, but now the dragon army and Vigo would come for them as soon as they crossed to Ashyer. The crystal began to glow fiercely with the power being channeled into it as Cidric started the machinery, and Cirrus began casting spells. Miraph took up a defensive position near her father as the afternoon waned into evening. Nightshade perched on the volcano's lip with her immense wings stretched in all their black glory. In her hand, she held the Blade of Kings. As the sun began to set, the gold on its edges started to sparkle, and it spoke in her mind, *victory my Queen!* Frost stood on the rim of the volcano opposite Nightshade with the Blade of the Forest in one hand and the dragonslayer in the other. Wisps of fog rose gently from the icy blade. On the beach, Ty laid darts in a row, readying them for use. Krenn stood by him with the Blade of Time and Space. On the sand, already glowing with immense heat, was the Blade of the Inferno. Victoria crouched behind an outcropping of rock halfway up the side of the volcano with her helmet off but both swords extended. Her long golden hair flowed like ocean waves as the constant wind rushed up the side of the volcano. She intended to speak to Vigo one last time. She still clung to love in her heart, but she really needed to remember what was forgotten. The memory was certainly the key to defeating the wizard.

D arkness fell across the land, and the sickly yellow color of the moonrise began to illuminate the horizon. They all looked toward the east as the yellow orb of the giant moon rose. There was an incredibly powerful *crack* from the distance and a shockwave rumbled deep in the ground—the time was nigh.

"There are two hundred and one creatures approaching from the southeast," the voice of Ghost Girl announced in the laboratory. The announcement brought chills to those who heard. Two hundred was an unbelievable number. Soon, they could hear wind from the middle sea, a sound resembling leaves tossed in the wind, only hundreds of times louder—definitely hundreds of dragons.

"It begins!" Nightshade shouted, taking to the air.

Ty donned the gauntlet, grabbed a dart, and touched it to the Blade of the Inferno. The dart began to pulse with heat. He nodded to Krenn, tore reality creating a rip close to the nearest visible spot on the horizon. Through the rip, they could see the scales of a dragon in flight, and Ty threw the pulsing dart. Krenn closed the portal. A great explosion flashed in the distance.

"One down!" Ty said while preparing the next dart.

Nightshade began to circle the volcano at great speed, recalling her battle in the valley of the yellow mist. She readied her sword for the task ahead. Below, she could see Cirrus begin the final incantation while Cidric started the great machine.

A yellow beam of light shot suddenly into the sky toward the moon. Several distant dragons who were in the path of the beam exploded. The ground began to shake as the beam reached the moon. Frost steadied himself on the now shifting terrain. In the distance, they could hear the mountains beginning to crumble as the world shook.

The bulk of the dragons arrived in force attacking with abandon. Dragonshade blacked the sky with flame as the beasts scorched the entire landscape. Their plan seemed to be utter obliteration. Nightshade blurred into the fray at full speed, decapitating dragon after dragon, always darting away just before being singed by the explosions or dragons' breath.

In the confusion, dragons began to attack each other. Frost used the power of the Dryad to extend a vine from the Forest Blade to a passing dragon. He lassoed and mounted it. Before the dragon could toss him off, he pierced it with the dragonslayer and used the vines to swing to the next target. Ty and Krenn continued to destroy dragons with their dart-portal trick. None of the dragons were aware of what was really happening below in the center of the volcano. Soon, the sky was filled with smoke as heavy as the morning fog. Explosions lit up the blackened air one after another, but the beam held steady.

Nightshade was hit with blasts of fire in the confusion and flew higher to get a better angle of attack. Smoke was roiling off her wings, but she was still in the fight.

Darts flew in all directions as Ty and Krenn worked at a blinding pace. Frost was nearly incinerated when a dart struck the dragon on which he landed. He saw the burning projectile strike and reacted with his own uncanny speed combined with the power of the Dryad, throwing himself off the doomed dragon a moment before the explosion. He sent out vines to ensnare another and was soon mounted again.

An ear-shattering roar rolled across the battlefield, and all fighting ceased momentarily as all looked up. The enormous Lord of the Dragons hovered in the sky, flapping his gargantuan wings. His roar cleared the smoke, and his size made an immense silhouette against the moon. He listened to the sounds and heard the beam. Floating below him was a black sphere with two white flames emanating from within.

The Lord Dragon roared a fiery command. "DESTROY THE MOUNTAIN!"

No one heard the approach of the *Azure Sphinx* during the battle. Now everyone, and every dragon, saw it as it plunged its front lance into the heart of the huge dragon. The explosion filled the entire night sky. Krenn and Ty hit the ground. Frost felt a desperate pull inside of himself and was encased in burning wood as he tumbled from another dragon's back. Nightshade plummeted from her height into the sea. The explosion was so great, other dragons were ignited by it and explosions ripped through the sky all around. Dragons began to bank and flee in all directions as the explosions continued, but the floating sphere remained. Victoria stood and faced it.

"Vigo! Reveal yourself!" she shouted.

The sphere became transparent, and Vigo was revealed. He floated inside Omegas' protective sphere with his dragon cloak and staff extended. Spellfire burned brightly in his eyes. "I am your Ruler. You must submit!"

"Please, my love, come back to your senses. You have lost. Your army retreats!" Victoria yelled while searching her mind for the missing memory.

Vigo seemed shaken by the words "my love." The sphere floated down to where Victoria stood, bringing them eye level with each other. He gazed into her eyes, old, long forgotten feelings flooding back.

"My floating boy in the forest," Victoria said with a tender smile.

His posture started to relax. He looked around at the devastation, and an expression of unutterable sadness started to overcome the stark lines of his face.

Then, he noticed the beam. He looked back at the moon, which was getting smaller in the sky, and roared, "FOOLS!" He raised his staff and flew like an arrow into the crater of the volcano toward the machine. As he approached, lightning began to issue from his sphere. "The machine must be reversed! We need the dragons to bring order to my world!" Vigo yelled, "Fools! You cannot understand the scope of history! We will not survive without order!"

Krenn, Ty, and a blackened Frost stepped through a portal next to Victoria and grabbed her. Krenn opened another portal, and all four stepped through, emerging near the machine. Cirrus was channeling magic fiercely into the crystal, and Cidric was operating the lenses to keep them focused on the moon. Vigo's sphere landed in the laboratory, settling him upon the ground but remaining as a field of force enwrapping him. Miraph crept up behind in the form of an all-white tiger. From above, Nightshade descended to join her comrades. She was streaked with blood—both the dragons' and her own.

Vigo raised his right hand and waved it at the crystal. The beam flickered for a moment, and the giant crystal flipped with a thrumming sound.

"The beam is reversed!" Cirrus yelled. He cast another spell and the crystal flipped again. Sweat was dripping from his brow. The room thrummed and shook badly. "Stop him at all costs!" Cirrus yelled to the others.

They converged on Vigo, swords drawn, claws out, darts flying. All were reflected back by the sphere. He did not seem phased by their attack. He was studying the device. Frost separated the Forest Blade into two swords and attacked again. Nightshade used the Blade of Kings on the sphere, and Krenn attempted to teleport inside. All their attacks were in vain. Ty ran and used the Blade of the Inferno to cut the floor around the sphere, but the sphere remained stationary, floating in place.

Vigo focused on Cidric and waved his right hand. A black blade appeared behind Cidric's head and flew into him from behind. Cidric fell dead instantly. Miraph lost her tiger form and began screaming. Vigo looked at the crystal and waved his now glowing right hand at it. Cirrus attempted to block the spell, but the collision of the two magics threw him into a far corner of the room. The clash also sent the crystal flipping end over end. The beam flickered faster and faster. The room shook violently, and the lava beneath the spinning crystal began to boil.

Miraph stood and screamed, "Damn you!" She waved her hands from the sky down toward Vigo. From above, a streak of light appeared, and before he could react, Vigo was hit by the meteor. The sphere was shattered by the collision. Rocks began to slide into the laboratory from above, and Ghost Girl was giving a warning that none of them could hear over the thrumming of the spinning crystal.

"My gods!" Cirrus uttered as he looked up at the moon. It had begun to fracture under the flipping pressure from the beam.

Victoria remembered in a frozen moment of clarity—as a girl, she saw Vigo fleeing through the woods. She noticed his right arm glowing when he flew into the air that first day. That must be where the power crystal was imbedded. She came back to the present and realized that Vigo was holding his staff up inside his cloak—he was going to shield himself.

"Krenn! Your blade!" Victoria yelled to Krenn and reached out. Krenn threw Victoria the Blade of Time and Space. Victoria caught it, and using the speed granted by the blade, rushed beneath the cloak an instant before it solidified and severed Vigo's right arm. Then, with the blue blade in one hand and Vigo's right arm in the other, Victoria escaped the pyramid that formed around Vigo.

At the same moment Vigo became trapped, the moon above exploded. The entire sky blazed yellow as the unsteady beam turned the once-distant world into dust. At the same moment, the crystal fractured and shattered in a huge burst of energy.

As the others looked up, Frost fell to the floor. Pain exploded down his spine. Under his cape, his steel string bow jabbed him as if a swordsman had split open his back. The floor was starting to melt above rising lava. Alarmed, Frost reached back for the bow, realizing there was but one hope. He carefully nocked the dragonslayer into the taut metal string, then used his legs to push the mighty bow forward while he pulled back hard on the string, the sword now an enormous projectile readied for launch. Frost arched his back, skewing the icy blade, his mighty limbs trembling from the strain. He took aim and let the dragonslayer fly. Just as the enchanted sword took to the air, the steel string snapped, cracking the bow into ruin. The cold, blue blade flew a deadly arc, striking the precise center of the eruption. One final tremor rocked the volcano. Frost's dragonslayer bled bitter cold into the scorching lava until the volcano was frozen solid. All fell silent except for the gentle sound of Miraph's weeping.

23. The empty throne

"brought sweet rolls!" Ty's voice came from the stairway in the tree.

Miraph always detected something a little forced in his voice now. She wondered if it was to cover desperation. "We're in the sitting room," she called back.

Ty entered the underground dwelling—glancing nervously up at the lake suspended above their heads, as he always did—carrying a wonderful-smelling sack in his hand.

He looked around as he came to the sitting room. "You cleaned up for me?" The sitting room was tidy with two chairs facing a hearth. The logs were barely smoldering, but the temperature was still pleasant—the crisp days of autumn were just starting to roll in. Ty glanced at the motionless figure of Frost in the other chair. "Sweet roll?" He offered one.

Frost languidly reached up and took it without moving his eyes from the dwindling fire.

Ty winced at the ribbon-like scars on the arm of his oldest friend, then turned to Miraph, who had been staring dreamily at fish swimming by outside the clear ceiling .

She shuffled over and flopped into the empty chair, gazing expectantly at the sack.

"Here you go." Ty handed her the rest.

Miraph noticed Ty's voice had lost all attempt at cheer. "Let's walk by the lake topside." She offered her hand to Ty.

An inkling of his old humor returned as he took her hand and said, "Yes, I've always preferred strolls by the lake to strolls *under* the lake."

He obediently followed her to the stairs and up through the tree, which now freely allowed the entrance and exit of any of Frost's guests.

As they walked, Ty stared morosely at the lake. He knew his friend and king was down below. King of the forest now—he was more and more coming to resemble a sentinel tree.

Frost had spoken less and less since the night the moon exploded. At first he seemed to keep his spirits up by helping Miraph through her grief over her father's death. But as Miraph returned to normal, Frost slipped away.

Ty looked up at the sky. Even in the daytime one could see the wondrous rings that now encircled the world of Ashyer. During the day it was possible to ignore them, but some nights they reflected so brightly that one could find oneself transfixed for an hour just staring.

Ty thought back to that night. The death of Cidric was terrible, but another death had occurred that none of the others knew of until Frost started to scream. When the Dryad shielded him from the Dragon King's explosion, it had killed her. None of them could have ever understood the internal relationship that Frost had with her, but they soon saw how complete the physical symbiosis had been. As Frost screamed, his skin began to tear and his armor was soaked with blood. Then, as if pulled by an unseen force, dead wood flew out of his body in all directions, and Frost collapsed. Miraph had administered healing spells to him at the tower in Olan for many months. But as the summer drew to a close, he insisted on returning to the lake.

Shaking off his own sullenness, Ty asked Miraph, "So, kid, how are you doing?"

"I'm okay. *Underlake House*"—which is what she had started calling their magical den of solitude—"provides for me, and there are many books I want to read."

"That's not quite what I meant," Ty said.

"I know. Sometimes I am sad. I don't know how else to put it. There are nights when he stays up and looks out through the bottom of the lake at the rings in the sky. I don't know if he is sad or angry, or just gone."

"You let us know if you want to leave," Ty said kindly. "Nightshade and I can come here. Cirrus has also said he would come and stay with him for a while."

She smiled knowingly. "You would come. Nightshade has been ruling in his place at the castle, even if she does not sit on the throne. And Cirrus? He is head of the wizards ... way too busy. I know they are building new airships. I will want to see them when they are complete. We will bring Frost to see them, won't we?"

"Of course," Ty said, defeated. "I would come here if you needed me to."

"I know. But let's be honest. Nightshade is with child now, is she not?"

Ty stopped walking abruptly. "Yes, but ... she ... how do you know that?"

"I know she thought it impossible, but she is. So, you need to be with her. Victoria and Krenn returned to Redim after relinquishing the Blade of the Inferno in Anden. They said they wanted to start the rebuilding of their home."

Ty nodded. "Yes, we see them sometimes when they teleport to Olan."

"But they were never as close to Frost as the rest of us. Sure, they'd die for him. But to live with him?"

Ty chuckled, and they continued walking, the conversation lapsing.

Then Miraph asked, "When is the baby due?"

Ty threw up his hands in surrender. "Can't keep anything a secret around here, can we? Midwinter is what we think, but Nightshade said there's no way to know, since none of her kind has procreated in over a thousand years."

Miraph took a moment to ponder this. "Then I shall start telling Frost that we will return to the castle before midwinter. That way, we will be there to see the new baby."

It was Ty's turn to ponder. "That … that could be bad. If the baby …"

"The baby will be fine, I promise." Miraph gave Ty a warm, reassuring smile. "We magical healing folks have our ways of knowing things."

Ty smiled back. "Well, my dear, enjoy the sweet rolls, and I will see you again soon."

He bowed and walked into the forest and toward the city.

As the months passed, Miraph reminded Frost of their impending move as she cared for him. She kept the strange dwelling clean and read all the books she could find to pass the time. Sometimes, she would look into the lenses of the Sphere of Global Observation and spy on tiny little people in different parts of the world. She watched as the people of Redim started to rebuild, and the people of Anden began to venture out of their city.

There were still dragon attacks at times. Countless had escaped the final battle and were now scattered around the world. She considered looking at the burned spot that was the laboratory, but always decided not to. It would only make her feel pain.

One night when she could not sleep, she turned to the sphere and observed something exceedingly queer. One small airship headed out from Anden, trailing a small group of dragons -- *What do you call a group of dragons?* she wondered. *A flock? A pack? A murder? No, a bonfire,* she remembered. The new airship followed the bonfire until they landed and nested down. Then, a black shape dropped from the airship while yet some distance away. She momentarily lost sight of it as it slipped through the shadows at superhuman speed, but she caught sight of it again, creeping right up to the dragons. Then, the figure moved in a blur so fast she could not follow it. In seconds, gouts of blood were spurting up from the necks of all three of the dragons, creating a veritable rain of blood. The dragons lashed about furiously, unable to find their attacker. Soon they all expired in their usual loud, colorful fashion—tiny little pops on the surface of the sphere, too small to be seen except through the powerful lens, though she knew that down there, the destruction to the surrounding forest would be catastrophic. Before they combusted, the shadowy assassin was already gone. He was sated. She remembered what the Vampire Emperor had said—he did not drink human blood. Apparently, he had developed an exotic taste for dragon blood.

Frost had laid the Forest Blade to rest on its stone table in the center of the hive-like home under the lake. As time went by, Miraph observed that it was rusting and losing its magical properties.

She had seen the black, human-sized pyramid in the city center of Olan, testament to the defeat of perhaps the most powerful wizard Ashyer had ever known. She also knew that it was actually an exact simulacrum of the cape that he had turned solid as a shield while Victoria cut off his arm. As one of the companions whose names would be sung in halls around the globe, Miraph was privy to many things—like the fact that the real tomb was hidden in the catacombs beneath the castle of Olan. This precaution was taken because no one really knew if Vigo was still alive inside. They only knew that no magic could penetrate the pyramid; and they assumed that without the power crystal embedded in his arm, Vigo himself could not undo the spell. She often prayed that it would prove to be the last spell he ever cast, and that the impenetrable material now contained only a rotting corpse. But she suspected Victoria had conflicted emotions about that.

When winter arrived, she watched as snow hit the surface of the water above, wondering if anyone else had ever seen snow melting on the surface of the water from the underside before. Within a few short days, the lake was completely frozen over, and Underlake became very gloomy. It was time. When Ty visited after the freeze, he found all of their things packed and Frost on his feet.

"Ready to go, old friend?" Ty asked him. Frost nodded his head slowly without looking at him.

Only two weeks later, in the newest chamber of the now sprawling reconstruction of Olan Castle, Nightshade gave birth. The crying echoed down the halls and was heard by all. Cheers erupted throughout the castle.

Miraph brought Frost into the chamber where Ty sat on a bed beside Nightshade. In Ty's arms was what looked like a bundle of white feathers. Frost looked down and frowned slightly, as if his eyes were only now coming into focus.

Ty looked up. "See him, Frost? He is our son, the first male angel born in thousands of years." At the sound of voices, the bundle of feathers moved. In a slow, languid motion, white wings unfolded, revealing a baby boy with black hair and Ty's eyes. "We have named him Necovis."

"He told me his name," Nightshade corrected. "He has my abilities, and we have been speaking for many months."

Frost stared for a long time at the boy with the white wings, until Ty began to grow a little nervous. Slowly, Frost began to smile. Rough from disuse, his voice was barely audible when he said hoarsely, "Welcome Necovis, to Ashyer, the wonderful ringed world."

Ty handed their son to Nightshade and rose to embrace Frost. There was commotion as Cirrus, Victoria, and Krenn joined the joyous event.

No one noticed that Miraph slowly receded back toward the wall in horror, and no one heard when she said in a monotone and automatic voice, "He sits enthroned in the dark place no more. He is born."

More Maps of Ashyer

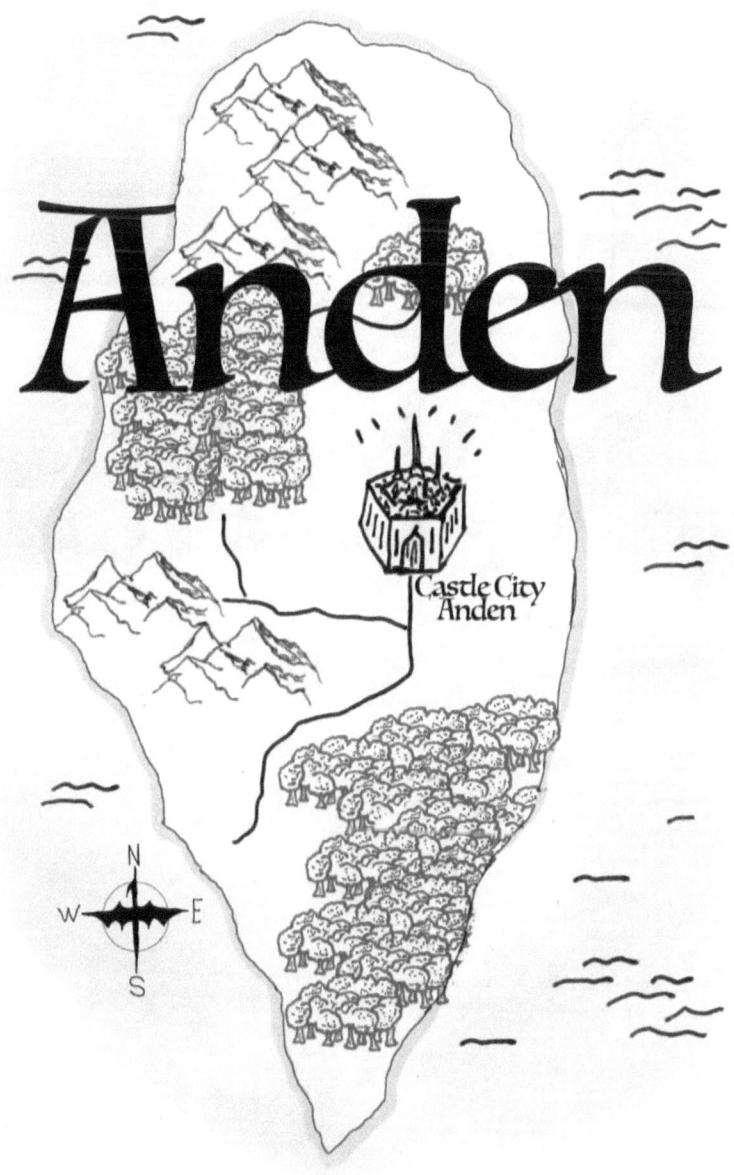

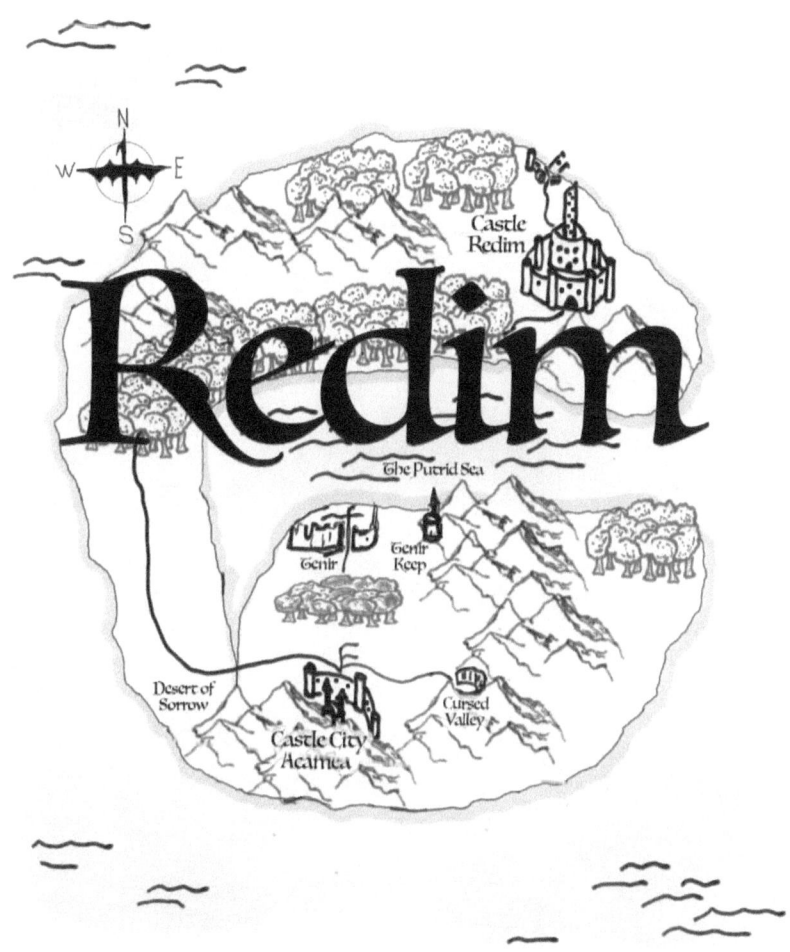

Acknowledgements

I want to thank Nick Ozment, who was not only a developer and editor, but an adventuring companion. We dove deep into the world of Ashyer and survived to tell the tale.

I also have heartfelt thanks for Tom Driscoll, Shipwreckt Books Founder. Thank you for being a mentor and teacher, Tom. Without you, my stories would be indecipherable ideas.

About the author

James Petrillo hails from beautiful Lanesboro, Minnesota, where he lives with his family. After his university studies, he worked in theatre, both children's and professional, before becoming a television producer. Upon returning to his home town, he independently released a novel, *The Darkwood*, a horror thriller. His true heart lives in the fantasy realm of magic, swords, and dragons, and he has written fantasy most of his life. *Ashyer* is his first full novel written with that true heart.